The Rancher
Next Door

CATHY GILLEN
THACKER

MILLS & BOON®
Pure reading pleasure™

First published in Great Britain 2008
by Harlequin Mills & Boon Limited,
Eton House, 18-24 Paradise Road, Richmond, Surrey TW9 1SR

ISBN: 978 0 263 86068 9

23-0908

Harlequin Mills & Boon policy is to use papers that are
natural, renewable and recyclable products and made from
wood grown in sustainable forests. The logging and
manufacturing processes conform to the legal environmental
regulations of the country of origin.

Printed and bound in Spain
by Litografia Rosés S.A., Barcelona

This book is dedicated to

Lukas Frederick Gerhardt , the "Third Musketeer,"
and the proof that wishes do come true.

Welcome to the family, little guy.
The joy you've brought us is indescribable.

And one more thing: if your two older brothers try to
give you the business...you give it right back...

CATHY GILLEN THACKER

married her school sweetheart and hasn't had a
dull moment since. Why? you ask. Well, there
were three kids, various pets, any number of cars,
several moves across the country, his and her
careers and sundry other experiences (some of
which were exciting and some of which weren't).
But mostly there was love and friendship and
laughter, and lots of experiences she wouldn't
trade for the world.

Dear Reader,

All parents want their children to be happy and have a good life. For Texans Luke and Meg Carrigan, this means marriage and a family. They didn't plan to become involved in their offspring's romantic lives, but, after years of watching their three daughters and one son lose in love, Luke has decided to become more proactive, and Meg is reluctantly putting in her contribution, as well.

Rebecca Carrigan, arguably the most head-strong and independent of the lot, is the first \to get the full attention of her parents when she comes back to Laramie to start her own alpaca ranch.

Rebecca tells Trevor McCabe there is no way she is going to date him, no matter what her matchmaking parents have – or have not – arranged. That's fine with Trevor – there is no way he is going to date Rebecca, either!

Unfortunately, life has a way of happening when Rebecca and Trevor are busy making other plans. Before they know it, their lives and fortunes are hopelessly entangled, and their emotions soon follow suit.

I hope you enjoy this book as much as I enjoyed writing it. For information on this and other books, please visit me at www.cathygillenthacker.com.

Best wishes,

Cathy Gillen Thacker

Chapter One

"I take it you've heard the rumors," Luke Carrigan said as he ushered Trevor McCabe into the study of his Laramie, Texas home.

Who in the county hadn't?

Tired of his three daughters' well-known aversion to commitment, Luke Carrigan had vowed to take a hand in introducing them all to "suitable" men, in what Trevor figured was a vain hope they would soon settle down and have families.

What was it about their parents' generation, Trevor wondered, dropping down into the wing chair Luke indicated, that made them think marriage was essential to a person's happiness? He was content living the single life, and saw no reason to change his own circumstances.

"Don't worry, that's not why you're here," Luke continued.

Trevor held back a sigh of relief.

Luke sat down behind his desk. "I did want to talk to you about Rebecca, though."

Trevor tensed. Luke's second-to-oldest child had been two years behind him in school. The two of them had nothing in common then—or now. He vaguely recalled

Rebecca Carrigan as a rah-rah type who had always been busy organizing something.

"She has a tendency to go off on—well, let's just call them tangents."

Trevor didn't know what Luke was getting at, but he was willing to hear the noted family physician out and settled more comfortably in his seat. "Last I heard Rebecca was in Asia."

"Actually, she's been all over the world with the tour company she worked for."

Trevor shrugged his broad shoulders. "That's one way to travel the globe."

"Don't get me wrong. I'm very proud of how hard Rebecca has worked since she graduated college. Even more delighted with the staggering amount of money she has saved in the past six years." Luke paused and looked at Trevor, his eyes full of parental concern. "What worries me is what she plans to do with it."

Trevor grimaced. "Dr. Carrigan, I really don't think this is any of my business."

"You may change your mind when you hear what my second-to-oldest daughter has planned."

Trevor doubted it. Honorable men did not step in the middle of other families' contretemps.

"You know that small ranch you've had your eye on?"

Trevor tensed at the mention of his neighbor to the west. The fifty-acre tract was definitely in his sights, along with the much larger property on the other side of it, The Circle Y. "I gather you're talking about The Primrose?"

Luke dipped his head in acknowledgement. "Miss Mim is planning to sell it to Rebecca."

Trevor swallowed a curse. His jaw set. "That can't be right." *He and Miss Mim had an understanding.*

"I'm afraid it is," Luke replied. He didn't sound happy.

Trevor forced himself to put emotion aside and think about this rationally. "Your daughter doesn't have a background in ranching," he pointed out. Growing up, she'd never been a member of any of the agricultural groups such as 4-H. She'd selected SMU instead of Texas A&M, where all the agricultural students went, for college.

Luke shrugged. "That won't stop Rebecca. She wants The Primrose. She's leveraging everything to get it. And that's what has me so worried, the lengths to which she's willing to go." Luke paused before continuing. "I need someone who's been there to talk some sense into her, make her realize that buying and starting up a ranching operation is no game. It's grueling, twenty-four hours a day, seven days a week, work."

And probably harder than anything she had ever done before, Trevor thought. He wondered how long it would take her to give up and sell out, like every other dilettante who had a romantic instead of practical view of the ranching life. *Hell's afire.*

Trevor exhaled in slow deliberation. "What makes you think she would listen to me?"

"Nothing, except you're her age and well respected in the ranching community."

"Are you sure your daughter is planning to work the property? Or just reap the financial rewards? After all, Miss Mim has never actually managed it. She's leased it out to me, and other ranchers who needed extra land to run their herd." Trevor wouldn't have a problem with Rebecca living "next door" if she continued the lease.

Luke tapped his fingers on his desk. "If the risky financial dealings she's concocted with that San Angelo bank go through—and I have to tell you, right now it looks as if they will—Rebecca plans to breed alpacas."

"Alpacas!" Trevor echoed, gripping the arms of the chair. "She plans to raise alpacas in the middle of cattle country?"

"That's what she says unless someone can convince her otherwise. Which is why—" Luke leaned across his desk and looked Trevor straight in the eye "—since you're going to be living right next door to her, I've summoned you."

REBECCA CARRIGAN was just turning the corner onto the street where her parents lived when she saw Trevor McCabe driving away.

"I don't believe it," she muttered to herself as she squinted against the brilliant April sun. She had warned her father not to try and run her social life—or lack thereof—the previous evening, or interfere in her new career. Obviously, he hadn't listened.

Which left her two choices. Ignore what she had just witnessed, wait patiently for Trevor McCabe to make his move and then shut him down.

Or give chase and set him straight.

Always one to take charge when opportunity presented itself, she drove past the big turn-of-the-century Cape Cod she, her two sisters and brother had grown up in, and followed the dark green, extended cab pickup truck through the center of town to the feed store.

Trevor McCabe parked his vehicle in front of the store, and before she could do the same, disappeared inside.

No matter, Rebecca decided, sliding her small yellow pickup truck into the last slot. She'd just follow him in and ask him to step out.

Keys in hand, leather carryall slung over her shoulder, she marched through the doors of the cavernous warehouse.

It was as busy as usual. Stacked sacks of feed took up the majority of space. The rest was occupied by shelves containing various home-veterinary supplies.

Half a dozen ranchers and hired hands stood at the cash register. Another five or six strolled the aisles, mulling over choices. In the middle of the action stood Trevor McCabe.

As always, Rebecca found the sight of the thirty-year-old rancher a little intimidating. It wasn't just that he was tall—he had to be six foot four—and buff in the way that men were who made their living through physical endeavor. It was the tough-but-smart aura he exuded, the cynical I-dare-you-to-try-and-put-something-over-on-me gleam in his hazel eyes. He'd had the same confidence back in high school, and it had only grown more daunting since. Not that she was going to let that stop her. Rebecca stepped right in front of him and tapped the toe of her boot on the cement floor. "Could I have a word with you?"

Trevor tipped the brim of his stone-colored hat away from his forehead and looked her up and down.

"Sure." He started to take her elbow.

Rebecca backed away. Suddenly, the thought of having a private conversation with this very grown-up version of Trevor McCabe seemed risky as all get out.

"Actually, I'd rather talk here," Rebecca said.

Trevor's lips compressed. "I don't discuss my private business in public."

No surprise there, given the fact that he probably didn't want everyone in town to know her father had just tried to convince him to make a play for her.

"Well, that's too bad because here and now is the only way we're ever going to converse." All Rebecca wanted to do was set the record straight. Let him know she was definitely not interested in him—romantically or any other way, no matter how ruggedly appealing he had grown up to be.

Their eyes met and held. Electricity sparked between them with all the unpredictability and danger of a downed power line. Rebecca caught her breath, deliberately held it. And prayed and hoped she would get what she wanted from him—a promise he would never meddle in her life, at her father's behest, or for any other reason. Independence mattered to Rebecca. She wanted Trevor—as well as everyone else in town—to respect and believe in her the way her family never had.

For a second, Trevor seemed tempted to hear her out but something—maybe it was the eyes of all the men in the feed store—had him doing otherwise.

"I don't think so." Trevor turned away.

Gosh darn it. What had her father said to him?

Unwilling to give up on this quest, Rebecca stepped closer. When he refused to acknowledge her, she tapped his arm. "I mean it, Trevor McCabe. You and I really need to talk."

His bicep flexing enough to get her to immediately drop her hand, he swung toward her once again. He spoke, carefully enunciating each and every word. "As I said, I don't think here and now is a good idea. I'd be glad to meet you later, however."

Rebecca just bet he would.

The sexual heat in his eyes said he wouldn't waste any time putting the moves on her.

She curled her fingers into a fist, to stop their tingling.

Noting he wasn't going to budge on this, and that everyone in the building was definitely staring at the two of them, she felt her temper getting the better of her, and snapped, "Fine, have it your way. I'll do all the talking."

Rebecca pointed a trigger finger at the center of his chest. "And you, cowboy, can listen."

His brow arched. All conversation in the feed store had died.

Trevor had just dared her to go on.

Feeling the temperature between them rise, Rebecca propped both her hands on her hips. Perspiration gathered at her temples, on the back of her neck, in the hollow between her breasts. "I don't care what my father said to you." She paused to let the emphatic words hang in the air. "I am not—I repeat *not*—going to date you."

He stepped in closer. Amusement glimmered in his eyes. "Is that so?"

Feeling as if she had picked the wrong man to humiliate, even if it had been by his choice, not hers, Rebecca angled her chin higher. "You can bet your cattle ranch, it is."

Trevor rocked back on his heels, ran the flat of his palm beneath his jaw. "Well, that's interesting."

His rumbling drawl sent shivers over her skin. "Why?"

"Because I hadn't planned to ask."

Deep male chuckles surrounded them.

To her dismay, Rebecca felt her cheeks turn a self-conscious pink. "Then why did you even go and see my dad," she asked, "if you weren't willing to be part of his plan to get all of his daughters married off?"

A plan that Luke had told her started with her, since she was the daughter currently in so much "trouble." Why did her father have a problem with her running a ranch anyway?

"If you want to know why I was talking to your dad this morning, ask him," Trevor said.

"I'm asking you!"

Resentment sparked in Trevor's eyes. He hooked his thumbs through his belt loops and rocked forward on his toes. "Well that's too bad," he said, lowering his handsome face to hers, until they were nose to nose, "because what was said was strictly between me and your father."

Rebecca rocked forward on her toes, too. "But it was about me. Wasn't it?"

To her mounting aggravation, Trevor said nothing.

A discreet cough made them both turn their heads.

Rebecca caught sight of a well-dressed thirty-something cowboy she didn't recognize, lingering in the doorway of the warehouse, listening and watching all that was going on. Everyone else was looking at him, too, in the same way, which meant he was not known to people in these parts. The handsome blond-haired hunk lifted a hand in greeting to one and all and headed in their direction.

The stranger smiled pleasantly. "If it were me, I'd tell you everything you needed and wanted to know, and then some." He swept off his hat and waved it at the crowd. "Vince Owen," he introduced himself to one and all. "Trevor and I went to college together." Vince clapped a hand on Trevor's shoulder, grabbed his hand and shook it heartily. "Good to see you, buddy."

Trevor nodded, the expression in his eyes unreadable. "Vince."

Vince Owen turned to Rebecca. Charm radiated from him like light from the sun, as his gaze fastened on her face. "And you're…?"

Rebecca smiled, switched her keys to her left hand, and stuck out her right palm. "Rebecca Carrigan."

Vince clasped it warmly. "Good to meet you, darlin'. If you need anything, I'm at your service. I just closed on a ranch in the area—The Circle Y. You heard of it?"

Aware that Trevor had gone stone-still with something akin to shock, Rebecca paused. Ignoring the man who had given her so much grief in so little time—what did she care what Trevor McCabe's reaction to the news was anyway—she asked Vince, "It's right next to The Primrose, isn't it?"

He nodded. "And one ranch away from Trevor's Wind Creek Ranch, although I could be his next-door neighbor if I can snap up The Primrose, too."

"I doubt that will happen," Rebecca said politely, not sure she should say more until the papers were actually signed by her and Miss Mim.

"I agree with Rebecca." Trevor gave Vince Owen a long, steady look. "Last I heard, The Primrose wasn't for sale."

Which showed just how much Trevor knew, Rebecca thought, a tad guiltily. Miss Mim had told her Trevor'd had his eyes on her place, too, for quite some time now. But that was neither here nor there.

Deciding she had wasted enough time, she tightened her hand on the thick strap of her shoulder bag and took one last look at Trevor. "I meant what I said. I don't care what bill of goods my father tried to sell you about me needing a man in my life, Trevor McCabe." She ignored the chuckles of all the men gathered around them. "I'm fine as is," she continued stubbornly, holding Trevor's testy gaze with effort. "There won't be any connection—any private talks—between the two of us. And I'm *sorry* if my father misled you otherwise."

Trevor flashed her a grin that was more of a come-on than an expression of mirth.

"You don't look sorry," he remarked.

Knowing this wasn't a conversation that she would ever have the last word in, Rebecca merely rolled her eyes, turned and walked away.

As TREVOR EXPECTED, Rebecca Carrigan had only to leave the warehouse before Vince Owen whistled. "That is one gal who needs a man to tame her."

Trevor had an idea what that would entail in Vince's opinion. Seething, he swung around on the man who had dogged his every step since the first day they'd met on the Texas A&M campus.

Trevor had vowed never to get tangled up in any of Vince Owen's cutthroat antics, no matter how much or how often he was baited. It had been a promise that had been easy to keep—until now. "Don't talk about her that way."

Vince offered the perverse smile Trevor had come to loathe. "If I didn't know better, I'd think you were sweet on her." Vince unclipped his BlackBerry from his belt and checked the screen, before hooking it back on his waist. "Not that it matters." Vince regarded Trevor steadily, his sick need to compete with Trevor as obvious and as powerful as ever. "Rebecca Carrigan is going to be mine before the month is out."

Trevor doubted Rebecca would fall for Vince's practiced lines, no matter how avidly Vince courted her. Although Vince would never show the sleazy side of himself to Rebecca. To Rebecca, Vince would be all Texas charm and helpfulness. Like a chameleon, Vince had a talent for blending in—when he wanted to be inconspicuous. Right now, however, Vince's compulsive competitiveness had exposed his arrogance. Instead of making the friends he ought to be, Vince was making a statement about his own superiority to all the other ranchers in the feed store. A mistake in a place like Laramie, where folks didn't let anyone's head get too big for his or her hat.

"I think Rebecca just might have something to say about that," Trevor said casually, walking over to sign for the special bags of organically grown grain he had ordered for his calves.

Vince followed. He leaned against the sales counter. "Oh, I'll make her happy," Vince stated, loud enough for everyone to hear. He paused to let his words sink in. "And before I'm done, I'll bet you I get a ring on her finger, too." Vince turned to the other ranchers gathered around. He removed his wallet from his back pocket, withdrew two crisp one-hundred-dollar bills. "Any takers?"

It was all Trevor could do to hang on to his temper. "We don't make bets on the women around here," Trevor said.

Vince looked around, obviously disappointed no one else was reaching for their money.

With a slimy smile, Vince slid his wallet back in his pocket. "That's too bad for me—although it's probably smart on you all's part, because I'm going to win this wager." Vince tipped his hat, looked every man there in the eye and sauntered out.

"We don't need that element around here," Nevada Fontaine, the feed store owner, grumbled in Vince's wake.

No kidding, Trevor thought.

"How'd you get to be associated with him anyway?" The farm equipment salesman, Parker Arnett, asked.

"We were both in the Aggie cattle management program at the same time." As much as Trevor had tried, there had been no avoiding Vince Owen.

Vince had set his sights on Trevor early on, and competed viciously with him ever since.

"You don't seem to be friends," fellow rancher, and esteemed head of the local rancher's association, Dave Sabado, remarked.

Nor would they ever be, Trevor thought, as everyone looked at him. Trevor knew this was his opportunity to tell everyone the whole sorry story. How ugly things had gotten before he landed the top honors of his program at A&M, how he'd lost the affection and respect of the only woman he had ever been serious about in his life, how he had figured once he graduated he could say good riddance to the fellow-ranching student who had made him a target of the unhealthiest competition Trevor had ever seen, only to find out the hard way that Vince Owen's obsession with besting Trevor was never going to end.

Unfortunately, that meant he'd be trashing another man's reputation in public and Trevor made it a policy never to do that. So he figured it best he keep his own considerable resentment to himself. The men here were smart enough not to fall prey to men of Vince Owen's ilk, anyway. "Vince has a history of buying and selling increasingly bigger ranches. No doubt his purchase of the Circle Y Ranch is just a temporary thing. He'll make some improvements, stay just long enough to sell it for a profit, and move on."

"And meantime?" Nevada Fontaine asked, signaling some of his help over to begin loading the feed Trevor had just purchased into his pickup truck.

"I plan to do my best to steer clear of him," Trevor said, with a shrug.

"What about Rebecca Carrigan?" Nevada asked.

"I'll keep her away from him," Trevor said. No way was Vince Owen hurting Rebecca the way he had hurt Jasmine.

"If she hears about the bet Vince Owen just tried to make…" Parker Arnett didn't need to finish the thought.

"She won't, as long as none of us tell her about it." Trevor looked each and every one of the men who had witnessed the attempted wager, in the eye. "Agreed?"

Slowly, the others nodded.

"Good." Trevor breathed a sigh of relief. "'Cause there's no use hurting Rebecca's feelings." And no use in putting her in the middle of the continuing clash between him and Vince Owen. She'd have enough to deal with when she found out the ranch she wanted to buy was not for sale after all.

Chapter Two

"What do you mean you sold the ranch to Rebecca Carrigan?" Trevor McCabe said, an hour later. He stood in the living room of the Primrose Ranch house, watching Miss Mim pack up the last of her cherished travel guides and books. The community librarian and veteran traveler was like a second mother to all the kids in Laramie, maybe because she'd never married or had children of her own. Trevor had grown up knowing he could confide in her. "You and I had an understanding."

Miss Mim handed him the dispenser of packing tape. As always, she was dressed in an outrageously colorful outfit that clashed with her flame-red hair. Moving more like a twenty-year-old than the sixty-eight-year-old woman she was, she patted him on the arm, then pointed to the box. "I think the 'understanding' was more on your part, dear, than mine."

Trevor bent to line up the cardboard flaps. The tape made a ripping sound as it left the spool. "What do you mean?" he demanded, pressing the adhesive on the box with the flat of his palm.

Miss Mim unfolded the last cardboard moving carton and turned it over so Trevor could tape up the bottom of the box. She smiled at him fondly as he assisted her. "You have no problem making up your mind. And you always tell people what you want."

"You just don't listen," Rebecca Carrigan said, coming into the room.

Trevor hadn't known Rebecca was on the premises. It figured she would be. He turned to square off with her for the second time that day, felt his senses kick into hihgh gear. It wasn't just that she was beautiful. It was the way she moved—with a kind of sexy, inherent grace. The way her lips curled softly and her chin tilted stubbornly. The slender curves hidden beneath the pink cotton shirt and faded jeans—along with her straight and silky honey blond hair, challenging golden brown eyes and delicate features—made it impossible for him to look away. Even though it was abundantly clear she wished he would disappear. "How would you know whether I pay attention or not?" he asked.

Rebecca shrugged in mute superiority and gestured at their surroundings. She took the deed out of her pocket and waved it in front of him like a matador waving a cape in front of a bull. "Case in point, cowboy, since this place is now mine, not yours."

Trevor felt like pawing the ground. Maybe because he had never been so ticked off, disappointed, and yes—humiliated. Figuring he would deal with Rebecca Carrigan later, he turned back to Miss Mim. "I told you I would buy The Primrose from you, at whatever price you deemed fair."

Miss Mim straightened and stated patiently, "And I said I would keep that in mind."

Trevor took over the job of fitting the last of her books into the carton. "And then sold it to Rebecca without giving me a chance to even make a bid?"

Miss Mim stood back, to watch Rebecca load the filled boxes onto a moving dolly. "She needs the land, dear. You already have a ranch."

Frowning—it went against his grain to let a woman lift things when he was there and could do it for her—Trevor brushed Rebecca aside. "A ranch that you know I would like to expand."

Miss Mim led the way to the front door and held it while Trevor pushed the dolly through. "Perhaps you can make the same arrangement with her that you've had with me, regarding grazing rights."

Rebecca followed them to Miss Mim's aging Cadillac. She fit the suitcases into the backseat, while Trevor set the cartons in the already-crammed trunk. Rebecca closed the door. Trevor shut the trunk. The warm April air was scented with primroses and the earthier smells of new grass, sunshine and grazing cattle. Despite this being one of his busiest times of year on the ranch, it was also the most pleasurable. Well, not this year.

Rebecca flashed him another provoking smile.

"Not going to happen, Miss Mim," Rebecca said with a defiant toss of her head. "In fact," her eyes claimed and held his, "I need Trevor to move his herd off my land as soon as possible. Hopefully, today."

Trevor did a double take. He'd expected trouble from Rebecca Carrigan, but not this kind. "You can't be serious."

Rebecca's smile faded. "Oh, but I am."

Miss Mim chuckled and got her car keys out of her handbag. "You two are going to get along splendidly!"

Like hell they were, Trevor thought.

"How soon can I expect you to move your cattle?" Rebecca asked, the moment Miss Mim had driven off.

Trevor turned back to Rebecca, a stunned expression on his face. "Where is she going?"

Trying hard not to think what it was going to be like having this sexy know-it-all for a neighbor, Rebecca replied, "Laramie Gardens Home For Seniors. She's the new social director."

"She's supposed to be retired."

"Yes, I know." Rebecca turned her glance to the three pastures located at the rear of the property. The square plots were each ten acres, and surrounded by an aging brown split rail fence. A ten-acre hay field sat behind that. The house, barn and detached garage were situated at the front of the property, on the ten acres nearest the road. The Circle Y and Trevor's Wind Creek butted up on either side of her. She was now living smack-dab in the middle of two extremely ambitious men, both of whom coincidentally wanted her property for their own. Wasn't this going to be fun?

"So why is Miss Mim taking another job?"

Rebecca reluctantly directed her attention back to her "visitor." What was it about the McCabe men that made them think they had to know everything? "Apparently, Miss Mim has done all the traveling she wants now, and sitting around all day isn't agreeing with her. A lot of her friends already live at the seniors' home."

Trevor folded his arms in front of him. He reminded her of a general surveying his troops. "When is she going to move the rest of her stuff?"

"They've given her a furnished apartment, as part of the job. So all she's taking is her clothing and personal affects. The rest she sold to me as part of the deal."

"I want to buy the ranch from you."

Rebecca blinked. "What?"

"Add ten percent to whatever you paid her for it, and I'll pay it to you."

"Only ten percent?" she mocked. "Vince Owen has already been here and offered an additional fifteen."

"You're kidding."

Rebecca let her too-sweet smile fade. "Do I look like I'm kidding, cowboy?"

The corners of his mouth took on a downward slant. "What did you say?" he demanded.

"The same thing I'm telling you," Rebecca shot back. "No."

She wasn't surprised to see that Trevor looked relieved about that. Which led her to the next item on her agenda. "Back to the cattle. I need you to move 'em as soon as possible. And you'll need to make sure you clean up after them, or in other words, remove all the dung. I want those pastures clean as can be when I put my alpacas out there."

"You're planning to use all three?"

Rebecca nodded. "One for the females, one for the herd-sires and another for the nursing crias and their mothers."

"How big a herd are you starting with?"

"Ten. But I expect to expand rapidly." Rebecca gave him a moment to absorb all that. "So, can I expect this will be done today?"

Trevor begrudgingly relented. "I'll have to get some temporary help. I don't employ anyone else on a regular basis." He paused. "That may take a few days to arrange."

She glanced out at the far pasture, where he had some thirty steers grazing. "Or you could start right now," she suggested with a discreet lift of her brow, "doing it yourself." Seriously, how long could it take?

His hazel eyes darkened. "I can see living next door to you is going to be a challenge."

She slapped him on the back, rancher-style. Strode off, calling over her shoulder, "Cowboy, you don't know the half of it."

AN HOUR AND TWO PHONE CALLS later, Trevor met up with Tyler and Teddy at his horse barn. He'd known he could count on his triplet brothers to drop everything and help him out of this predicament, just as he had assisted them on numerous occasions, emergency and otherwise. The three of them were more than brothers and confidants; they were best friends. Their two much younger brothers, Kurt and Kyle, were growing up the same way.

"That totally sucks," Teddy said, after Trevor had finished filling them in on everything that happened that day.

The ever-practical Tyler shrugged. "Should have had a contract with Miss Mim."

Trevor brought out the lassos and handed one to each brother. "We've never had a contract on any of our arrangements. I just told Miss Mim what I wanted to do. She always said okay. When she needed something, she let me know, and I took care of it for her. I knew she'd want to sell the land eventually—she'd been thinking about moving into town for some time. I just figured when the time came she'd sell it to me."

Tyler carefully cinched his saddle. "When it comes to women, I've learned the hard way, never assume anything."

Trevor squinted, grinned. "You talking about women in general or Susan Carrigan in particular?"

Teddy swung himself up into the saddle. "You ought to just go ahead and admit it, Ty. There's never going to be another woman for you but Susan."

Tyler guided his horse between Trevor's and Teddy's. "Susan and I don't get along."

"Sometimes you do." Trevor winked, thinking how smugly content his veterinarian-brother could be when his relationship with Rebecca's older sister, Susan happened to be humming along. And how miserable Ty was at times—like now—when it was "off."

"The two of you should just quit all the drama and get hitched," Teddy agreed, as they rode toward the pasture.

"You should talk," Tyler grumbled, with a sharp look at Teddy. "Since you've never had eyes for anyone but Amy Carrigan."

"Amy's my friend," Teddy muttered.

Trevor stopped at the pasture gate and dismounted to open it. "I don't see you dating anyone else—at least not for long."

Teddy turned his glance toward the cattle they were going to have to move. "That's because I've been busy getting my horse-breeding operation up and running."

Trevor knew how hard he'd worked. The Silverado was fast becoming known in Texas as the place to get quality, affordable quarter horses. "Now if you could only train a woman as well as you school a horse," Tyler teased Teddy.

Trevor frowned, his thoughts jumping back to the problem that had brought them all together on such short notice. "I could sure use a few tips on how to handle Rebecca Carrigan," he said, closing the pasture gate, before taking the reins once again.

"Burr under your saddle, huh?" Teddy replied.

Worse, Trevor felt responsible for protecting her, since it had been Trevor's lively public exchange with Rebecca at the feed store that had brought her feisty presence to Vince Owen's attention.

Rebecca didn't know about the bet the conniving jerk

had tried—and failed—to make about her that morning. If Trevor had his way, she never would. What worried him was the thought that Vince was going to be living—at least part of the time—on The Circle Y Ranch, on the other side of Rebecca. If Vince were true to form, he'd soon be using his proximity to Rebecca every which way but Sunday in order to get to Trevor.

Vince's efforts to annoy, distract and otherwise make miserable were already working. Trevor's mind was on anything but the business he was supposed to be running on the Wind Creek cattle ranch.

Instead, he kept waiting for Vince to start up the ugly cutthroat competition again, via Rebecca, as a way of punishing Trevor for succeeding academically, professionally, romantically, where Vince had not. Knowing Vince, he'd probably go after the financial success of The Primrose Ranch and the Wind Creek cattle ranch before he was finished, too.

Unfortunately, the only way Trevor would be able to protect Rebecca and her newly acquired property was by befriending her first, a task not made easy by the fact that she thought, erroneously—her parents actually wanted the two of them to start dating. And was, of course, absolutely opposed to having anything at all to do with him. Now or in the future….

Aware his brothers were waiting on Trevor's response to his pretty new neighbor, he frowned and said, "You're right about that much. Ms. Rebecca Carrigan is going to be one royal pain."

As a kid she'd had a reputation for never listening to anyone in a position of authority. From what he could tell so far, that had not changed.

Tyler slowed his mount's pace as they reached the

opposite side of the Wind Creek pasture and the gate that separated it from the Primrose Ranch pasture, where alpacas would soon be grazing. "Not to worry about it, bro."

Teddy winked and continued the ribbing, "If any man can handle her—"

And that was a mighty big if, Trevor thought grimly.

"—you can," Tyler said.

"REBECCA, DEAR, I've already thought of at least half-a-dozen things I forgot to get from the house," Miss Mim said.

"No problem, Miss Mim. I'll get them for you." Rebecca picked up the chalk from the tray on the message board in the kitchen. "Just tell me what they are and I'll make a list."

"My favorite vase, on the dining room table."

"Check."

Miss Mim rambled off four more items while Rebecca wrote. "And I was going to ask you for my binoculars on the hook by the back door, but I've changed my mind. I thought you might want to use those to keep an eye on your new neighbors."

Rebecca rolled her eyes, even as she took the binoculars and looped them around her neck. "Very funny, Miss Mim."

"I'm serious, Rebecca. Those two men are going to be vying for your hand in marriage in no time. Just don't make my mistake and say no to romance, like I did. When you get to be my age, you'll find you regret it."

Rebecca knew that was true.

Although Miss Mim had been "family" to every parent and child who'd come through the Laramie Public Library, lately she'd been regretting the road not taken. Fortunately, Rebecca was saved having to respond by muffled voices on the other end of the connection.

"Dear?" Miss Mim was back. "The canasta game is about to start. I'll phone you later."

"When would you like me to bring the items by?"

"Two days from now—say around seven in the evening? I'm going to be busy prior to that."

"No problem."

Rebecca hung up the phone.

She walked around the house, gathering the requested items and slipping them into a cardboard box, all the while admiring her new home. It was hard to believe fifty acres of prime Texas acreage, never mind the pretty white stone ranch house with the rose-colored shutters and dark gray roof, was all hers now.

Miss Mim had inherited the seventy-five-year-old homestead from her parents and had taken loving care of it during the forty-two years she had resided there. Handsome dark pine floors shone beneath the delicate antique furniture. Upstairs, there were three bedrooms and a large old-fashioned bath with a claw-foot tub and pedestal sink. In the master bedroom there was an old-fashioned four-poster, matching wardrobe, chest of drawers and vanity. The second bedroom was a sewing room and the third, a study.

Downstairs, a formal parlor and dining room, suitable for entertaining, encompassed the front of the house. In the rear was a big kitchen, complete with trestle table and six Windsor chairs, fireplace and white stone hearth. Black marble countertops gleamed next to state-of-the-art stainless steel appliances and antique white cabinets. The combination laundry room and spacious food pantry were tucked behind panel doors.

Across the front of the house was a wide front porch. Instead of a patio or deck out back, there were steps down to the grass, and a flagstone path that led to a white stone gazebo, surrounded by primroses.

Beyond that was a big red barn and a good distance away from that, a white stone detached garage. Rebecca intended to park in the lane in front of the house and convert the garage into the official farm office, where ranch business would be done.

Figuring she should go down and take another look at the interior of the barn to see what if anything needed to be done before she brought animals onto the ranch, Rebecca headed out the back door.

She had just passed the gazebo when she saw three men on horseback cantering across Trevor McCabe's land, and onto hers.

Wondering whom he'd gotten to help him move cattle on such short notice, Rebecca picked up the binoculars from around her neck and stepped back into the gazebo.

It took a little focusing—and a minute for her to get a vantage point that avoided the stands of cedar and live oak trees between her and them—to get a good view of what was going on out on her land.

Rebecca smiled, identifying Trevor and his two oldest brothers.

When Trevor, Tyler and Teddy were younger, everyone had trouble telling the McCabe triplets apart. These days, it was no problem, despite the fact they all dressed in typical cowboy garb of hat, jeans, boots and cotton shirts. Although they all had broad shoulders, slim hips and fit, muscular physiques, their appearances differed. Trevor's thick reddish-brown hair was clipped so short it was barely visible beneath the brim of his hat. Tyler's hair was on the long side and brushed his collar. Teddy's hair was midway between the two and tended to kink up on the ends. Their differing personalities set them apart, as well. Trevor had a commanding air about him Rebecca found hard to ignore. Tyler was more aloof and had a gentle, assessing manner. Teddy exuded friendliness and a willingness to go the extra mile to help out a friend.

Hearing the phone ring, Rebecca went back inside. It turned out there was a problem with one of her alpacas. But at least she knew where help could be found. Assuming, of course, Rebecca thought as she picked up the binoculars and headed back to the gazebo, that Trevor and his two brothers hadn't left yet.

To Rebecca's relief she could easily make out Tyler and Teddy on horseback, moving the herd. Trevor McCabe, however, was nowhere in sight. Unless, Rebecca thought, getting down on one knee, he and his horse had disappeared behind that distant grove of trees....

Frustrated because she still couldn't locate Trevor, Rebecca adjusted the lens to the highest magnification.

A chuckle to her immediate right had her turning swiftly in alarm. Binoculars still resting on the bridge of her nose, she found herself close up and personal to a denim-clad zipper. Rebecca gasped and dropped the lens.

Smug amusement in his eyes, Trevor McCabe sauntered forward. "Find anything you like?" he drawled.

"YOU HAD NO RIGHT to sneak up on me that way!" Rebecca scrambled to her feet, glad the two of them weren't as close as her initial view had seemed to indicate.

Trevor tipped the brim of his hat back. "Isn't that a little like the Peeping Tom calling the spy nosy?"

She told herself it was the heat of the spring day making her sweat. "I am not a Peeping Tom!"

"Well, you're not a spy, either." He abruptly changed

from flirting cowboy to more sober rancher. "Which leads us to the question of why you're using binoculars on me and my brothers."

Rebecca ignored the heat of awareness rising up between them and forced herself to return his level gaze. "I need to talk to you about borrowing your livestock trailer tomorrow morning. I just got a call from the breeder. I have to pick up one of my alpacas tomorrow morning."

He lifted a brow. "Just one?"

"Blue Mist is pregnant. The vet in San Angelo doesn't want her traveling past tomorrow. He thinks moving her too close to her due date could jeopardize the cria—the baby."

"Why not pick up the rest of the herd while you're there, then?"

Rebecca inhaled the scent of man and sun and horse. "I'm not ready for them yet. But I can go ahead and pick up Blue Mist."

"Sure you want to do that?" he asked. "Alpacas are pack animals."

Now he was sounding just like the saleswoman she had just gotten off the phone with. Fortunately, Rebecca knew a hard sell when she heard one.

"That can wait until early next week." Rebecca knew she would have her hands full just managing one alpaca on her own. That went double for a pregnant alpaca. Besides, she wanted to make sure Blue Mist was completely comfortable and settled in before she brought in the other nine animals she'd bought. And then there was the matter of the balance due when she took possession of the animals. The temporary operating loan she had negotiated for start-up of the ranch was barely adequate. And she'd used most of her own savings on the down payment and mortgage fees for the ranch. She still had her credit card, but she didn't want to max out on that unless she absolutely had to. The remaining balance was her only safety net. And she still had so much to do before the Open House in less than two weeks.

"So can I borrow your livestock trailer?" Rebecca continued.

Trevor frowned. "I'd have to charge you for it."

Despite her tricky finances, Rebecca wouldn't have it any other way, since she absolutely did not want to be beholden to him. "I'd expect to pay a reasonable rent," she said hoping it wouldn't be too much.

"My price is one home-cooked meal."

Rebecca had been prepared to dicker over dollars. She opened her eyes wide, sure she couldn't possibly have heard right. "What?"

Trevor lifted his hands. "That's the arrangement I had with Miss Mim. Whenever I did a favor for her, helped her prune trees, or clean the shutters or whatever, she repaid me with a home-cooked meal and that is what I want from you, too."

Rebecca bit her lip as she tried to figure a clever way out of this that would not shut down all the help she was bound to need from him—in the short haul anyway. "Miss Mim is a fabulous cook." *So was she.* Trevor McCabe did not need to know that, however, lest he make a regular practice of demanding her culinary skills. She'd much rather exchange money or any other less personal commodity—like mucking out the pasture—with him.

"How well I know that," Trevor recollected. He ran the flat of his palm across his jaw. "That's what made working for her such a treat."

Rebecca could see he'd made up his mind about what he wanted from her. "I would prefer to pay cash."

"I don't take money from women. Or in other words—" he paused long enough to give his words an aggravating connotation "—my favors are not for sale."

Refusing to let him ruffle her, Rebecca tilted her head to one side. "And mine are?"

"I don't know," he replied. He leaned toward her and whispered conspiratorially, "Are they?"

Rebecca bit down on an oath. "Stop trying to get under my skin."

"Why," he countered, "when it's so much fun?"

For the second time in ten minutes, Rebecca found herself fighting a self-conscious blush. "Is there anything else you'd be willing to barter?" she asked.

He took a moment to consider.

Sexual chemistry arced between them, hotter than ever.

She held up her hand in halting fashion. "Never mind." Pulse racing, she shook her head in silent regret, mumbling just beneath her breath, "Forget I asked that." She forced herself to meet and hold his decidedly mischievous gaze. "When do you want to get your dinner?" she asked.

Her irritated tone brought a provoking smile to his lips. "You make it sound like I'd be picking up a meal through a drive-through window."

"Pretty close, although to be generous, I will be delivering it to you." That way she could do at least that much of it on her terms.

He stepped closer, purposefully invading her space. "I don't think you get what I'm saying to you. When I say I want a home-cooked meal from you in return for borrowing my trailer, I'm talking about the two of us getting to know each other and sitting down to break bread together."

Just why he was suddenly so determined they be chums, she didn't know. But she didn't trust his newfound interest in her any more than she trusted whatever it was he had secretly been discussing with her father this morning.

Taking her time, she cocked her head and played with the ends of the braid falling over her shoulder.

Channeling Scarlett O'Hara—or maybe it was Calamity Jane—she batted her eyelashes at him coquettishly, asked sweetly, "I can't just put the food on the table and run?"

He stood, legs braced apart, muscular arms folded in front of him. "You only wish I were that easy to deal with."

No kidding.

He looked her up and down with lazy male confidence. "If you want my help, you have to sit down with me and regale me with your charming company every bit as graciously as Miss Mim always did. And in turn—" his gaze slid past the delicate hollow of her throat, past her lips, to her eyes "—I'll regale you with mine."

"Geez." Rebecca made a great show of blowing out an exasperated breath. "You drive a hard bargain."

He inclined his head in arrogant agreement. "Always."

It was time to get back to business. "I'll need the trailer at seven tomorrow morning," she said.

Trevor tipped the brim of his hat at her. "I'll be here, ready to go."

"I didn't mean you had to come with me!"

"That's the only way you can have use of the livestock hauler since I'm the only one insured to use it." Again, he appeared about as flexible as a thousand pound steer.

She took a deep steadying breath, tore her eyes from the masculine contours of his chest. "It's going to take half a day or more to do all the business with the breeder, talk to their vet, load up Blue Mist and get back here."

He shrugged his broad shoulders. "Then you better fortify me tonight with your culinary skills."

Once again, Rebecca found herself stunned by Trevor McCabe's temerity. "You expect dinner here tonight?" She'd been hoping to put it off at least a couple of days.

He declared victory with a sexy wink. "We'll just call it payment in advance."

Chapter Three

"Mom and Dad wanted to be here, too, but they both have to work evening hours at the hospital," Amy Carrigan told Rebecca an hour later.

Her three siblings had stopped in to congratulate her. They'd also brought housewarming gifts. Sunscreen and lip balm from Susie, who worked outdoors as a landscape architect and garden center owner and knew the importance of protecting skin. An indoor herb garden from Amy, who owned her own ranch and plant-growing business. And a deluxe first aid box from Jeremy, a family physician at Laramie Community Hospital.

"They said they'd be by later in the week," Jeremy continued.

"Right," Rebecca said.

Susie understood the hurt Rebecca felt—maybe because she had encountered resistance, too, when she had decided to eschew lucrative job offers and go into business for herself, right out of college. She and Amy had both been remarkably successful eventually, but there was no denying their first few years out of the gate had been so lean financially that their parents had worried constantly. Susie had taken the brunt of it, since she had been the first to take the leap.

"Just give them time. They'll come around, once they see you making a go of it," Susie encouraged, for once being more supportive than overly protective.

"And that Open House you're planning in two weeks to get your business off the ground will help," Amy added.

Rebecca hoped that was the case. Now that she was actually residing at the ranch, for all of…six hours…she was beginning to feel slightly overwhelmed by everything that had to be done, despite the steps Miss Mim had taken to make the transition easier for her by leaving the pantry, fridge and freezer stocked with fresh food and homemade entrees.

Lucky for her, Miss Mim had loved to cook for others.

"Just be glad you're not in my position," Jeremy lamented, "since everyone at Laramie Community Hospital still thinks of me as Luke and Meg's kid."

It had to be hard, Rebecca figured, taking a position at the same hospital where their physician father was Chief of Family Medicine and their mother an RN who supervised the entire nursing staff.

"You want to trade positions with me?" Rebecca teased. She stood on tiptoe to retrieve a glass casserole dish, then set it on the counter. "I'll be glad to let you cook dinner for Trevor McCabe."

"I still don't get why you agreed to that," Amy said.

"Yeah. Why didn't you just tell him to go jump in Lake Laramie?" Susie sipped the iced tea Rebecca had poured for everyone.

Rebecca shrugged and opened a foil-wrapped single serving packet marked Tex-Mex Chicken Casserole. She dumped the rock-hard concoction into the dish. "I have to borrow a livestock hauler from somebody. He has one that isn't being used tomorrow. He lives right next door to me. He had no problem being neighborly."

Jeremy watched as Rebecca unwrapped another packet. "Maybe I should try his approach. It's certainly a novel way to get a date."

Rebecca regarded her siblings, her brows arched. "This isn't a date."

"Then what is it?" Susie persisted.

Rebecca popped the casserole into the microwave and punched Defrost. "It's an opportunity for me to start setting some boundaries with that handsome cowboy."

Amy tilted her head. "Interesting way to refer to your neighbor to the north."

"Come on," Rebecca huffed. "You all know what I mean."

"The question is, do you?" Jeremy asked.

Rebecca studied the dish in the microwave. "Trevor needs to understand I am no Miss Mim."

Her only brother chuckled. "I think he's got that part down already, giving how fast he's moving in on you."

The microwave dinged. Rebecca grabbed a pot holder and removed the dish. "For the last time, Jeremy, Trevor McCabe is not staking out any kind of claim on me tonight."

"If you say so." Jeremy looked over her shoulder. "And if I were you, I'd use about four of those if you don't want Trevor McCabe to leave hungry. Those are lady-sized portions." Jeremy patted his stomach. "I figure I could put away at least three of them, so he probably could, too."

"Good point." Rebecca went back to the freezer and emerged with two more single-serve packets. "I wouldn't want him to leave hungry."

Susie studied her, ready to jump in, if necessary, and save Rebecca from herself. "That gleam in your eye means trouble," Susie said.

"Does it?" Rebecca asked innocently, wondering when

Susie would finally realize that Rebecca could survive just fine without any sisterly—or parental—help?

Ever the peacemaker, Amy said kindly, "You could always ask us to stay for dinner, too."

Rebecca slid the extra portions on a plate, put them into the microwave and pushed Defrost once again. "If I did that," Rebecca replied, peeved Amy was now starting to meddle a bit, too, "Trevor McCabe would think I was hiding behind you."

"And what's wrong with that?" Susie demanded.

Rebecca reached for the herb garden and broke off sprigs of mint, cilantro, oregano, basil, rosemary, parsley and thyme. She got out a cutting board and began dicing up everything but the cilantro. "I am not afraid to spend time alone with him."

Amy frowned. "You realize you just mixed all those herbs together."

"Indeed, I do." Rebecca took the plate out of the oven, added the contents to the casserole dish, then picked up her spoon, and prepared to get to work. "And soon Trevor McCabe will, too."

THE GUILT STARTED as soon Rebecca opened the door. She hadn't bothered to do more than wash her face and brush her teeth to get ready for her company. Her hair remained in the two loose braids she'd put it in that morning. She was still dressed in a T-shirt, jeans and boots.

Trevor had obviously showered before driving over. He was wearing a clean pair of jeans, a freshly ironed white Western shirt and dress boots. He smelled of soap and cologne. His reddish-brown hair was still damp, parted neatly on one side.

To make her feel even worse, he hadn't shown up

empty-handed. He had a large wicker gift basket jammed with all manner of sauces and condiments, all bearing his mother's company's name—Annie's Homemade—and a plate of homemade ranger cookies.

Behind her, a less-than-appetizing smell filled the air. Rebecca tried not to think how the doctored casserole was going to taste.

To his credit, and her increased annoyance, he didn't react in the slightest to the rather unappetizing aroma scenting the ranch house. "My mom and dad sent you a housewarming gift, welcoming you to the neighborhood."

Rebecca studied the array of labels gratefully. She already knew Annie's barbecue sauce, ketchup, hot sauce, mustards and salad dressings were first-rate. "I didn't realize your mom had expanded into jams and jellies, too," she said. There was everything from boysenberry to apricot fruit spreads, as well as jalapeño jelly and chipolte pepper mayonnaise.

Trevor smiled. "Seems she's always perfecting some new recipe." He set the plate of cookies down on the kitchen table. "Better be careful or she'll have you acting as a taste-tester, too."

Rebecca nodded at the dessert plate. "Your mom make those, too?"

"No." Trevor took off his hat and hung it on a hook near the back door.

Rebecca studied the cookies. Golden-brown, perfect in size and texture. Her mouth watered, just looking at them. "Bakery in town?"

Trevor shook his head.

"Grocery?"

"Does it matter?" He was beginning to look a little annoyed. "I can vouch for 'em. They're good."

Rebecca slid one out from under the cover of plastic wrap. They smelled delicious, too. "I'm just curious." She bit into the confection, and found it rich and buttery and full of crispy rice cereal, oatmeal and coconut.

"I made 'em."

It took all her concentration to swallow. "You?" she sputtered, amazed.

Trevor shrugged. "My brothers and I all know how to cook. Even Kyle and Kurt."

"The younger two," Rebecca said, remembering.

"They're only seventeen and eighteen but they can grill a mean steak, scramble eggs. Throw together a salad. All the basics."

Maybe doctoring the food hadn't been such a good idea. She could have cooked normally and he likely would have been disappointed. Now, well, it was obvious what she had done....

"Anyway, I hope you like oatmeal and coconut...."

Like 'em? She was addicted to both. Even more annoying, it looked as though he was a better cook than she was, if the cookies were any indication.

"Can I help?"

Rebecca shook her head. Gestured for him to have a seat at the trestle table. She'd put herself at one end, him clear at the other. Four places and a vase of primroses stood between them. Aware the lettuce was beginning to wilt over the heavy application of buttermilk ranch dressing she'd layered it with a good half hour before, she set the wooden salad bowl on the table and went to the oven to get the casserole.

"I never knew you wanted to ranch," Trevor remarked.

Rebecca set two steaming plates on the table and sat down opposite him. "That's because I never confided my ambition to anyone but Miss Mim. She used to help me find books at the library."

"But you didn't study agriculture in college."

Deciding to start with her salad, Rebecca twirled a soggy piece of lettuce on her fork. "That's because I couldn't see myself breeding cattle or horses, or heaven forbid, pigs! I can't say chickens appealed to me much, either."

Trevor dug into his first course with an enthusiasm that made her wince. "So instead you took the job with that tour company and headed overseas."

That had been due more to a quarrel with her sister Susie and her father, over their outright betrayal of her in a romantic matter, than anything else. But Rebecca wasn't about to get into that. Especially since her relationship had never really been the same with her sister Susie, or her father, since.

Rebecca shrugged. "I'd always longed for adventure. The job provided that, and more." Plus, since she'd always been working and traveling and hadn't had to pay apartment rent, she'd been able to bank nearly her entire salary.

"I still don't see how you got from there to breeding alpacas." Trevor finished his salad, and took a big bite of Tex-Mex chicken casserole.

It was all Rebecca could do not to gag herself as Trevor swallowed and followed his first bite of the main course with a gentlemanly sip of water.

She continued to play with her salad. "One of the European tours went to an alpaca ranch. I fell in love with the animals almost the moment I saw them, and when I found out how valuable their wool is—it's the finest in the world—I knew I'd found my calling."

"Sounds like you've given this some thought." Trevor

got up and walked over to the gift basket. He came back with a bottle of Annie's Homemade Ketchup, with the familiar blue-and white-gingham label. He sat down and poured a liberal dose over the entrée.

"More than you could ever know," Rebecca replied.

He studied her while he ate. He didn't need sips of water now.

Rebecca on the other hand had all she could do not to gag on the mixture of incompatible herbs that she had added to the casserole.

Which served her right, she figured, for having done such an immature and bratty thing to begin with. She knew better than to treat a guest—even a self-invited one—this way.

"It's okay to be nervous about a new business venture," Trevor said eventually.

Finished with the meager portion she had put on his plate, he helped himself to some more, added ketchup, and—to her complete astonishment—dug right in.

"What makes you think I'm nervous?" Rebecca groused, not about to deal with one more naysayer in her life.

Her parents' worries, combined with her three siblings' unvoiced skepticism, had been more than enough.

Not that anyone had bothered to listen to the entirety of her plan. No, she usually lost them when they heard about the second loan she'd taken against the first, and the balloon payment due two weeks after closing.

Oblivious to the calculated financial risks she was taking, Trevor regarded her with a gentleness she didn't expect.

"You have the same look in your eyes that I had in mine when I closed on Wind Creek."

Rebecca couldn't figure out whether he was being straight with her or not. What he'd said did not sound like the Trevor McCabe she knew. "You. Mr. Big Shot Cattle-man. Were nervous."

"Oh, yeah," Trevor replied. "As was my brother Teddy when he started up The Silverado." Trevor finished his second helping, and went for a third. "It's the same thing everybody feels when they buy their first car or home or pet, or accept a job. That what-have-I-gotten-myself-into-now panic. Buyer's remorse, some call it."

Rebecca added ketchup to her dinner, too, and found the condiment delicious and the casserole beneath just as unpalatable.

She toyed with the food on her plate, suddenly glad he'd brought this up. She needed some encouragement. "When does the panicky feeling pass?" she asked him.

"As soon as you get going." He flashed her a sexy smile. "Which is why it's probably good you're going to pick up the start of your herd tomorrow. Once you get busy caring for your alpacas, you won't have time to think."

Not thinking sounded good.

Rebecca started to relax.

Trevor smiled at her.

Too late, she saw the unexpected had happened...they were becoming more than neighbors...they were becoming friends.

"YOU DIDN'T TELL ME you had a puppy," Trevor remarked a few minutes later as they cleaned up the dishes.

"I don't."

"Then you've got a visitor."

Rebecca followed his glance to the bank of kitchen windows overlooking the backyard. Sure enough, a choco-late-brown Labrador retriever was alternately nosing the ground and trotting briskly toward the house. When he reached the stoop, he let out a sound that was half bark, half whine. "Oh my goodness. He barely looks old enough to be away from his mama."

Trevor caught the puppy before he could dart past Rebecca, into the house. He lifted the squirming Labrador to chest level. "It's a she. And I'd guess, from the size of her, that she's about nine, ten weeks old, which means she probably just left her mama and the rest of her litter."

Interesting. "Does she have tags?"

"Nope." Trevor looked. "Just a collar."

She sure didn't look scared or lost. "Anyone around here have puppies recently?" Rebecca asked.

"Not that I'm aware. And this is a purebred, which makes her worth a pretty penny."

"You got that right," a male voice concurred.

Rebecca and Trevor turned.

Vince Owen strode toward them.

"This is Coco. I just got her today. I was bringing her over to meet you and she got ahead of me. Trevor." Vince nodded.

Trevor nodded back, looking, Rebecca noted, no more pleased to see the Circle Y's new owner than he had earlier in the day.

"Rebecca." Vince leaned forward, and before Rebecca could stop him, kissed her cheek in Southern-style greeting.

Rebecca didn't know why she was annoyed. Having grown up in Texas, she had received many a casual peck on the cheek as hello over the years. None had ever bothered her. This one rankled. The way he subtly moved in between her and Trevor seemed meant to annoy his old college classmate. She didn't like being used as a pawn in anyone's game.

Trevor handed Coco to her new owner with a cynical look.

"I hope I'm not interrupting something," Vince said.

Rebecca sensed Vince wanted an explanation for Trevor's presence and perhaps an invitation to hang out for a while, too. She was just as inclined not to give it. Intuition told her that despite his smooth manner and cordial appearance, the handsome, blond Vince Owen was nothing but trouble.

Trevor looked at Rebecca, checking, she figured, to see if she needed him to stay. Knowing it would be easier to get rid of Vince and back to what she needed to be doing in preparation for the morning, Rebecca let Trevor know it wasn't necessary.

To her relief, Trevor took the hint, albeit with barely concealed reluctance.

Trevor slipped back inside the house to get his hat. "I've got an early day tomorrow. I better get going. Vince." Trevor dipped his head in polite acknowledgment.

Vince nodded back. He waited until Trevor climbed into his pickup truck and drove away, then turned back to Rebecca.

"Like to hold her?" Without waiting for a reply, Vince thrust the puppy into her arms.

The chocolate-brown pup looked up at Rebecca with dark liquid eyes. As always, when confronted with puppies, Rebecca felt her heart melt a little. They were just so sweet, vulnerable, eager to please...

And given the packet of investment information she had yet to pull together for future customers of the Primrose alpaca operation, she really did not have time for this.

"My cattle won't be delivered for a few days. I've got two hired hands sitting idle. Should you need anything, be sure and let me know. I could send my cowboys over to help," Vince said.

"That's a very generous offer," Rebecca replied. But not, she figured, without strings. What kind, she wasn't sure she wanted to know.

"What are neighbors for?"

Rebecca petted Coco's head. She was a beautiful dog. Rebecca smiled as Coco licked her forearm with her velvety rough tongue. Too bad her new owner didn't seem half as smitten with the puppy as Rebecca was.

"You don't work the cattle yourself?" Rebecca asked.

Vince Owen shook his head. "I've got two other properties around the state. Have to ride herd on all of them." He withdrew a business card from his wallet, handed it to her. "Here are all my numbers. Should you need anything at all, just call. Meantime, as long as you and I are getting acquainted—" he paused to flash her a salesperson's winning smile "—I've got two tickets to the Laramie County Rancher's Association Spring Fling."

Rebecca already knew about the black-tie dinner-dance at the community center on Friday evening. "Thank you for the invitation, Vince, but I'm already planning to attend."

"With McCabe," Vince guessed, a hint of unpleasantness coming into his eyes.

Rebecca gave him the "attitude" she reserved for too-persistent men. "Alone," she corrected.

Relaxing, Vince gestured affably. "If we went together, you could introduce me around."

Reluctantly, Rebecca handed his puppy back to him. She didn't want anything or anyone interfering with her efforts to network and promote her new business. Vince could easily do just that, as could Trevor McCabe. "Laramie is a very friendly place. You won't have any trouble meeting people on your own."

Vince took her rejection with a graceful shrug. "Another time, then."

Not, Rebecca thought, if I can help it.

The tension between Vince and Trevor aside, there was something about Vince Owen she just didn't trust.

"SO WHAT'S THE STORY between you and Vince?" Rebecca asked Trevor the next afternoon, after they had returned. Her first stock purchase, the cornerstone of her alpaca breeding operation, Blue Mist, had weathered the trip back well, and was now grazing in the shade.

Trevor's hands tightened on the pasture gate. Up until now, he hadn't asked her anything about her other visitor from the night before, but she had felt his curiosity as surely as her own. "Why?" Trevor tipped the brim of his hat away from his face. "What did he say?"

"Nothing about you."

Trevor rested an elbow on the top rail. He looked out at the pregnant alpaca. "Then why are you asking?"

Rebecca finished filling the water trough and shut off the hose. "Because clearly the two of you are not mutual admirers."

Trevor tilted his head. "Happens sometimes."

She tilted her gaze in the same direction. "Usually, for a reason."

He raised one eyebrow. "Anyone ever tell you you're nosy?"

Her pulse picked up. "Anyone ever tell you you're maddeningly private?"

"All the time." He tapped her playfully on the nose. "And you didn't answer my question," he said.

She tried hard not to stare into his eyes as deeply as he was gazing into hers. "Inquisitive was the word Miss Mim used, I believe," she murmured, feeling her cheeks heat. "And yes, she said that all the time." She held up a finger as if lecturing to a student. "And you know what that means."

He waited.

"Once I have a question in my mind, I have to discover the answer." She paused for effect. "No matter what it takes."

"Threats don't work on me," he told her mildly.

She wrinkled her brow, the way she always did when working a puzzle. "Is that what Vince Owen did to you? Did he threaten you someway, somehow?"

Trevor scoffed. "You've been watching too many mystery shows on TV."

"But something despicable is going on here, nonetheless. Otherwise you and Vince wouldn't give each other those looks."

Trevor's expression remained impassive. "Looks," he echoed, as if he hadn't the slightest idea what she was talking about. Even though she knew he did.

"Like you can't stand each other but you're going to be polite because you've ended up living and working in the same place and to do otherwise would make everyone else even more uncomfortable and that would be ungentlemanly, and you were brought up, as a McCabe, to be a gentleman."

"Well, now that you've got it all figured out…"

"Okay. Don't tell me." Rebecca pivoted. "I guess I could always ask your mother."

He clamped a hand on her shoulder, brought her back around. "Why do you care?" he demanded.

She made her eyes go wide. "Because in case you haven't noticed, cowboy, I live between the Circle Y Ranch and the Wind Creek Ranch, and that puts me right smack-dab in the middle of you two guys. And although you might be willing to let that go, I assure you, Vince Owen will not."

Resentment warred with the curiosity on his handsome face. "Did you ask him?"

Why hadn't she? She could have. "I wanted to hear your side."

"And not his?"

Rebecca tried not to think why she automatically trusted Trevor in a way she couldn't seem to honor Vince. "Are you going to tell me or not?"

"Vince and I met at Texas A&M," he told her brusquely. "We were both studying cattle management. I was at the top of my class from the beginning—probably because I grew up on a cattle ranch and worked side by side with my dad, who happens to be one of the best cattlemen around."

It was more than that, Rebecca knew.

Trevor had a way with animals. An immense capacity for hard, physical, down and dirty work. And a need to achieve as deep as her own.

From what she'd seen thus far, Vince seemed driven by the outward trappings of success. Instead of being content with one ranch in one area of the state, he wanted three. He managed instead of ranched. And he already had his eye on the local social scene.

"Vince wanted to be the top student in our department. He was upset when he could not best me on exams and labs."

Okay. "And that's it?"

"Obviously, you've never had anyone continually competing with you. It grates on a person."

She studied him. "You think that's why Vince Owen bought a ranch so close to yours, don't you?"

Trevor clenched his fists in frustration. "It's not just this ranch. He dogs me all the time. I was asked to be a speaker on a ranching seminar last year. He found out and unbeknownst to me, got on the program, too. He found out what kinds of cattle I was breeding, started breeding that type, too. Bought a herd of heifers out from under me. Bought that land on the other side of you—the Circle Y—out from under me. I had offered the asking price to the previous owner, when he was ready to sell. Next thing I know he has accepted an offer from an intermediary for ten percent more. When I heard it, I had a sinking feeling who the new owner might be, but I didn't know for sure until Vince Owen walked into the feed store yesterday morning."

She glanced sideways at him. "Wow. No wonder you're annoyed."

Trevor dropped his hands to his sides and shrugged. "I just don't want to see you get hurt."

"I won't. I knew right off he wasn't the kind of guy I wanted to have as a friend."

"That doesn't mean he won't use you to get to me," Trevor warned.

"To use me, he'd have to get me to give him something. I have no intention of doing that. Now or ever," Rebecca said flatly. "I do want to thank you, though, for helping me go get Blue Mist this morning."

"No problem. I haven't been around alpacas since I was in college. I had forgotten how beautiful they are."

Interesting he would say that, Rebecca thought. It mirrored her feelings exactly.

As if realizing she was being talked about, Blue Mist ambled toward them.

The fawn-colored animal stood at almost five feet. With her gentle demeanor, long, sloping neck, sturdy giraffe-shaped body and dense, soft and fluffy wool coat, she lent a pastoral quality to The Primrose. Her cute oblong face and intelligent dark eyes only added to her appeal. Rebecca stroked her wool.

"How much do you know about shearing?" she asked Trevor.

He grinned. "I haven't tried it on my cattle."

"I'm going to have to do that once I get the entire herd on the property. It has to be done before it gets too hot."

He rubbed Blue Mist behind the ears. "You shear them once a year?"

Rebecca nodded. "In the spring."

Trevor dropped his hand as Blue Mist moved away once again. "One question. How did an alpaca with light brown wool get the name Blue Mist?"

Rebecca had been wondering if and when Trevor would ask that. "She was born on a foggy morning, and when the owners first saw her, she was rising up out of a blue mist."

"Ah."

"It's a good name, I think. Prophetic."

"You mean romantic," he teased.

Rebecca couldn't afford to be thought of as anything less than business-minded. "I mean it spoke to me when I heard it. And when I met her, saw how gentle she was, and found out she was already with cria, I knew she was the start of my herd."

"Speaking of which…you and I need to talk about the fence around your pastures."

"Why?" Rebecca braced for news that would cost her more than she'd already spent. "What's wrong with it?" she asked in trepidation.

"The wood is breaking down in places."

She cocked her head. "You had your cattle in there."

His lips twitched. "Circumstances are different now. We're going to have my thousand-pound steers on my side of that fence, and your one-hundred-pound alpacas on the other."

"Are you saying your cattle are going to bother my alpacas?"

His hazel eyes glimmered seriously. "Not under normal circumstances, but we have to be prepared for the unusual."

She wished she could say he was joking. "Such as?"

"Predators getting in the pasture with your alpacas."

She would have laughed at the statistical absurdity of the statement had it not been for his warning expression. "Are you trying to give me a hard time?"

"I'm trying to explain to you that even a stray cat or dog could spook your alpacas, and if they get spooked and start running and upset my cattle, we could have a stampede on our hands."

So it was back to the alpacas and cattle don't mix theory of ranching. An old wives' tale if she'd ever heard one. She planted her hands on her hips. "I think you're exaggerating."

He let his gaze drift slowly over her before returning to her face. He leaned down so they were practically nose to nose. "And I think you need mesh fence on the inside of the split rail borders, for safety's sake."

She dropped her hands and stepped back. "I can't afford to do that right now, Trevor."

He shrugged, as unconcerned with the financial details of the situation as she was obsessed. "Then I'll help you out."

His matter-of-fact offer sounded like a mixture of pity and charity. If she accepted either, word would get out, and she would never have the other ranchers' respect.

Rebecca shook her head, promising, "I'll get to it as soon as I can, but until then we're just going to have to make do."

Silence ticked out between them. "You sure that's a chance you want to take?" he asked eventually.

What choice did she have? She was on such a tight budget as it was, at least for the next month or so, the slightest catastrophe could catapult her into bankruptcy. Once she'd attracted outside investors, though, her situation would ease quickly.

Gulping around the anxiety rising up within her, she tried to smooth things over while still stubbornly holding her ground. "Look, Trevor, the rest of the herd won't be here for another ten days or so. As soon as I get past the Open House I'm having for potential investors, a week from Sunday," and get past the balloon payment that is due on my operating loan, "I'll take care of the fence. I promise."

Trevor looked like he wanted to continue debating her, but when he finally spoke it was only to ask, "Where are you going to house your herd at night?"

"In the stalls in the barn. Which reminds me. I've really got to get cleaning if I want Blue Mist and that cria she's carrying to have somewhere to sleep tonight."

Trevor took the hint, and left to tend to his own herd.

Three hours later, Rebecca had scrubbed down the central cement corridor and two of the ten wooden-sided stalls. She was filthy from head to toe, and bone-tired to boot. Deciding to check on Blue Mist, she walked out to the pasture, and stopped in her tracks at what she saw.

Chapter Four

"Blue Mist doesn't appear to be in labor," Rebecca told veterinarian Tyler McCabe over the phone, minutes later. Struggling to recall everything she had read on the subject in preparation, and wishing her many books and articles—which were still on the moving truck due to be delivered any time now—were already in her possession, Rebecca continued describing the behavior of her prized alpaca. "She's pacing, but not rolling around in the pasture. What concerns me more than the humming sound she's making is the way she's drooling, how tense she is. The way she's stomping her feet and grinding her teeth."

"Her behavior is probably due to the fact she's been separated from the herd and placed in a new environment. But I'd like to take a look at her tonight anyway. I'll run by as soon as I finish up office hours here. Probably around seven or seven-thirty if that's okay."

"That'd be great. Thank you, Tyler."

"No problem. And let me know if anything changes."

"I will." Rebecca cut the connection on her cell phone and dialed again. She got the breeder, Helen McNamara, on the first try, and spoke with her, too. Helen suggested several ways to improve the situation, and offered her help.

Forgetting her own timetable for getting her ranch up and running, Rebecca took Helen up on all of them this time.

Their plans set, the two women said goodbye.

Wishing she had listened to Helen's advice sooner, Rebecca pocketed her cell phone. She turned when she heard the sounds of wheels on gravel.

To her disappointment, it wasn't the moving truck she was expecting. It was the two people she least wanted to see at that moment.

She waited while her father's Suburban made its way up the drive to the house. "Mom. Dad." Rebecca nodded at Meg and Luke as they emerged from the vehicle.

Her mom was dressed in a light cotton dress and sweater, perfect for the warm spring weather, her dad a knit shirt, and slacks. They looked fit and trim. Regular visits to the salon kept the gray out of Meg's red hair, but Luke's sandy-blond hair was threaded with silver these days.

"We came by to see the ranch and see if you wanted to go to dinner with us," Meg said.

"Thanks for the invitation, but it's not a good time. I'm pretty busy."

"So we see." Luke looked past her disheveled appearance, toward the pasture. "That your first alpaca?" he asked, already heading toward the aging split rail fence.

As they neared, Blue Mist backed up and hummed and stomped even louder.

"Is something wrong with her?" Meg asked in concern.

"We think it's just homesickness, the fact she was separated from the herd. Tyler McCabe's coming out to check her this evening. The rest of the herd is going to be delivered tomorrow afternoon. She'll probably calm down when she sees the rest of her 'family.' In the meantime, it's

been suggested that I go ahead and get her settled in a stall
with food and water, so…"

"Is there anything we can do to help?" Meg asked.

Rebecca snatched the leather lead from the hook next
to the gate, where she'd left it, and shook her head.

Talking softly, the way she'd been taught when she'd
taken a seminar on the care and feeding of alpacas in
Europe the previous year, Rebecca attached the lead to
Blue Mist's halter and led her toward the barn. The animal
relaxed almost immediately when she entered the six-by-
ten confine with the high wooden walls. She settled onto
the recently scrubbed cement floor with a sigh and
"kushed" or lay down on her side. Rebecca removed the
lead, then talked to her a little more. When she was satisfied Blue Mist was settled, Rebecca backed out of the stall
and closed the gate.

Rebecca turned, to see her parents, watching. "Good job
with that," her dad said, looking impressed.

Meg nodded in agreement. "I had no idea you were this
good with farm animals."

"Even so, you think I'm crazy, undertaking this." Rebecca
knew from the look on her father's face that his opinion
hadn't changed in the least. Meg's probably hadn't, either.

Luke glanced at the interior of the barn. It hadn't been
used to house animals for thirty years.

Meg walked out into the warm spring evening. The
scent of flowers filled the air. Until now, she had kept
silent on the subject, leaving the "heavy lifting" to Luke.
Rebecca sensed that was about to change.

"We're so glad to have you back in Laramie again,
Rebecca, and we applaud your desire to be independent
and run your own business, but we'd be lying if we said
we weren't worried about what you're trying to do here."

Luke nodded. "I've done some research on alpacas."

"Then you know that compared to most types of livestock, they are very gentle and easy to raise."

"I also know what they cost. And I'm guessing you paid more for Blue Mist than for your brand-new pickup truck."

Rebecca didn't deny that was the case. "I'll make the money back and more. And I'll show you how I'm going to do that when I have my Open House the Sunday after next."

"All we're saying is that maybe you should slow down," Luke continued. "Take on a few animals, see how that goes before you invest every penny you have in this endeavor."

"You could start your own travel agency," Meg chimed in. "With your experience…you've been so many places. You would be great at it. You could still live on The Primrose. Have one or two alpacas for pets. You just wouldn't have to…"

"Labor like a farm hand?" Rebecca guessed where this conversation was going.

"Exactly," Luke said.

Rebecca was saved having to reply to that suggestion by another vehicle moving up the gravel lane that served as her driveway. "If you'll excuse me, I need to show the movers where to put my boxes."

Rebecca lifted the cross bar on the swinging wooden doors and opened up the detached barn-style garage that would soon be turned into the farm office. She greeted the driver and his assistant and indicated where she wanted the boxes stacked. The two men had just gotten started when a third vehicle drove up the lane.

"When it rains it pours," Rebecca mumbled, not all that

sorry Trevor McCabe had taken this moment to drop by, too. She could use whatever distraction her neighbor provided, and then some.

Trevor drove past the movers and parked next to her parents' vehicle. Rebecca watched as he strode toward her and her parents. He said hello to everyone then grinned at her disheveled state. "Looks like you've been busy," Trevor drawled.

Rebecca noted he also looked a little worse for wear, as if he'd spent the day working, too. "Then that makes two of us."

"I stopped by to see if you wanted to borrow my pressure washer to clean out the barn," Trevor said. "I could show you how to use it, if you've never handled one."

Aware her parents were hanging on every word, Rebecca said, "I'd appreciate that. Thanks."

"Want me to go and get it for you now?" Trevor asked. "That way you'll have it when you need it."

"I'll ride over with you, if you don't mind," Luke said. "I've never seen your ranch."

Trevor's surprise faded as quickly as it had appeared on his face. "Sure."

Rebecca stepped between the two men. "Smooth, Dad. But you can stop trying to set up Trevor and I. He's already told me in no uncertain terms that he has absolutely no interest in dating me."

TO TREVOR'S RELIEF, Luke didn't even try to deny his supposed matchmaking before heading off to the Wind Creek with him. "Is that true?" Luke demanded as Trevor turned the vehicle around and headed toward the rural two-lane highway.

"Rebecca misunderstood why I was talking to you yesterday morning." Trevor eased back out onto the road.

"Did you tell her I asked you to talk her out of ranching?" Luke studied the feed corn growing in the field to their right.

"Nope," Trevor said as he turned into his own drive.

"Thanks. She wouldn't appreciate the behind-the-scenes interference."

He stopped to get the mail out of his box. "No kidding."

"I know you think I'm wrong for trying to change her mind about this."

Trevor shrugged and continued driving. "She's a grown woman."

"Who is still capable of making a mistake."

Trevor parked in front of the barn and cut the engine. "Maybe it should be hers to make. Look, Dr. Carrigan, I know you mean well. But Rebecca has a right to live her life any way she pleases."

Luke hit the release on his safety belt and pushed from the vehicle. "Even if it costs her six years of savings?"

Trevor led the way into the state-of-the-art facility. It smelled of disinfectant and spring air. "This venture of hers is not going to do that. Ranch land around here is only going up in value. Alpacas, while expensive, are a much sought after commodity, not just in Texas, but in the entire United States. There's a ban on importation. She's going to have to breed wisely to get the maximum value from her investment, but even if she doesn't, it's unlikely she will lose money, given the demand for the animals." He retrieved the pressure washer out of the tack room and carried it to his pickup.

Luke lounged against the pickup's gate. "That could all change if demand declines."

"True, but since it takes eleven months to produce a single alpaca, and alpaca wool is wanted world over, it won't happen any time soon."

Luke stuck his hands in the pockets of his slacks. "I heard what happened at the feed store with Vince Owen."

Trevor shut the gate. "Then you also know there were no takers for the bet he tried to make about Rebecca."

Luke exhaled. "Does she know?"

"No, and everybody there agreed she shouldn't. It would only hurt her feelings. Make interaction with him all that much harder. And since Vince owns the ranch on the other side of her now…"

Luke rubbed his neck. "Have the two of them met?"

"Yes." Trevor propped an arm on the side of his truck. "She doesn't like him."

Luke's posture relaxed in relief. "She's always had good instincts about people."

"About a lot of things, from what I see," Trevor concurred. He understood why Luke was protective of his second-oldest daughter, but protection wasn't what Rebecca needed.

Luke studied Trevor a long moment. "I never thought of you as a potential boyfriend for my daughter," he said. "But I want you to know, should you ever decide to pursue her, you have my blessing."

Trevor accepted the announcement with the respect it had been given. "I appreciate that, sir, but I would prefer you not mention this to Rebecca. It would probably blow whatever slim chance I have of getting her to go out with me."

A quizzical lift of the brow. "And do you want to go out with her?" Luke asked.

Trevor shrugged. "I don't think she wants to go out with anyone right now. She's got her hands full starting up her operation."

"Which is exactly why she needs someone like you in her life."

"Be that as it may, that's up to her to decide," Trevor said. "And with all due respect, sir, I suggest you back off and give her room to do it."

"SO WHAT'S REALLY GOING ON between you and my dad?" Rebecca asked Trevor the moment the movers and her parents had left.

He turned and gave her a look that was pure innocence. "What are you talking about?"

So you're going to make me spell it out. "He obviously wanted to speak to you about something. Otherwise he wouldn't have ridden over to your ranch with you."

Trevor's hazel eyes took on a gentle expression. "He's concerned about you. I told him he didn't need to be. You're going to be a fine rancher. Yeah, there are bound to be difficulties, but there are people like me and my brothers and my mom and dad around to help you get acclimated to ranch living."

Trying not to notice how masculine and capable he looked in the dusky light, Rebecca propped her hands on her hips. "Why would you want to do that?"

He sauntered closer. "Same reason I'm loaning you my pressure washer." He playfully tugged at the end of one of her braids. "Because it's the neighborly thing to do." He paused, let his hand drop back to his side. "Ranchers help each other, Rebecca. That's the rule. You don't have to like your neighbor, or even know 'em, to lend a hand. And the expectation is that they'll help you back, when the opportunity arises. Otherwise, no one would be able to prosper. We'd all be taken down—financially and otherwise—by one emergency or another."

That made sense. Rebecca studied him. "I still feel like there's more going on here than I know."

The corners of his lips curved upward. "There probably

could be." His glance sifted slowly over her face, lingering on the flush in her cheeks and bare lips before returning slowly to her eyes. "Did you know you've got cobwebs in your hair?"

Rebecca headed for the closest place to check her reflection—the side-view mirror on his pickup truck. She groaned at what she saw. "Not to mention dirt on my face! Why didn't someone tell me?"

He lifted one broad shoulder in an indolent shrug. "I'm guessing your parents didn't want to embarrass you."

Tingling all over for no reason she could figure, she demanded, "What was your purpose for keeping that info to yourself?"

The mirth in his eyes increased. A sexy rumble emanated from his chest. "I think you look kind of cute all dirtied up like that."

Loath to track any of the dirt into the house, Rebecca headed for the outdoor faucet. She turned on the water and washed her hands, then did the same to her face. "You make it sound like I was mud-wrestling."

Looking as if he wouldn't want to be anywhere else, he lounged against the side of the house, watching as she scrubbed her face with damp hands, rinsing and rubbing, until her fingertips came away clean. "Nah, just cleaning a barn. There are days when I've got muck on me an inch deep. That's why I put a shower outside my barn. You ought to think about it."

"You'd like that, wouldn't you? Me, naked as a jaybird, standing out in the open, under a steamy spray."

Trevor couldn't deny the notion had its appeal any more than he'd own up to his desire to watch over her and make sure she was safe. Ruthlessly, he pushed the steamy image her hot-tempered words had evoked away. He jabbed a thumb against his chest. "First of all, my outdoor shower has high wooden walls and a lock on the inside, insuring privacy. Second, I wasn't the one using binoculars on my neighbor last night. That was you, as I recall."

A fiery blush emphasized the sculpted curves of her cheeks. With a glare, she spun away, reminding, "I explained that!"

He had a fine view of her backside as she leaned over to shut off the faucet. And what a fine backside it was. "Mmm, hmm."

She marched right back to square off with him. "What do you mean, mmm, hmm?" She angled her chin at him.

Unable to resist, he tilted his head and ribbed her a little more. "I think you just like looking at me."

The humor left her eyes. "Don't flatter yourself."

If he hadn't struck a nerve, she wouldn't be half this upset. "Someone's got to."

She tossed her head. "You can leave anytime now."

"Not," Trevor countered, answering the challenge in her golden-brown eyes, "before I do this."

She had time to get away. They both knew it. Even as they both realized she didn't really think he would do it. And it was the dare that had him stepping forward and wrapping an arm about her waist. He heard her soft gasp of surprise—and delight?—as he cupped his other hand beneath her chin and tipped her lips up to his.

The first contact was brief, like the flash of a Fourth of July sparkler.

"What was that for?" she asked, dazed.

"Heck if I know," he murmured, bending his head once again.

Their lips met, held. He felt heat, softness, but frustratingly, no surrender.

"I think there ought to be a reason," Rebecca gasped, coming up for air.

Desire roaring through him like a river after a heavy spring rain, Trevor brought her nearer still, until the length of her body was flush against the length of his.

Happy to be finally getting somewhere with her, he moved his hand around to the back of her neck, tilted her head up even more.

"And I think," she whispered as their lips brushed slowly, inevitably once again, "you ought to tell me."

Trevor'd never been one to dissect his desires. He wasn't about to start now. "Wanting you," he confessed, looking deep into her eyes, "is the only reason I'll ever need…."

The world narrowed to just the two of them, and that's when Trevor heard a low, irritating voice come out of the silence behind them.

"If I were you, Rebecca Carrigan, I'd ask for a heck of a lot more than that."

EMBARRASSED TO BE CAUGHT on the verge of totally making out with the man, Rebecca shoved at Trevor's chest then whirled to find herself looking at Tyler McCabe, vet bag in hand.

"Hate to interrupt, but maybe it's a good thing for you I did." Tyler winked at Rebecca and tilted his head at his brother. "Rumor has it Trevor's harder to catch than a rodeo bull."

Trevor shook his head at his sibling. "You're one to talk since you can't seem to stay with or away from Susan Carrigan."

Tyler's easygoing expression did not falter. "Susie and I are old friends."

And sometimes lovers, Rebecca knew. As long as Ty

was in Susan's life, there wouldn't be room for any other guy. Problem was, Tyler seemed no more inclined to make any sort of lasting and/or romantic commitment to Susan than Susan was to Ty. So like dancers on a stage, they moved endlessly toward and away from each other, for reasons only the two of them knew.

"But enough about our love lives or lack thereof," Tyler continued. "I'm here to see Blue Mist."

"She's in the barn." Rebecca led the way.

Tyler and Trevor followed.

Blue Mist was still kushed on her side, humming softly. Ty examined her. "She's not in labor."

Rebecca breathed a sigh of relief. Trevor looked pleased about that, too.

"But this kind of stress definitely isn't good for her cria," Tyler continued, listening to her heart and lungs.

Feeling almost as nervous as the mother alpaca herself, Rebecca shoved her hands in the back pockets of her jeans. "The rest of the herd is being delivered to me late tomorrow morning."

"That's good." Ty removed the stethoscope from his ears. "I imagine that will calm her immensely."

Rebecca hoped so.

"In the meantime, you might want to just keep her in here tonight." Trevor put the instruments back in his vet bag. "Check on her periodically through the evening. Then if she's calmer tomorrow, you can try and put her in the pasture once again."

Ty ran a hand down the alpaca's side one last time, then stood, and let himself out of the stall. He and Rebecca went over the regimen of vitamins and supplemental feed required for the mother-to-be, as well as the vaccination schedule for the rest of the herd.

"I'll get copies of all the records to you by the end of the week," he said. Tyler handed her a business card. "That's got my pager and home number on it. Don't hesitate to call if you need anything or have any questions."

"Thanks."

"And do yourself a favor. Watch out for this guy." Tyler kidded his brother and was rewarded with a playful punch to the bicep, reminiscent of their childhood when the three McCabe boys were the scrappiest, most mischievous guys around. "I heard he can be Trouble with a capitol *T*."

TROUBLE WAS RIGHT, Rebecca found herself thinking, long after both men had departed, haunted by the sweet, hot kisses she and Trevor had shared. She hadn't been even half this physically attracted to Grayson Graham, and she knew how poorly that had ended. Plus, there were disturbing similarities to the two situations. Grayson had participated in private talks with her father, then refused to divulge what had really been said until the day he dumped her, and by then it had been too late. Her heart had been broken, her pride wounded so badly she'd had to leave Texas to begin to get over the betrayal.

Worst of all, her father still didn't think he had done anything wrong in keeping her in the dark. Luke thought—then and now—he had only been doing what a father should. Protecting her.

She would bet her ranch something similar was going on now between Trevor and Luke, Rebecca thought.

The question was what.

If Luke hadn't asked Trevor to pursue her socially, what had he asked him? she wondered as she showered and changed. Was Trevor looking out for her simply because

Luke had asked him to do so? If that were the case, it somehow diminished everything Trevor had done thus far. And why would Trevor keep that a secret from her anyway?

Because she would have refused his help outright, on principle, that was why.

Rebecca sighed and went down to the kitchen to forage for some dinner. Too tired to cook, she made herself a sandwich and a cold drink, then finished off the meal with an apple and a handful of green grapes.

It had been an hour since she had checked on Blue Mist so she pulled her boots on and went out to the barn. Rebecca'd left a battery-powered light on a hook on the opposite wall, which cast just enough light to let the sweet-faced alpaca see where she was yet not interfere with her rest. It also gave Rebecca enough light to check on the expectant mother.

Blue Mist looked up at Rebecca as she entered the stall, her big dark eyes wide and serious. "How are you doing, sweetheart?" Rebecca asked gently.

Blue Mist responded by humming louder. But she relaxed into Rebecca's touch. A good sign, Rebecca thought. It meant Blue Mist was beginning to understand that she would be the one caring for her from now on. "The rest of your buddies are going to be here tomorrow, so just hang on, you won't be alone much longer."

Rebecca talked to Blue Mist a few minutes more, made sure she had water, then let herself out of the stall. A glance at her watch showed it to be barely nine o'clock and already she was ready for bed.

Rebecca headed for the ranch house. She heard the phone ringing as she stepped inside.

"Rebecca, it's Vince Owen, I'm glad I caught you. Coco seems to have run off."

"What do you mean, run off?"

"I let her out into the backyard to take care of business about forty-five minutes ago. She disappeared into the darkness. I haven't been able to find her. I've been calling her, but I'm not getting any response. I thought—hoped—she might have shown up at your place, since she was there the other night. I hope she's not on the road, although I've got my two hired hands out there looking for her."

The thought of the sweet little puppy getting hit by an unsuspecting motorist was more than Rebecca could bear. "I haven't seen her, but I'll get my flashlight and go out and look around."

They agreed to take their cell phones—should one of them find her, they'd let the other know. Rebecca checked around the house, just to be sure, then headed out into the pastures, her powerful flashlight spreading a wide beam. She could see another flashlight, probably Vince's, coming across the property line onto her ranch from the Circle Y. Toward the two-lane road that fronted all three ranches, two more flashlights could be seen, probably those of Vince's hired hands.

Beginning to feel a little frantic, and worried about what would happen to the puppy if she got around the cattle on Wind Creek property, Rebecca flipped open her cell phone and dialed Trevor McCabe.

"What's going on over there?" he asked without preamble.

Figuring he'd seen the flashlights, Rebecca told him.

"I'll check around my property, too," Trevor promised.

Rebecca kept looking. Kept calling. Finally, she heard a small but distinct whimper, followed by a loud, pleading bark.

Chapter Five

Trevor turned his flashlight toward the sound. An arc of yellow light bathed the chocolate brown puppy as he scampered across the pasture toward Rebecca's kneeling figure. She welcomed the quivering animal into her arms while Trevor walked across the pasture to see what had attracted the puppy to the corner of the fenced-in area in the first place.

As Trevor suspected, Coco's presence on Rebecca's property was not coincidental. Trevor knelt to pick up three remaining nuggets of dry dog food hidden in the six-inch grass, and slid them into his pocket.

Scowling, Trevor headed back toward the action.

Vince came up to stand beside Rebecca. "You found the little scamp," he said.

"I think he scared himself, wandering so far away like that," Rebecca said, cuddling Coco closer, and laughing as the puppy licked her gratefully beneath the chin.

Trevor joined them.

"What are you doing here?" Vince asked Trevor.

"Trevor came over to help with the search." Reluctantly, Rebecca handed Coco back to her owner.

"I'll have to keep a better eye on this little one," Vince promised.

"You should," Trevor agreed, looking Vince in the eye. "Had Coco ended up in a cow pasture, instead of this one, she could have been trampled or kicked in the head by a steer."

Rebecca shuddered at the thought. Vince appeared unmoved and unconcerned. "Well, now that the calamity is over, I think I'll go back to the house," Rebecca said. She bade them both good-night, then headed for the ranch house, her long legs eating up the ground.

"Butting in where you don't belong, aren't you, fella?" Vince said, his flashlight still at his side, spreading an arc of illumination in the grass around them.

Trevor withdrew the dog food from his pocket and held it in his palm. "With good reason, apparently."

Vince shrugged, all clever innocence. "I don't know what that is supposed to mean."

Trevor put the kibble back in his pocket. "You planted that puppy in her pasture with a pile of kibble to keep it busy until Rebecca could find it. You're just lucky she didn't see the lengths to which you'd go to manipulate her."

Vince set the puppy down in the grass between them, where she nosed around, looking for more food. "So why didn't you tell her?"

Trevor's innate protectiveness heightened. Not sorry he had spared Rebecca the worry, Trevor glared at Vince. "She's got enough on her hands, getting her ranch up and running. She doesn't need you bothering her."

Vince smirked. "I don't know what you think is going on here, McCabe, but no one, least of all Rebecca, has appointed you her protector."

Trevor took a step forward, even as Coco roamed an increasingly larger area around them. Trevor clenched his fists at his side. "I am not going to let you hurt her."

"The only thing I plan to do to her is pleasure her. The same way I pleasured Jasmine."

It was all Trevor could do to keep from punching Vince in the jaw. Knowing a free-for-all on Rebecca's property was exactly what his nemesis wanted, Trevor remained where he was, temper boiling, violence held in check. "You have a gripe against me then you come after me, but you leave Rebecca alone."

"Or?" Vince taunted.

Trevor scooped up Coco and handed her back to her owner, before the puppy could get lost again. "You'll have more trouble on your hands than you ever imagined."

"DON'T TELL ME you slept out here."

The low sexy voice dragged Rebecca out of a heavy sleep. She opened her eyes to the sight of Trevor McCabe, leaning into the open window of her pickup truck.

Stifling a yawn, she said, "It was easier than trekking from the house to the barn to check on Blue Mist." Which she'd done every hour or so for the first half of the night, then gotten the idea to park her pickup next to the open barn door and sleep with the windows open, easily alert to any further trouble that might come up with her prize alpaca.

"Speaking of Blue Mist…how's she doing?"

"Better." Rebecca grabbed the steering wheel, moved her legs from the bench seat to the floor on the passenger side, and struggled to sit up. She felt as if she could have slept another ten hours or so.

Rebecca shoved the hair from her eyes and gave Trevor the latest news. "Blue Mist calmed as the night wore on although she was still making that humming noise about half the time. I'm sure she'll settle down when the rest of the herd gets here." Muscles aching, head still a little groggy, she got out of the pickup and tried not to notice how good Trevor looked in the early-morning light, even in worn jeans and an old concert T-shirt. "What are you doing here?"

Half his mouth crooked up in a tantalizing smile. "I came over to give you a hand with the power washing of the interior of the barn in exchange for a free meal."

Somehow, she'd never figured Trevor McCabe as a glutton for punishment. "Sure you want to do that after the dinner I cooked the other evening?" she teased.

"What was wrong with dinner?" he asked.

"It was awful."

He palmed his chest. "I ate all mine."

Yes, he had, with nary a complaint, a fact that made her like him all the more, since he had no way of knowing— yet—that was hardly an honest effort on her part. She headed back into the barn, feeling ridiculously happy when he fell into step beside her. She slanted him a sideways glance, wondering what it would be like to interact with Trevor like this every day. Even as friends slash mutual annoyances it was a tantalizing notion. "By the way, you didn't have to come over here last night," she remarked casually.

His expression grew resolute. "I thought we'd established neighbors take care of each other in the Lone Star State. And that goes double for ranching neighbors."

That was the problem. She could see herself getting used to him looking out for her, way too easily.

Wishing she'd had a chance to brush her hair and wash her face before meeting up with him, and change out of her rumpled T-shirt and jeans, Rebecca led the way to the first stall. Blue Mist was lying down on the cool and clean cement floor. The animal's soft humming picked up as Rebecca let herself inside. The feed she had left for her prized alpaca looked barely touched, but she needed more water.

"I hope she starts to eat soon." Rebecca stroked her soft woolly flank, then went to get more water from the spigot outside the door.

Trevor hung out next to the open stall door, patiently watching over the alpaca.

When Rebecca returned, Blue Mist was standing next to the feed bucket, eating. "How'd you get her to do that?" Rebecca asked in amazement, noting Blue Mist was no longer humming.

"Actually, I think it's something you did."

Rebecca set down the water bucket. "If that were the case, she would have been eating last night." She relaxed opposite Trevor, hands flattened on the wood behind her. "You sure you're not Dr. Doolittle or something?"

Amusement glimmered in his hazel eyes. Blue Mist stopped eating long enough to drink. "I can't talk to the animals...yet. My brother Tyler might be able to, however."

"Because he's a vet," Rebecca guessed, wondering how she ever could have had trouble telling the three guys apart. The triplets, though still identical, were so very different, Trevor so much more appealing than the other two, in so many ways....

"Because Ty's spent so much time around them," Trevor corrected, dragging her attention away from the masculine shape of his lips and back to the conversation. He gave her a hard look, as if wondering where her thoughts had drifted. "There are a lot of other ways to communicate with animals besides language," he continued.

As Blue Mist headed back to her food, Rebecca slipped

from the stall. Trevor followed her. "A look, a touch..." She guessed.

"Right."

Trying not to think about the way Trevor looked at her—as if she were suddenly the most fascinating woman on the planet—and what the proprietary, light touch of his hand beneath her elbow meant, Rebecca led the way across the yard to the ranch house.

"I hope you don't think this is going to become a habit." She went to the sink and washed her hands. She had decided to take him up on his offer and cook for him because having help with such an arduous task like cleaning the barn interior was worth the aggravation of having him around.

Tall frame radiating barely leashed energy, Trevor waited until she was finished, then stepped to the sink. "Nah, of course not." He lathered up to his elbows with gusto. "Once you get it cleaned, that barn'll only need a power washing once or twice a year."

Pretty sure he wasn't that dense, Rebecca rolled her eyes. "I meant having breakfast here."

He rinsed his powerful arms one at a time. "I suppose we could always have it at my place."

Rebecca knelt to hunt for her favorite skillet. She pulled it out with a clatter. "Why would I be there?"

He watched her shut the cabinet door with her foot. "To help me with my chores?"

Rebecca released a long, slow breath. "I don't know anything about cattle."

Pleasure teased the corners of his lips. "I imagine you could learn if you wanted."

An answering satisfaction swept through her. She really shouldn't be enjoying these unexpected interactions with him quite so much. "How do you want your eggs?"

"Same way you're having yours."

"Migas it is, then."

"Want me to do anything?"

"Yeah, you can make the coffee and pour some juice for us."

"Toast?"

"If you wouldn't mind."

They worked in companionable silence. Rebecca whipped half a dozen eggs together in a bowl, added salt and pepper, and then cooked them in a skillet, waiting until they were almost scrambled before she added crushed tortilla chips and grated cheddar cheese. By the time she plated the eggs, and topped them with salsa and avocado slices, he had everything else on the table.

They sat down kitty-corner from each other this time. "For someone who has no interest in dating me you're sure hanging around a lot," Rebecca noted.

Trevor cleaned his plate, sat back in his chair. He studied her over the rim of his coffee cup. "That kiss yesterday has me thinking I might've been a little hasty."

A distracting shiver swept through her.

Tyler had been right.

Trouble with a capitol *T.*

"That kiss, cowboy, is exactly why we shouldn't date."

NOT EXACTLY THE RESPONSE he had been hoping for, although it was pretty much the one Trevor had been expecting. He'd figured out in the last twenty-four hours that nothing about romancing Rebecca would ever be easy. But then, nothing worth having was ever easy, either.

"I don't follow," Trevor said, wondering if Rebecca had any idea how beautiful she looked, with her hair all mussed, her cheeks pink, eyes sparkling with a fiery light.

Her jeans and the navy T-shirt she'd slept in might have been rumpled but they still clung in all the right places. And she still smelled of soap and shampoo....

"Then allow me to explain it to you," Rebecca began. "One embrace and you're suddenly all proprietary, coming over here last night, staying around even after we found the puppy and I headed inside, subtly but surely making sure Vince Owen felt your presence." She stood and began to clear the table.

Figuring cleanup should be a fifty-fifty proposition, too, he put the dishes in the dishwasher. Turned to see her wiping down the table and counters.

It was clear she had looked back at some point after going inside the house the previous evening, noticed he and Vince squaring off in the pasture and knew it hadn't been a social chat.

"It looked like you needed my help. Would you have rather I stayed away?"

"This isn't a competition." Finished wiping the counter, she headed for the door.

Tell that to Vince, Trevor thought.

He followed her outside. "I never said it was."

"Look, all three of us are neighbors. I'm smack-dab in the middle of the properties. I don't care whether you two like each other or not. I plan on being friends with both of you."

He crossed the yard with her. "Good luck with that." Vince had never been good at being anyone's friend, which was part of what made him so jealous and envious of others who did have friends.

"Oh, I'll manage, I assure you," Rebecca said, shooting him another defiant look. "What was it you said to me yesterday? We ranchers don't have to like each other or even know each other all that well to help each other out?"

He snapped his fingers in regret. "Brought up short by my own words of wisdom."

"You've got to live by them, too."

She snapped the lead on Blue Mist and led her back out to the pasture.

Aware she was right—he couldn't afford to be the hypocrite among them—Trevor set up the pressure washer and vowed to do better at managing his reactions to Vince Owen.

The next few hours were spent cleaning out the interior of the barn. By the time they had finished, the musty odor was gone, replaced by the clean smell of the bleach and water solution. A gentle breeze blew through the doors. Rebecca was just as much a sight as she had been the previous day. Dirt smudged her face and hands and stained her clothes. But she looked happy and satisfied as she studied the stalls, as if her irritation with what she saw as his overprotectiveness were all but forgotten.

"What kind of cooling system do you have in your barn?" she asked.

Glad to have the conversation moved back to neutral territory, Trevor shifted closer. "Thinking about the summer heat?"

She nodded, looking around reflectively. "It's fine in here at night right now, but it's only April. By the time we reach July…"

Or even the end of May, Trevor thought, aware her ranch insurance agent would be bringing this up to her, too. "You're going to need a way to move the hot air out."

She nodded. "Alpacas carry the heat in the belly, so to cool them off you need to run fans at floor level. I'm thinking that it would be smarter to keep the temperature down overall and not have to worry about how to safely set up ten floor-level fans."

"For cattle we use a system of misters and fans mounted on the ceiling of the barn."

"The same has been recommended for alpacas. Did you install your system yourself?"

"Yes, but it wasn't easy. If you want my help on that—"

"Thanks, but I'm sure if you can do it I can manage to do it, too."

"Honestly, I wouldn't mind."

"And honestly, I think I've leaned on you, and your pressure washer, enough."

"You're kicking me out?"

She took his elbow and guided him toward the open barn door. "I'm sure your cattle miss you."

Trevor doubted that, since he'd tended to them before coming over here.

He lifted his hands in surrender. "Never let it be said that I can't take a hint."

"So how are things going out at The Primrose?" Miss Mim asked, hours later.

"Great, actually." Rebecca set down the box of forgotten belongings Miss Mim had asked her to bring to her on the public library information counter.

Although no longer the head librarian for Laramie branch of the Laramie County Public Library system, Miss Mim still volunteered on Thursday evenings. "The herd was delivered today." Already, Blue Mist had settled down, as had all the other alpacas. "I pastured the two males in the pasture furthest from the house, five of the females in the second, and Blue Mist and one other female in the one nearest to the house. I was a little worried about putting them in the barn for the night, but they all went right into their stalls, no problems, and settled right down."

"That's wonderful."

"Yeah." Rebecca grinned. She was exhausted, and her braided hair was still wet from her steamy shower and shampoo, but she had a deep sense of accomplishment, too. "I'm beginning to feel like a real rancher. But I need your help." No one could find information quicker than Miss Mim. "I have to put a mister and fan cooling system in the barn as soon as possible. I need to know which one I should purchase, what it costs and where I should go to get it."

"I'd be happy to help you look that up, dear." Miss Mim swiveled around to her computer, which was already logged on to the Internet. "But wouldn't it have been easier to just ask Trevor? I know he's put one in his barns. He told me all about it, at the time."

"I'd rather not."

Miss Mim raised a brow in silent inquiry.

"I feel I've leaned on him too much as it is. And while you're at it, can you price pressure washers for me? I need to purchase one of those, too."

Miss Mim found the Consumer Satisfaction Web site on ranch equipment, printed the appropriate pages and handed them over. "Networking is important, dear, no matter what profession you're in. There's a lot to be learned from your more experienced counterparts, and a lot you will someday be able to pass on to others, too. Which is why I hope you're planning to attend the Laramie County Ranchers Association Spring Fling at the community center tomorrow evening."

"I am." For advertising reasons only. She needed people to know about her upcoming Open House.

"Who is escorting you?"

Miss Mim might never have married but she had very

definite ideas about what was proper, and what wasn't, when it came to social activities. Rebecca was pretty sure that young ladies driving themselves to black-tie dinner-dances was not an acceptable option in Miss Mim's view.

"No one," Rebecca responded airily. "I'm taking myself."

Disappointment mingled with the hope in Miss Mim's blue eyes. "You could ask Trevor."

Enough already about Miss Mim's favorite ex-neighbor, Rebecca groused inwardly. Smile fixed on her face, Rebecca reported stubbornly, "He's already asked me, as did Vince Owen." She paused to look Miss Mim in the eye. "I'm not going with either of them."

"Any particular reason why not?"

Yes, and a very good one. "I don't need a man in my life."

Miss Mim smiled and wagged a teasing finger Rebecca's way. "Ah, but do you want one?"

MISS MIM'S QUESTION haunted Rebecca all the way back to the ranch. Did she want a boyfriend? Up until Trevor McCabe had kissed her, she could honestly say she hadn't cared, either way. If a guy came along who interested her, she usually went out with him, until it became clear they weren't suited for each other after all. At times that realization took one date, some times half a dozen. But always there were difficulties that could not be overcome. She and "Mr. Wrong" realized they either had zero chemistry or wanted very different things out of life, and they parted ways.

Now, finally, she'd met a man whose kisses rocked her to her very core. He was a Texan who wanted to ranch and live in Laramie County, same as she. He had family in the area, to whom he was obviously close. He even lived next door.

He was also bossy, opinionated and way too protective of her. He seemed to have a problem letting her do things herself, her way. Yes, he had offered to help her out with ranching matters when needed, for a price, but deep down, she had the feeling he was just waiting for her to fail, so he could buy the ranch he'd already stated he wanted, and had planned to buy before she'd purchased it out from under him. And worst of all, he'd already had two private conversations with her father that she knew about. There might have been more.

That reminded her of Grayson Graham. No way did she want to be made a fool of again.

It had hurt too much the first time around.

And then there was the niggling unpleasantness between Vince Owen and Trevor, the undercurrent of competition that kept cropping up between them. Trevor had told her that Vince was the one competing with him, and given the fact that Vince had purchased a ranch in the vicinity of Trevor's home turf, that seemed to be true. But she also got the impression that Trevor didn't want Vince befriending and/or romancing her, and that Trevor—who'd initially announced he had no interest in dating her—would even put himself in the running for her boyfriend rather than see her hook up with Vince. And if that wasn't being competitive on Trevor's part, Rebecca didn't know what was.

The only safe route for her to take was to try and stay "neighborly" with both men, while keeping both at arm's length.

Maybe it was time for her to be thinking about having a boyfriend again. But for all their sakes, it wouldn't be either Vince Owen or Trevor McCabe.

"IF I HADN'T SEEN YOU getting out of your pickup truck, I don't think I would have recognized you," Trevor teased, falling into step beside Rebecca.

Rebecca picked up the skirt of her glittering turquoise evening gown as she made her way through the dozens of vehicles crowding the community center parking lot.

"I could say the same about you," she replied. She had never seen Trevor McCabe in formal attire and was unprepared for just how good he looked. The cut of the black tuxedo jacket and pants played up his fit masculine physique, while the snowy-white shirt contrasted nicely with the suntanned hue of his skin and the rusty brown of his short hair. He'd shaved closely and smelled of soap and sandalwood and leather cologne. His hazel eyes missed nothing as they took her in. Suddenly acutely aware of her exposed shoulders, the décolletage of her strapless gown, she turned her glance toward the door.

The dance had started nearly an hour ago.

Late getting home, even later taking care of her herd, she'd wondered at one point if she was going to make it at all.

"You had me wondering if you were even going to be here," Trevor remarked.

Rebecca stepped carefully up onto the sidewalk. She waved to someone else she knew. "I got caught in traffic en route home from San Angelo."

"What were you doing there?"

"I was purchasing a misting system for my barn." An action that had seriously depleted the remains of her operating loan. But with a searing heat wave now predicted for the middle of the following week, she didn't think she could wait.

He looked across his shoulder at her. "When's it going to be installed?"

"Whenever I get around to it."

He slid his arm beneath her elbow. "You're planning to do it yourself?"

Aware that anyone who saw them coming into the dance that way would think they were hanging out together this evening, she slipped away. "The salesperson said it isn't that hard."

He shrugged and held the door for her. "Maybe not if you're used to doing electrical and/or plumbing work yourself."

She turned sideways. Her dress brushed him as she passed. "The instructions are self-explanatory."

He smiled down at her and fell in step beside her. Once again his hand was on her, this time pressed to the middle of her spine. "Take it from someone who's done it, it's not as easy as it looks."

She flushed, heating at his light touch, aware they were already getting curious looks. "Thank you for the vote of confidence," she said sarcastically, giving him a narrow-eyed look.

He leaned down to whisper in her ear. "I'm not trying to undermine you."

She sucked in a breath. "Could have fooled me."

"Rebecca. Lovely as ever." Vince Owen joined them. He leaned over to kiss her cheek.

Something in her recoiled but aware others were watching, she forced herself to maintain a smile. "Hello, Vince."

"That gown new?"

Rebecca stepped back, away from both men. "I've had it for a while."

She had a closet full of evening wear left over from her career as tour director. She would have little excuse to wear any of the outfits again, yet she didn't have nearly enough blue jeans and denim work shirts.

"Well, you look lovely," Vince said.

"Thank you. Now if you'll excuse me…" Rebecca

threaded her way through the crowd to Greg Savitz, her ranch insurance agent.

A few years older than she, the happily married father of four had taken over his father's business the previous year.

"How are things coming?" Greg asked. He led the way through the buffet line.

"Great." Rebecca picked up a plate, too.

"Good. As I told you on the phone, I can only give you a grace period of forty-eight hours. Now that you've got the herd out there, I'm going to need a check from you as soon as possible, as well as specifics on the herd, including health records, valuation and description of each alpaca you want covered."

"You're aware I want to go with monthly instead of bi-annual payments."

"Can't blame you for that."

Her insurance on the animals alone was going to run her several hundred dollars. That didn't include the land, the ranch house, barn and garage.

Greg gave her a sympathetic look. "I know it sounds like a lot, but with your herd alone valued at over one hundred thousand dollars, you can't afford not to insure them."

"I know."

"And speaking of the herd, I should have told you earlier that in order to go with the lowest possible rate, you're going to have a cooling system installed in your barn."

"I'm already ahead of you on that. I bought it today. I'm going to install it right away."

"Great."

As Rebecca headed for one of the tables, she ran into Elliott Allen, a banker with Laramie Savings and Loan.

"Hey, I heard you went with a San Angelo bank for your financing on the property."

Rebecca nodded, aware Elliott Allen's bank had been the one most frequently recommended to her. Unfortunately, they were also very fiscally conservative lenders. "I needed to go an unconventional route, to get started."

"I understand." Elliott pressed a business card in her hand. "But if you ever want to refinance, give me a call." He winked and went on his way.

Well, that at least was positive, Rebecca thought as she found a seat at a crowded table. She chatted up her ranch while they all ate dinner. By the time she had finished, the dessert tables were being set up, and the dance band had started.

Rebecca passed out invitations to her Open House to everyone at her table, then rose to do more of the same.

No sooner had she started working the room, than Trevor and Vince were back. Vince approached her first. "I can see you're busy networking, but I need to talk to you about the fence on our property line."

Rebecca held up a hand, already knowing where this was going, thanks to her discussion with Trevor McCabe. "You don't need to worry about that. I'm planning to install mesh fencing inside the split rail as soon as I can."

Vince looked confused. "Why would you want to do that?"

"Because alpacas and cattle don't mix?"

"My cattle are not going to bother your alpacas. And I doubt your alpacas are going to want anything to do with my steers, when I get them in the pasture."

"Which will be?"

"The hired hands are going to start moving them in tomorrow." Vince took her elbow, and instead of guiding her to the side, as she expected, he escorted her onto the dance floor.

The next thing she knew, the two of them were dancing, and eliciting more than a few curious looks. "Who told you that you needed mesh fencing?" Vince tried to bring Rebecca close.

She used the pressure of her forearm on his chest, to push him away. "Trevor."

Vince shook his head. "Sounds like him. Take it from me, you don't need it. In fact, you don't need a lot of things people are going to try and sell you, like full insurance on your animals and a misting system for your barn."

"I wouldn't feel comfortable without either."

"Suit yourself, but it pays to surround yourself with like-minded business people, risk takers like ourselves, not naysayers. I admit I'm sometimes unconventional in my approach to things, and ridiculously old-fashioned in others, but bottom line, I now own three ranches instead of just one. My net worth is probably four or five times that of Trevor McCabe's and every other rancher in this county."

Rebecca didn't know about that. Trevor's uncles had been in the ranching business for years and owned some very prosperous ranches.

"If you want me to show you how to get maximum return on a ranching business with minimal cash outlay, I'd be happy to sit down with you and show you how, and it starts with alternative financing. But then, I gather you already know that, since you didn't go with the bank in Laramie."

"How do you know that?"

"I saw Elliott Allen trying to drum up business with you—he already did the same with me. Like you, I went elsewhere for funding where they had more competitive rates."

What had seemed like a good idea at the time, was now beginning to make Rebecca feel very nervous. "Speaking of ranching, I really need to continue to tell people about the Open House I'm having."

"I presume I'm invited, too?"

Why was her instinct to say no, when she needed every bit of outside financial investment she could get? "Certainly." Rebecca withdrew another small invitation from her purse and handed it to him.

No sooner had the dance ended, then Rebecca turned around, and found herself running full steam ahead into Trevor McCabe's chest. "My turn," he said, wrapping an arm around her waist as the music began once again.

"You really don't have to compete," Rebecca said.

"Who's competing?" Trevor replied, staying a respectful distance away, as they two-stepped to the beat of the popular country song the band was playing. "I want your attention. I've got it."

Rebecca tried not to think how right it felt to be held in Trevor's arms. "I don't want to be a pawn used in this rivalry between you and Vince."

He sobered abruptly. "I don't want that, either."

Looking into his eyes, she could almost believe him. Until Vince tapped on Trevor's shoulder and smoothly cut in, taking Rebecca back into his arms. Aware people were beginning to stare at them, Rebecca forced a smile, and firmly but surely extricated herself from Vince's arms. Only to find herself in Trevor's once again.

Then Vince's.

Trevor's.

Vince's.

"Hold it!" Rebecca wriggled free. Evaded Trevor's arms.

She lifted both her forearms, held them in front of her. "No more. Please. From either of you. Now if you'll excuse me…" She turned and headed for the dessert table.

"Wow, only back in town a week and already you've got two guys fighting over you," Amy remarked, joining her.

Rebecca made a face at her youngest sister, who was there with her pal since kindergarten, Teddy McCabe. The two enjoyed a platonic relationship, but filled in for each other when one of them was currently unattached and needed a date for a function like this.

"Let's not talk about that," Rebecca said with a roll of her eyes. She looked at Teddy. As usual, he exuded friendliness and was always willing to go the extra mile for a friend. "How's your horse ranch doing?"

Teddy moved down the table, filling his plate with sumptuous treats as he went. "The Silverado is coming along nicely, thank you very much." He slanted her an affable glance. "How are things out at The Primrose?"

"Gearing up. In fact, I'm having an Open House from ten till four Sunday after next. I'd love it if you could come by, take a look around." Rebecca winked. "Maybe think about the financial advantages of owning—or leasing—an alpaca or two of your very own."

Teddy grinned, amused but not entirely opposed to the idea. "I'm not sure how well they'd do with horses," he said.

"No problem. I'm planning to board alpacas, too. That way you'd be able to breed your adult female to one my herd sires, sell the cria or offspring and reap the monetary rewards without doing any of the work. For a fee, of course."

Teddy studied her with the expertise of a person known for making sound investments, on and off his own ranch. "I assume you'll have a sales pitch ready?"

Rebecca nodded. "I'll be working on it all next week."

"In the meantime, how about giving Susie and/or Mom and Dad and Jeremy a call?" Amy suggested. "We haven't seen or heard much from you since you've been back in Laramie. We miss you."

Rebecca missed them, too. More so now that she was close enough to visit whenever she wanted. Aware Trevor was still watching her, from a distance now, she looked away, admitting, "It's still awkward." As Rebecca looked in the other direction, she discovered Vince Owen watching her, too.

Her sister Amy, however, was not distracted.

Amy gently touched Rebecca's arm. "It's not going to get better unless you confront the problem head-on. Talk it out. Deal with it. Fight, scream if you have to, do whatever you have to do to move past what happened with that whole Grayson Graham mess once and for all."

Rebecca looked away, her emotions in turmoil. "I'm not sure I can, Amy." Her father and sister's betrayal of her still felt so acute. Made more so by whatever her father and Trevor McCabe were keeping from her now.

Chapter Six

"Talk about the perfect end to a less-than-perfect evening," Rebecca muttered as her pickup truck lurched to the side of the two-lane county road and skidded to a halt.

She slammed the door of her truck and made her way around to the right front tire. Just as she'd thought. It was flat. And here she was, out in the middle of nowhere, dressed in an evening gown, without an auto club membership to her name.

Her frustration erupted in a string of invectives. She kicked the tire with the heel of her evening sandal. Lost her balance. And would have fallen over had she not been able to grab hold of the passenger door handle.

Naturally, her temper tantrum did not go unnoticed.

Headlights bathed her in a yellow spotlight as another pickup truck slowed and pulled over, parking behind her vehicle.

Trevor McCabe got out and strode toward her. He'd left his motor running, hazard lights blinking, headlamps on. The light bathed his tall, muscled form. "Need some help?"

She didn't even have to think about it. "Nope."

He narrowed his eyes. "You can't fix a flat in an evening gown."

Want to bet? "If you can do it in a tuxedo, I can do it in a dress."

Trevor stood with his hands in his pocket. "Ever think your stubbornness is more trouble than it's worth?"

Rebecca marched back to get her jack, then realized she couldn't recall where it was stowed. Not about to admit that to him, or stand there reading her owner's manual while he watched, she lowered the tailgate and climbed up into the bed of the truck—a little less gracefully than she would have liked. Figuring the compartment that held the spare had to be there somewhere, she walked back and forth, looking for a latch.

"If you're looking for the spare, it's underneath the truck," Trevor said, retrieving something from his own pickup, and walking toward her once again. "Now, the only question is are you going to let me use this?" He held up a can of Fix-A-Flat. "Or are you going to force me to do it the hard way?"

Time is money, Rebecca reminded herself. "Fine. Use the can. What does it do anyway?"

He squatted down beside the air gage. "It inserts a complex liquid into the tire. The leaking air instantly polymerizes it to plug up the leak. And it also inflates your tire."

"Wow." Rebecca watched as her tire resumed its normal shape.

Finished, Trevor stood. "If there is a nail in there, this may not hold all that long. But it should be good enough to get you back to The Primrose."

"Thanks."

He smiled at her as if coming to her rescue yet again was all in a day's work and swaggered back to his truck.

Just to be on the safe side, Rebecca drove slowly.

Trevor was right behind her the entire way.

Instead of going on to his driveway, however, he followed her down the lane and parked just behind her, cutting the motor, but once again leaving his headlights on.

She met him in the lane, halfway between their two vehicles, wishing he didn't look so damn good. "You can go home now."

"Job's not done." He took off his coat and tie, and rolled up the sleeves on his pleated white shirt.

What would it take to make this man realize her difficulties were not his problem? "Yours is."

"How long do you think it will take you to change this tire?"

She tore her eyes from his brawny forearms. "Couple hours, I guess. I don't know."

He reached around beneath the truck. Half a minute later, both the jack and the tire were on the ground. "It'll take me fifteen minutes."

She had to admit it looked as if he knew what he was doing thus far. "It's not your responsibility," she repeated.

He patted her on the top of her head. "Anyone ever tell you graciousness is not your strong suit?"

Rebecca paced back and forth, the folds of her long silky skirt swirling around her legs. "I suppose you're going to want another meal for this."

He set up the jack and worked it like a pro. "Actually, what I'd really like is a cold beer when I finish."

A cold beer sounded amazingly good to her, too. "And that's all you want?"

He flashed her a crooked smile. "Well, if you're offering…"

Rebecca stilled him with an equally presumptuous look. "A chilled beverage is all I'm offering."

He slid his eyes to the hollow of her throat, to her lips

and then her eyes. All innocence once again. "Then a chilled beverage is all I need."

She told herself the evening would definitely not end with her kissing him again. "Then you'll leave?"

He dipped his head in a gallant bow. "Then I'll leave."

Aware her pulse was racing as if he had made another pass at her, Rebecca left him to his work and went into the house. Five minutes later, she had changed out of her evening dress and back into her jeans, boots and a snap-front Western cowgirl shirt. By the time she had walked out the back door onto the lawn, he already had the damaged tire off and was fitting on the spare. She headed for the barn, checked on her herd. All were resting peacefully, even Blue Mist.

Rebecca made sure all of them had plenty of water to get them through the night, then she walked back out of the barn.

Trevor put the jack and the tire in the bed of her truck and turned off the headlights on his vehicle.

"In the house or out?" she asked.

"How about the gazebo? It looks like a nice place to have a drink."

"I'll meet you there."

Rebecca slipped back inside, got two beers, twisted off the caps and walked back outside.

To Rebecca's surprise, Trever stayed just long enough to have a drink with her. She told herself she was relieved when he left—and not disappointed.

THE NEXT DAY SHE ROSE early and headed for town. The first order of business was dropping by the insurance office to give Greg Savitz a check, the second, a stop at the vet's to pick up the prescription sedatives she was going to need for her alpacas when she undertook shearing later in the week, the third, Murphy's garage.

"So how did this happen?" Rebecca asked Mr. Murphy.

Mr. Murphy handed her the bill. "It looks as if the tire was punctured with a sharp object."

Rebecca reached for her checkbook. "You mean there was no nail in it."

Mr. Murphy nodded. "Just a small leak."

"How could that happen?" Rebecca asked.

"Sounds to me like it was deliberate," Vince Owen said, coming up to the counter. He had two cans of motor oil and a pair of windshield wiper blades in his hand.

"Could have been," Mr. Murphy agreed with a shrug. "Though why anyone would want to do that to you, Rebecca…"

Why indeed, Rebecca wondered.

Trying not to think how quickly her bank account was being depleted, she finished paying Mr. Murphy, then walked back out to her truck.

She was about to climb behind the wheel when Vince caught up with her. "I think I have an idea how that happened last night," he told her. "And it all has to do with me. And you."

"What do you mean?"

"Trevor probably told you the rivalry between us goes one way. Don't you believe it. He's just as competitive as I am. Otherwise, why would he have changed his mind about pursuing you?"

Vince's question was a good one.

A chill went down Rebecca's spine as she recalled that first morning in the feed store. What was it Trevor had said to her when she had accused him of being party to her father's matchmaking and let him know she wasn't going to accept a date? *"Well, that's good because I hadn't planned to ask…."*

There had been no doubt in her mind that Trevor had meant what he said.

And yet, mere hours later, he had started his sure but subtle conquest of her, inviting himself to dinner, turning on the charm...insisting they be friends as well as next-door neighbors. Vince had her attention now.

"According to the guys at the feed store, McCabe couldn't have been less interested in making you his woman—*until* I made it known that I wanted to date you," Vince continued. "And now here he is, doing everything and anything he can to publicly claim you. Including coming on strong at the dinner-dance last night, then co-incidentally swooping in to your rescue right after."

Rebecca shook off the implication. "Look, it doesn't matter what Trevor does or says. The fact of the matter is I don't want to date anyone right now. And that includes you, too, Vince."

"That doesn't make me any less interested in you, but I can accept that. I tend to put business first, too. And I can see you have your hands full, making The Primrose opera-tional. I'm not sure I can say the same thing about Trevor McCabe. Especially since..." Vince's voice trailed off. Frustration etched his features. He took off his hat and swept his hands through his sandy blond hair.

"You might as well spit it all out."

"Trevor wants to steal you the way he thinks I stole Jasmine from him, back in our college days. When the truth is Jasmine left Trevor after finding out what a cheating, lying, SOB he was. And then, she left me, too."

REBECCA SPENT THE REST of Saturday alternately tending to her herd and painting the interior of the business office the light primrose-yellow she intended to use on all ranch correspondence. By nine that evening, the large cement-floored room looked less like the interior of a garage than it had, but it still had a long way to go.

During the day she would be able to open up the old-fashioned barn-style doors for light and ventilation, but at night, the single overhead bulb was not going to do it. So she went back to the house, got a couple lamps from the living room and got ready to give the walls another coat of paint.

She had just dipped her roller into the pan when the sound of a pickup rumbled in her driveway. Seconds later, Trevor strode in. He stepped around the towers of moving boxes in the center of the room. "Is there some reason you're not answering your phone?"

She straightened, and her grasp on the handle tightened. "I'm answering it."

"I've called ten times today. You didn't pick up once."

She studied the buttons on his starched tan work shirt. "I wonder why that would be."

For a long moment he didn't say anything, and she forced her gaze to his face. It wasn't just the aftershave clinging to his jaw—she could tell he had just shaved. He also looked ready to go out. Not surprising, since he was single and it was Saturday night.

He continued to study her as if trying to figure something out. "Are you mad at me?"

Emotion bubbled up inside her. Relentless. Unmanageable. She tapped a finger to her chin, realizing too late it had paint on it. "Gee. Let me think. Yes. I believe I am."

He looked around, spotted a clean cotton rag on one of the boxes and handed it over. "Why?"

Embarrassed by her clumsiness, Rebecca dabbed at her chin. "Why do you think?"

He strode a little closer, still examining her like a specimen under a microscope. "I've no idea."

Rebecca scowled. Turning her back to him, she resumed painting. "Sure you do." She brushed the walls with harder than necessary strokes. "Just think a little harder."

A big hand captured hers. "If you're accusing me of something…"

Rebecca kept painting. "Now, you're getting the picture."

The pressure of his grip kept the roller from moving any farther. "I'd like to know what."

Rebecca swung around. "I found out what happened to my tire was no accident." Deciding that trying to paint and argue was a dangerous proposition, she set the roller carefully back into the pan, and paused to wipe her hands on the rag. "And I know all about Jasmine Whatever-Her-Last-Name-Was, too."

He didn't comment but the sudden way he let go of her and the lift of his brow said it all.

"Vince thought I should know how you make a woman think she needs help and then swoop in to rescue her. Apparently, it's your MO in the romance department."

The corners of his mouth turned down. "I don't know what you are trying to imply, but I did not damage your tire."

"Well, someone did."

He lowered his voice. "Did you ever stop to think that someone might be Vince?"

She'd never been the sort of person to accept gossip at face value. Yet something—maybe it was the strength of her attraction to Trevor—had her looking for any and every reason not to get further involved with him. Even if she knew said reason was flat-out wrong.

A guilty flush rose from her chest, to her face. Aware she was reacting presumptively, but unable to help it, she shrugged. Reminding herself that the only person who had come along to see her with that flat tire, the only person who had benefited from her "distress" had been Trevor McCabe, knowing the best way to get at the truth was to feign more knowledge than she actually had while simultaneously provoking emotion, she lobbed yet another outrageous remark his way. "Vince told me you'd blame it on him."

"Maybe," Trevor allowed slowly, bitterly, "because if your tire was indeed sabotaged Vince probably did it."

"And yet Vince didn't show up to rescue me and be my hero, did he?"

Trevor rocked back on his heels. "That would have been a little obvious, don't you think?"

A trickle of unease sifted through her.

Trevor had a point about that. Rebecca lifted a hand, then paused to level him with her gaze. "Truth to tell, at this point I don't think I care which one of you it was. Just know that I have no intention of becoming the next 'Jasmine.'" The two men could compete over someone—something—else.

His resentment filled the space between them. "Good to know you're interested in my side of the story."

She drew a conciliatory breath. "I'm listening."

He made a scoffing sound. "Too little, too late."

"Trevor." She moved to block his way. The hurt and outrage in his eyes flooded her with remorse. Too late, she realized if she wanted to put distance between them, she should have found another way to do it. "I want to hear your side."

Again, he was silent for a few moments. "So you can decide what's true and what's not."

"Yes."

"Thanks." His eyes narrowed. "I'll pass."

"What do you mean, you'll pass?" Who didn't want to

have their side heard? Especially in one as messy as the one Vince had described?

"I thought you and I could be friends as well as neighbors," he drawled before turning and heading for the door without so much as a backward glance. "Looks like I was wrong."

REBECCA SPENT THE REST of the evening alternately pushing away guilt and painting. Exhausted, she took a shower, and climbed into bed with the installation instructions for the misting system for the barn. It didn't take long for her to realize she was going to have to find a faster way to keep her alpacas cool before the midweek heat wave. So once again she revised the work schedule she had devised to help her get ready for the Open House.

Fortunately, her brother and two sisters had meant what they said about lending a hand, and gave up their Sundays off to come over. Rebecca handed out the construction masks. First up was Blue Mist. Because she was with cria, they had opted not to give her the sedative all the others had been given with their morning's breakfast. Susie cradled the quivering alpaca's neck and rubbed her behind her ears while they used an air hose to blow the dirt and grass out of her fleece. Jeremy held Blue Mist's hind legs, Amy her front. Rebecca manned the clippers, shearing the alpaca's tummy first, where the most valuable, softest fleece grew, then moving around to her back and sides, and finally her neck and legs.

With five inches of wool removed, she looked much skinnier. "She's got to be much cooler now," Amy noted, as they let the alpaca stand again.

"She'll feel even better once she delivers," Rebecca said as she put the valuable fiber into a plastic bag.

"When is she due?" Susie asked.

"Another two weeks."

Rebecca praised the alpaca for her cooperation and gave her a treat, then led her back to the pasture and got another female. As she led Midnight back to the barn, she couldn't help but notice Trevor, working the fence line closest to his ranch. He was too far away for her to tell what he was doing.

Unlike Blue Mist, who'd been relatively calm throughout the procedure, Midnight turned skittish the moment she saw the air blower.

"I'm surprised Trevor's not up here helping you," Susie remarked.

He would have been if I'd asked him, Rebecca thought.

"Did you ask if he wanted to lend a hand?"

"Yeah, with his experience with cattle, he'd probably be a lot better at this than we are," Jeremy said as he coaxed a recalcitrant Midnight onto the barn floor.

Aware her siblings were waiting for an answer, Rebecca shook her head. "I'm not really in a position to ask Trevor for any favors right now," she said.

"How come?" Susie asked.

Midnight flinched and moaned as Rebecca moved the clippers over her belly.

Briefly, Rebecca explained.

"Trevor McCabe would not sabotage your tire, just so he could come to your rescue later!" Amy said.

"I know that."

"Then why did you accuse him?" Jeremy asked.

"Easy," Susie cut in, as she sat, cradling Midnight's head in her lap. "Because he's getting too close, too fast. And Rebecca can't have that."

As much as Rebecca would have liked to tell her sister she was wrong, she couldn't. She had learned the hard way not to rush. Not to get too physical too soon. Not to confide, not to trust, not to open her heart up to lust and love, without putting on the brakes often and long, first.

Like it or not, Trevor McCabe made her want to do away with caution altogether.

He made her want to lean on him, go to him, include him in her life.

And she couldn't have that.

She had fought hard and long to be able to achieve financial independence and start up a ranch on her own. She was finally living her dream. Or trying to, if only the financial realities would stop getting in the way.

And yet she couldn't stop thinking she had been unfair to him. Really unfair. And that bothered her more than anything.

TREVOR HAD NEARLY FINISHED installing mesh fencing along the Primrose-Wind Creek property line when he looked up and saw Rebecca Carrigan marching his way. As usual, she was dressed in a T-shirt and jeans that attested to her willingness to get as down and dirty as the business of ranching required. A flat-brimmed hat shaded her face from the worst of the Texas sun. The pink in her cheeks deepened as she came to a halt just short of him.

Trevor kept right on working.

Rebecca propped her hands on her hips.

"I thought I told you I wasn't ready to put up a mesh fence," she said.

Wondering when he would stop wanting to haul her in his arms and kiss her once again, Trevor straightened slowly, tipped the brim of his hat back to better see her face. He rested an elbow on the top of the split rail wooden fence Miss Mim had installed, years before. "This mesh isn't on your property, it's on mine."

"I thought we were going to split the costs—and the decisions about this."

"Obviously—" Trevor pounded another five-foot metal stake into the ground, and attached another section of the rolled mesh fencing to the post "—after last night, that's not going to work."

She stomped closer. Her cheeks grew even more flushed. Her tongue snaked out to wet her lips. "About that—"

"I think you've said all you need to say." Trevor tried but could not quite keep the exasperation from his low voice. "I got the point."

As the seconds drew out, her lips formed a delicious pout. "I was wrong. I know that."

Now, this was interesting. Trevor wiped the sweat off his brow with the sleeve of his shirt. In no hurry to let her off the hook, he studied her a good long time. "Wrong to what?" he demanded gruffly.

Abruptly she looked as frustrated with him as he still was with her. "To jump to conclusions." Her soft hands lifted in a conciliatory manner. "To even tell you what I'd heard in the first place."

Trevor dropped his sledgehammer onto the grass and reached for the cooler of water. He opened the spout and tipped the jug against his lips. None of this was as easy as she wanted to make it. With his free hand, he swept off his hat and let it rest against his thigh. "You think I want you keeping secrets from me, is that it?"

"No." She folded her arms in front of her contentiously and glared at him. "Of course not! Nor do I want you keeping vital information from me!"

"Vital information, huh?" he repeated in a tone meant to annoy her. He closed the spout with a snap and dropped the jug back into the grass. He dropped his hat and stepped forward, not stopping until he towered over her. "And just what vital information would that be?" he asked, ignoring the erratic intake of her breath and the clear definition of her breasts beneath the clinging light blue cotton T-shirt.

She tilted her chin at him and slapped her hands on her hips. Expressive brows lowered over her long-lashed eyes. "I still want to know about Jasmine."

He regarded her with silent derision.

Undeterred, she continued impatiently, "This is what I know thus far. You had a girlfriend in college named Jasmine. You were serious about her. Your senior year, Jasmine caught you making out with another woman in the university lab, and she dumped you and turned to Vince. Vince and Jasmine started dating. And you've never forgiven Vince, even though Jasmine eventually dumped Vince, too. And that's what the rivalry between you two guys is really all about."

Leave it to Vince to twist things just enough....

Aware that she looked as miserable as he had been feeling since they'd had words, he told her tersely, "You've got your facts wrong."

She shrugged and kept her eyes on his. "So enlighten me."

He studied her brooding expression. "I wasn't with another woman."

She wanted to believe him. He could see that. She just wasn't sure she should.

Rebecca dug the toe of her dusty boot in the grass. "Vince said you were kissing someone named Valerie when Jasmine and he walked in that night."

Trevor had never been one to shift the blame for his mistakes, but in this instance, he knew he wasn't at fault. Stupidly naive, maybe, but not unfaithful.

He tugged off his leather work gloves, let them drop to the ground, knowing before he spoke how lame this was all going to sound, even years later….

With a weariness that went soul deep, he began. "Vince told Valerie I had a secret thing for her, that I was just waiting for some sort of sign from Valerie that she was interested, and as soon as I got it, I was going to break up with Jasmine and go after her."

Something in his words must have clicked, because he saw a flicker of recognition or acceptance in Rebecca's eyes.

Trevor pushed on. "Vince arranged for Valerie to be in the lab the same time I was that night, then made sure that Jasmine was there, about the same time." He shook his head, recalling, "Vince and Valerie must have had it timed down to the second, because the moment Valerie grabbed me and planted one on me, Jasmine and Vince walked in. Vince had already told Jasmine I was fooling around on her, so when Jasmine saw Valerie making her move, she assumed everything Vince had told her was true. I tried to explain. She refused to listen to a word I had to say. So we broke up, and that was that." And Trevor had vowed to never again become entangled with a woman who did not trust him and believe him to be honorable.

"Just like I didn't want to hear your side of things last night," Rebecca murmured, looking distraught.

For a moment, Trevor's heart went out to her. Rebecca didn't deserve to be in the middle of any of this.

Had Vince not picked up on Trevor's attraction to her or wanted Rebecca's recently purchased property for himself, Vince wouldn't be pursuing her and causing mischief, now.

It was his fault, Trevor knew, that Rebecca had become a target for one of the most devious people Trevor had ever met.

"What else did Vince tell you?"

Rebecca took her hat off, too, and let it rest against her knee. She looked at it a moment before returning her glance to his face. "That you were only interested in me because you knew he was interested in me."

Rebecca took a deep breath and let it out. "Is it true?" she demanded.

Trevor knew he could sour Rebecca's view of Vince permanently simply by telling Rebecca about the bet Vince had tried to make about her.

But somehow that didn't set well with him, either.

If for no other reason than it would send Rebecca right back to Vince to discover the truth of that.

Figuring she couldn't be hurt by what she didn't know, hopefully would never know, Trevor shrugged. "I admit I don't want you involved with Vince Owen," he said. "I don't want to see any woman involved with Vince." His hands came up to cup her shoulders, and he pushed an errant strand away from her cheek. "But that sentiment has nothing to do with why I kissed you or helped you out."

Her palms flattened against the front of his shirt. "Then why did you do those things?"

Loving the warmth and softness of her as much as the spring sunshine overhead, he pried the hat from her fingers, tossed it in the grass and wrapped both arms around her. He pressed his lower half to hers. She surged against him. Everything that had been wrong righted. "Haven't you figured it out?" he teased, backing her up against the fence.

A shiver of desire swept through her, weakening her knees. Caution mingled with the yearning in her soft eyes. "Trevor…"

That was all the encouragement it took. He lowered his mouth to her and gave her a full-on kiss filled with passion

and need. She gasped in surprise. He grazed her earlobe
with his teeth, touched his mouth to her throat, the underside of her chin, her cheek, the tip of her nose, before
moving once again to her lips. And this time, when he fit
his mouth over hers, she was ready for him. Her mouth
softened under his, opened to allow him deeper, wider
access. She made a sexy little sound in the back of her
throat, and then her hands were coming up, to cup his
head. She was standing on tiptoe, pressing her body into
his, tangling her tongue with his.

Rebecca hadn't figured she'd end up kissing Trevor
when she'd come out here to talk to him, but now that she
was in his arms, she couldn't think of anywhere else she
would rather be. My heaven, the man was magic, his body
hot and hard and she was the reason. He shifted again, flattening his hand down her spine, pressing her closer still,
until there was no doubting how much he wanted her. Her
body registered the intense pleasure, even as she generated
more of her own, and she reveled in it, and wanted more.

Had he moved to take her then and there, she could
hardly have said no.

Instead, he slowly, inevitably, let her go, and lifted his
head.

"If we're going to do this," he said gruffly, looking
down at her, "we're doing it right."

Chapter Seven

Rebecca drew a jerky breath. Trevor was right. They couldn't continue this out in the middle of a field, where anyone who happened to be driving by could see.

"Your place or mine?"

He kissed her throat. "I don't reckon it matters. I'm sure we'll work our way to both eventually."

So he planned ahead.

So should she.

And paramount was keeping him from breaking her heart.

Wishing she had her hat on so she could shield her eyes from his probing gaze, she strengthened her emotional armor. "I'm just talking about a fling."

He ran his fingers through the sides of his hair. "One time," he repeated thoughtfully.

She nodded, aware her heart was still racing, her lips still tingling from the feel of his. "To get it out of our systems." Quench the desire building deep inside her.

His brows climbed.

"End the mystery of what it might be like and all that."

"I knew you were curious." His eyes alive and shining with suppressed devilry, he picked up her hat, settled it ever so slowly on her head. The corners of his mouth quirked upward. He focused with laser accuracy on her mouth, then teased, "I didn't think the need-to-know extended to this arena."

Not that he was protesting, mind you. It was clear from the evidence of his continuing arousal, pressing up against the front of his jeans, that at least part of him would be only too happy to discover what it would be like to be twisted up in the sheets with her.

Trying not to imagine how it would feel to have him buried deep inside her, she stated as casually as she could, "I don't make a habit of this." And that, in a nutshell, was the problem. She hadn't done this in forever.

Enter Trevor, with his sexy, oh so male presence, and what-I could-do-to-you-if-I-only-had-the-chance hazel eyes.

She found herself at the melting point of butter on a hot stove. And damn it all, if the rancher next door wasn't hot as could be.

"I expect you don't, either," Rebecca continued stiffly, aware she was making a fool of herself by acting so uptight and methodical instead of loose and free as the spring breeze.

Worse, he saw right through her pragmatic act.

"You're right," he told her drily, calling her a liar with everything he didn't say. "One night—or maybe I should say one afternoon—stands aren't my thing."

"Then we agree, this—us—is an exception?" she plodded on determinedly. The kind of exception-to-the-rule that made life great.

He chuckled. "We're an exception all right. But this chemistry between us is not going to end with a bang and a fizzle. When I make you mine—"

When, not if.

Rebecca focused on the words.

"—once isn't going to be enough." He lightly clasped her chin. "I can wait until the time is right." He leaned forward to brush her lips. "I trust you'll let me know when that is."

He paused to look deep into her eyes.

"But for now," he continued softly, knowing full well he'd just stolen her breath, again, "you and I both have work to do."

REBECCA DIDN'T KNOW whether to be impressed with his chivalry, relieved he'd had enough sense not to let them stray into territory they had no business exploring without some sort of commitment to each other, even if it was only for an ongoing love affair. Or frustrated she was going to go to bed once again with an ever-expanding To-Do List for company.

Maybe it was time she got a dog.

A puppy, like Coco, who'd be company for her, someone she could love and be loved by in return without having to worry about the complications a romance with a man brought.

As soon as she got her finances straightened out, Rebecca determined, and could afford the extra vet bills and food, she'd talk to Vince Owen, find out where he'd gotten his chocolate-brown Labrador retriever. And see about getting a "Coco" of her very own.

In the meantime, she had to take the fleece from the shearing to the local weaver recommended to her.

A quick call confirmed it would be okay to take it by for weighing and purchase that very evening.

So Rebecca showered, changed and drove off.

Unfortunately, the fleece didn't bring nearly as much as she had hoped. She'd only averaged eighty ounces per animal, instead of the maximum of one hundred and twelve. She'd gotten three and a half dollars per ounce, which was better than the low of two dollars per ounce, but less than the maximum of five.

"The more you pay for an alpaca," the weaver explained, "the better their fleece, and the more you'll get for it."

But the flip side of that was that a premium alpaca could fetch as much as four hundred thousand dollars per animal, and those animals were way out of her league, at least for now.

"You've done really well for a first shearing," the weaver said, as she handed over a check.

Unfortunately, "really good" wasn't going to cut it, Rebecca realized as she sat up late that night, going over her ranch books thus far.

Everything had cost more than she had anticipated when she had first drawn up her business plan two years before.

There were expenses—such as the mister and fan cooling system—she hadn't realized she would need, having done her preliminary training at alpaca farms in a much cooler environment over in Europe. Last summer's drought had pushed up the price of feed. Rising interest rates had ended up costing her more in closing costs on both her ranch mortgage and the financing package she had gotten on her herd of alpacas. And now she had a balloon payment due on her temporary operating loan that, although still payable, would leave her with exactly one hundred dollars in her bank account.

That wouldn't pay her mortgage for May or her utilities or gasoline for her truck or feed and supplements for her herd or the vet bills.

She was going to have to go back to the San Angelo

bank where she had gotten the financial deal that had allowed her to start up her ranch and ask for an extension on the balloon payment on her operating loan.

So first thing the next morning, Rebecca took care of her herd and put them out to pasture. Then, armed with the facts and figures she had been up half the night preparing, got in her truck and drove to San Angelo.

Leigh Meeks, the loan officer, met with her right away.

But it wasn't to hear Rebecca's pitch, as it turned out.

"I'm sorry, Rebecca," the young woman in the pin-striped suit said. "We can't give you an extension. Our bank no longer holds your loan."

Rebecca blinked. "What are you talking about?"

"Your loan was sold to a venture capital group in Dallas last week. Edge Investments. They specialize in unconventional financial opportunities. They put out the word last week they were looking for alpaca ranches to purchase. Your whole loan package was transferred to them by close of business Friday."

"No one asked me!" Rebecca declared, upset.

"Read the fine print on your loan papers. We don't have to ask you. No one does. Edge Investments is free to sell your loan at any time, too." Leigh flashed a reassuring smile. "This happens all the time, to regular mortgages, too. I'm sure it will be fine."

Rebecca felt as if she'd had the wind knocked out of her. It wouldn't be fine if Edge Investments refused to give her an extension on her balloon payment, and she was left with nothing in her bank account to pay her monthly expenses. She wouldn't be able to take care of her herd properly. Or pay her mortgage on the ranch. Without cooperation from her lender, she could be facing foreclosure and bankruptcy by summer! "How will I get in touch with them?"

"They're going to be contacting you."

"I can't just go ahead and call them?"

Leigh shook her head. "They need time to put your information into the system. I'm sure you'll get a letter in the next day or so, telling you who your new loan officer is. But I have to caution you, Rebecca, I very much doubt they will grant you an extension. They're in the business to make money, not give it back to customers. Your best bet, if you can't make that payment on schedule and have anything left to run your ranch is to try and refinance the whole package before the balloon payment is due, and just pay off the loan Edge Investments now holds in full."

LEIGH'S ADVICE MADE SENSE, so Rebecca drove back to Laramie and stopped at the bank. She had gone to high school with the loan officer, Elliott Allen, and he was glad to see her there to do some business. He listened to her problem, and agreed to look at her situation, see what he could do.

Unfortunately, it wasn't much.

"You're aware you leveraged way too much with this first set of loans," he said, studying the figures. "Worse, the interest rate on the operating loan is variable and written so that every time the prime rate increases, or your credit rating takes a dive, your rate goes up."

Rebecca hadn't worried about the latter, because she was the kind of person who always paid her bills on time.

"I knew it was a risk. But I needed to get in and get going, and I still think once I have my Open House on Sunday afternoon and get some outside investors to lease or buy some of my alpacas, and board them at The Primrose, that I'll be in good shape." Finances would still be tight for the first six months to a year, but after that...

"Tell you what," Elliott said. "You get some contracts

signed over the weekend that will demonstrate you have a good income generated by your business and come back here first thing next Monday, we'll give your situation a second look. But you're still going to have to make that twenty-thousand-dollar balloon payment to Edge Investments, also due next Monday."

"Any chance I could get a loan for that folded into my new mortgage?" Rebecca asked.

Elliott Allen lifted a brow. "It might be possible to set up a line of credit against the ranch, once you can demonstrate you have some income coming in, not just money going out, but again that all depends on a revised business plan and a good showing at your Open House." Elliott stood to show her out. "If I may, I'd like to suggest you talk to Trevor McCabe. He's an ace at putting ranch projections together. He did one not too long ago that had us agreeing to lend him the money for two more ranches."

"The Primrose and…?"

"The Circle Y. Of course those sold to you and Vince Owen. But the bank still stands ready to lend him that amount should he find a comparable property."

No wonder Trevor was so irritated with Vince. On top of everything else, Vince had purchased the property Trevor had his eye on, to help him expand Wind Creek. "Is he still looking—do you know?"

"I don't know. I spoke to him at the dinner Friday night, and he indicated he still hadn't gotten over losing out on the land adjacent to him."

Which meant what? Rebecca wondered as she said goodbye to Elliott Allen and walked out the bank doors, to the parking lot behind the building. That Trevor didn't just want her, he still wanted her ranch, too?

Could that be part of the reason he was pursuing her

after telling her at the feed store he wasn't the least bit interested in dating her?

Rebecca scowled at the thought.

"That bad, hmm?" a low voice asked.

Rebecca glanced up to see her father standing in front of her. Obviously on his lunch break from seeing patients at the Laramie Community Hospital office complex, he had a stack of papers in his hand.

"I was afraid of this." Hand on her shoulder, he guided her to a shady place on the sidewalk, where they could talk, uninterrupted. He looked down at her compassionately. "It's not too late for you to take a more cautious approach to this whole ranching business."

Rebecca braced herself for the lecture sure to come. "Meaning?"

"It's clear you're in way over your head. But there is still time to back out or cut your losses."

Rebecca started to brush a hand through her hair, then recalled she'd put it in a sophisticated knot at the nape of her neck for her business meetings. "How do you suggest I do that, Dad?" she asked in exasperation.

"You could sell most of your herd, just keep one or two alpacas, to start. Get a job in town. Life would be a lot easier." Luke paused. "I happen to know they are looking for a new social director for the community center. Or you could train to be an occupational therapist at the hospital."

What was it Vince Owen had told her?

"Stay away from the naysayers…. Surround yourself with like-minded people."

Vince had certainly been right about that.

He had also said, *"Big risks lead to big rewards. Forget conventional when it comes to pursuing your goals. Take*

*every shortcut you can. The important thing is getting
what you want, when you want it."*

Well, Rebecca knew what she wanted.

"Or even go back to leading day tours around Texas,"
Luke continued helpfully.

Rebecca did her best to contain her hurt. "You have
every right to your opinion, Dad. Just as I'm entitled to go
after what I want, with no holds barred. While I'm fighting
this battle, you have to back off."

Luke sighed, looking as if he wished he could give her
a great big hug and instantly make everything better for
her, the way he had when she was a kid. "That's exactly
my point, Rebecca. It shouldn't be a battle. It shouldn't be
this hard for you."

"DON'T YOU LOOK LIKE you just lost your best friend,"
Trevor said.

Rebecca spread drop cloths over the garage floor. She
had changed into an old souvenir T-shirt that had shrunk
the first time she washed it, so it was much wider than it
was long, ripped jeans and equally battered sneakers.
"What are you doing here?" she asked, for the sake of her
pride pretending she wasn't glad to see him at all.

If ever she'd had a day that left her feeling in need of
rescue, it had been today. But she had the feeling if she let
Trevor swoop in and help her with a revised business plan,
among other things, that wouldn't be all he'd end up helping
her with. And right now she had way too much on her agenda
to even think about beginning a love affair with a man who
had designs on her ranch, and the ranch next to her.

Trevor watched her move two sawhorses onto the center
of the cloth, some five feet or so apart.

Like her, he was dressed for work, in a light blue

chambray shirt and worn jeans that were frayed around the edges. He hadn't yet shaved, and the stubble gave him a rugged, sexy look.

Something hot and sensual shimmered in his eyes. "I came over to see if you wanted to go to a movie with me tonight."

Memories of the way he had kissed her the last time they'd faced off like this sent a burning flame throughout her entire body.

Mentally, Rebecca forced herself to douse the fire of desire.

She turned her attention away, and struggled with the unfinished wood door she had purchased at the home improvement center. "As in…a date?"

Trevor helped her situate the door across the sawhorses, his strong hands brushing hers. "If you want to call it that, sure."

She'd be a fool not to recognize all the pheromones flowing from his tall studly body. Rebecca was no fool. Mouth set in an uncompromising line, she nailed the door to the sawhorses. "I can't."

Laugh lines crinkled at the corners of his hazel eyes. "Because you're building furniture or because we didn't…?"

Pleased he had immediately figured out the use for the "desk" she had just made for her ranch office, Rebecca slanted him a glance meant to send him on his way. Better to get it all out in the open than stand around playing games. "Have sex?" she queried lightly, as if she hadn't been thinking about that possibility at all.

He moved lazily toward her. "Make love," he corrected, not stopping until he was close enough she could see the heat in his eyes.

It just figured he'd pursue her with romance.

Romance being the one thing she hadn't experienced in what seemed like forever, romance being the one thing that would leave her vulnerable, the one thing she couldn't afford to indulge in when her whole world was crashing in around her—financially, anyway.

"So back to why you can't?" he prodded, looking as if he wanted to do nothing more than take her in his arms and kiss her again.

"Because I have way too much to do."

And nothing he said or did was going to change that.

Finding the garage suddenly too intimate a setting for comfort, Rebecca went next door to the stable. She slapped a straw hat on her head, picked up a bucket of nutritional supplements disguised as treats and strode across the grass to check on the herd.

Trevor walked beside her. Blue Mist came over to the fence to investigate and Rebecca handed her a treat.

Trevor reached out to pat the alpaca's side. "She looks good."

Rebecca thought so, too. She took the hose from the pumping station next to the pasture and topped off Blue Mist's water trough.

"Nervous?"

Rebecca walked on out to the next field over, where the other females were pastured.

"How'd you know?" She tried to pretend she didn't appreciate the company.

Trevor tilted his hat back. "First time I birthed a calf, I was pretty edgy."

When they stopped at the fence, the other alpacas came over to get their supplements, too.

"How old were you?" Rebecca asked.

Trevor leaned against the four-foot-high mesh barrier

he'd erected on the other side of the wood fence. As much as Rebecca was loath to admit it, adding the extra barrier of finely tempered steel did give her an air of serenity she hadn't expected. Doubling up on the fencing between his cattle and her alpacas had been a good idea. Mentally, she vowed to continue it on the other three sides of fencing for her pastures as soon as she could afford to do so.

Trevor smiled, recalling. "Fourteen. My mom and dad were off on Annie's Homemade business and Dad had left me in charge of the cattle. A thunderstorm blew up, and a tree was struck by lightning in the pasture where the cows that were ready to give birth were staying. The rain put out the fire in the tree, but the cows were completely spooked, next thing I knew one of 'em was in labor."

Rebecca imagined the harrowing chaos that had ensued. "Naturally, again, all did not go as planned."

"The calf was breech and the cord got twisted around its neck," he told her, his voice a little rough. "I had to reach in and pull it out."

"And it survived."

Trevor's gaze moved over the size of the pasture. "As well as the rest of the calves that were born that day." Trevor turned back to her with a smile. "Like I said, that lightning strike really scared 'em. Several of 'em went into labor that day."

The two of them ambled down to the last pasture, where the herd-sires were kept, the warm spring breeze ruffling her hair.

"Well, I guess I know who to call if I run into any trouble with Blue Mist," Rebecca teased.

Trevor watched as Rebecca dispensed the treats to the males. He returned her sidelong glance. "My brother Tyler?"

"He is my ranch vet."

Aware she'd slipped and started flirting with Trevor again Rebecca forced herself to adopt a more businesslike attitude as she looked over at the Circle Y. Two large cattle haulers were backed up to the pasture, farthest from the house, bawling cattle pouring out onto the field, their large muscular bodies crowding each other and kicking up clumps of dust and grass.

Rebecca'd grown up around a lot of ranches. She couldn't recall any looking that chaotic. "That been going on all day?" she asked Trevor.

"Since midmorning."

Rebecca frowned. "It looks like a lot of cattle to be putting in one pasture." It reminded her of rush hour in the city.

"Yep."

She studied his expression. "You're not surprised."

Trevor shrugged. "Vince likes to squeeze every penny out of everything he does."

"No matter the cost in other terms, I'm guessing."

Trevor said nothing. Just turned his glance back to his own ranch.

Rebecca pivoted to survey the Wind Creek. In contrast, Trevor's place was downright pastoral, with the rolling green tree-lined pastures dotted sparingly with healthy-looking cattle, his white mission-style ranch house with red tile roof and white barns and outbuildings gleaming in the afternoon sun. "You don't run that many cattle in one pasture."

"And I won't. It's too hard on the grass, and bad for the cattle to be squeezed in that way."

"I'm guessing Vince Owen doesn't agree?"

"I push the envelope in one direction, he pushes it the other."

Admiring the restraint in Trevor's voice, Rebecca turned back to the Circle Y. From this distance, the cattle on the Circle Y versus the cattle on the Wind Creek didn't look all that different from one another, except for the obvious—they were different breeds. And different colors. Trevor's were white Charolais, Vince's Black Angus. "They don't look like they're suffering—yet anyway. I mean they're all pretty good sized."

He set his jaw. "He administers growth hormones and powerful antibiotics on a regular basis."

She studied him. "I'm guessing you don't."

"Mine are brought up on organic feed. No hormones. No antibiotics. Got fewer of them, but they sell for top dollar."

Which probably meant Trevor made as much as, if not more than Vince.

Trevor turned in the direction of the road. He inclined his head at Susie's green landscaping truck, turning into the drive. "Looks like you've got company."

Rebecca headed back toward the garage and Susie met her next to the barn.

Rebecca knew immediately that something was up.

"Dad told Mom about running into you at the bank today, and Mom told me."

"Great." Rebecca scowled. That was all she needed, her father spreading word of supposed impending failure as a rancher and a businesswoman.

"I came by to see what I could do," Susie continued, with her usual air of expertise.

Trevor started to edge away.

Knowing Susie would temper her remarks somewhat if someone else were there, Rebecca grabbed Trevor's shirt-sleeve. Getting the message, he stopped trying to make a graceful exit.

Unable to hide her resentment, Rebecca told her sister, "There's nothing you need to do."

"It's not about need. There's plenty I *can* do for you if you'll let me," Susie said, with the too-helpful look that had irritated the heck out of Rebecca for as long as Rebecca could remember. It was the look that said Susie knew better, the exasperated but concerned look that conveyed Susie had to rescue her stubborn little sis yet again. And once again, in Susie's estimation, it was too late, the damage was already done.

With effort, Rebecca pushed back years of pique and tried to be as civil as she had promised herself she would be, in her dealings with her successful older sister.

Susie had been through a lot.

In some respects, Rebecca knew, Susie *was* wiser than her years.

But not, Rebecca told herself firmly, in this instance.

Rebecca plastered a pleasant smile on her face. "Assisting with the shearing yesterday was help enough, Susie."

"Your Open House is this Sunday, Rebecca. Today is Monday."

"Believe me, I know how much—or how little—time I have left."

Susie gestured at the garage that was supposed to be the ranch business office. "You're not going to get it all done alone."

Rebecca's spine stiffened. "You don't know that."

"I know this. If you were to scale back on what you were trying to do, between now and then, you'd have a much better chance of success on Sunday. Your operation has to inspire confidence, Rebecca, to attract investors. It has to state that the business is firmly under your control. At the time you have guests here, nothing can remain undone."

Trevor coughed and gave Susan a look that wordlessly instructed her to back off.

Rebecca glared at Trevor. "I can handle her."

Trevor lifted his hands in wordless surrender. Still facing them, he stepped away.

Predictably, Susie began to lose her temper, too. "You don't need to handle me, Rebecca. You need to listen to me. I know ways you can increase your cash flow immediately without having to get any more loans."

That sounded appealing but letting Susie get involved and tell her what to do would mean Rebecca was no longer in charge of her operation, Susie was. Rebecca couldn't have that. "Thanks, but no thanks," she told her sister flatly.

Susie blew out an exasperated breath. "You are so stubborn."

"And you," Rebecca volleyed right back, "are always barging in where you don't belong, telling me how to act and what to think. Except of course the one time that you should have told me everything…"

"You're talking about Grayson Graham."

"Who else?"

"Dad and I apologized for that!"

"And it was too little, too late, on both counts."

Susie blew out an exasperated breath. "We were trying to protect you."

Rebecca folded her arms in front of her. "Then, as now, I don't need your protection. I need you to treat me as a capable adult."

Susie glared at Rebecca, frustrated as always when a situation—or a person—was out of her control. "Add sensible to your list and you might actually get somewhere," Susie muttered.

In her younger days, this would have been the perfect point to throw an all-out temper tantrum. "You know what your problem is? You just never had any faith in me," Rebecca told her sister calmly. "You still don't."

Susie started to reply, then stopped, brushed a hand through her blond hair. She sighed, abruptly looking as hurt and disappointed as Rebecca felt that it had come to this—again. "Believe it or not, Rebecca, I did not come over here to fight with you," Susie informed her sadly.

Bitterness welled up inside Rebecca. Some things, it seemed, would never change. "Well, you failed on that count, didn't you?" Rebecca asked softly.

TREVOR WATCHED as Susie drove away. He turned back to Rebecca, like a principal chastising an errant student. "That was uncalled for."

"Who asked you?" Rebecca marched past him.

"She was trying to be *nice*." He fell into step beside her.

"She was *trying* to butt in." Rebecca slammed into the house, via the back door.

He strode in right after her. "Maybe you need her to butt in. She runs her own business. She started it from scratch. As a landscape architect who had to convince people to trust her from a young age, she knows a thing or two about presentation."

Rebecca stalked to the sink and pumped liquid soap into her palm. "More than you?"

"I don't have to sell people on trusting me with their money. Susie does." Trevor's voice gentled. He stepped in beside her to wash his hands, too. "What's going on with the two of you anyway? And who the hell is Grayson Graham?"

Rebecca blotted her hands on a towel, handed it over to him. "My college boyfriend."

Trevor took a moment to compute that. "Is he the guy

everyone said you were about to get engaged to your senior year?"

Rebecca couldn't believe he remembered. "Yep."

"What happened?" Trevor lounged against the counter as she went to the refrigerator. "Did he have eyes for Susie?"

Rebecca set the pitcher of lemonade on the counter. "Not quite."

"She make a play for him?"

Rebecca aimed a lethal look his way. "No."

"Then…?"

"He was using me." Rebecca was so agitated she sloshed liquid over the rim of the glass. "Susie knew what he was up to, and she didn't tell me. She told *my dad* instead."

Trevor came to the rescue with a paper towel. "I don't follow."

Rebecca rummaged around underneath the sink for the spray cleaner. "Grayson Graham went out of his way to befriend Susie her senior year in college. Susie couldn't figure out why, since they didn't have much in common. Turned out Grayson knew my dad was on the admissions board for the UT–Dallas medical school, and Grayson wanted Susie to get him entrée to our dad. Susie refused. Apparently—" Rebecca calmed down as she began to clean "—Grayson had been told his MCAT scores were outstanding, but his grades from college were not. Without a certain grade point average, there was no way any med school in Texas was going to let him in. Grayson, who was brilliant but lazy, figured the only way to get around that was to get someone with influence—like my dad—to give him such a high recommendation the med school would have no choice but to admit him. When Susie refused to help him, Grayson asked me out."

"And Susie didn't tell you," Trevor guessed.

Rebecca added ice to both glasses. "Susie told me not to date him," Rebecca admitted reluctantly. "She *didn't* tell me why."

Trevor's hand brushed hers as she handed him the glass. "Would you have believed her, even if she had told you?"

His probing irked her. Rebecca lifted her brow. "That's not the issue."

He looked at her over the rim of his glass. "In other words, you would not have."

"The point is, I would have had the information." Rebecca gulped her drink and wiped her mouth with the back of her hand. "I could have decided for myself. At least, I would have been on my guard."

Thankfully, he did not argue that. "Where does your dad come into this?" Trevor asked.

Wishing she had on something other than the misshapen T-shirt and jeans, that would allow her look as pulled-together on the outside as she felt on the inside, Rebecca sighed. "Susie told him, too."

The look on Trevor's face said he knew what a mistake that was. "My dad agreed I needed to be protected, so the two of them concocted this plan to have Grayson come home to meet the family for a weekend." She flushed, recalling the stinging humiliation of that terrible time. "Fool that I was, I thought everyone was finally coming around to this wonderful college senior I was dating. And Grayson was so excited, so willing to become a member of the Carrigan clan, when he told me he wanted a private audience with my dad over the weekend, I thought he was planning to ask my dad for permission to marry me."

Trevor gave her a look that was so full of compassion she wanted to weep. "So you told everyone you knew…."

"Yes," Rebecca uttered miserably. She scraped the toe of her boot across the linoleum.

Trevor moved close to her side.

Rebecca continued looking at the pattern on the tile. "Grayson came home for the weekend, everything seemed to go great. My parents tried hard to get to know Grayson. Then, before we left, Grayson and my dad had their private meeting." Restless again, Rebecca began to pace. "I didn't know what was said, but I could tell—even though Grayson was all polite and everything—that Grayson was upset by whatever had transpired during their man-to-man talk. When we got back to school, I confronted him. I figured my dad had told him I was too young to be engaged. And I was all ready to comfort him, to tell him all we had to do was be patient."

"But that wasn't it."

"No. Grayson told me my whole family were jerks. I questioned how he could possibly have come to that conclusion when everyone had been so nice to him, and the whole story came tumbling out. By the time he had finished telling me his side of things, it was clear he had only pursued me to get entrée to my dad and he dumped me."

"And broke your heart in the process." Trevor's expression was grim.

Rebecca nodded, set her empty glass aside. "The worst part of it was that Susie and my dad both insisted they had only been doing what was right for me."

Trevor finished his lemonade in a single draft. "And you've been mad ever since."

Rebecca nodded. "For a long time, I was."

"Which was why you took that job after college with that tour company."

She gestured aimlessly. "That was part of it. The other part was I wanted to go off and see the world."

And she had.

Trevor came toward her, not stopping until they stood toe to toe.

Rebecca stood with her back to the counter, facing him, studying the strong column of his throat. "I thought things were going to be different now. I thought if I let them in on my dream, if I bought this ranch and started my own business they would stop treating me like a child."

Only it wasn't working out that way, she realized, more discouraged than she could remember feeling in a very long time. Not nearly.

She looked up at Trevor.

Expecting sympathy, she was surprised to see none.

Chapter Eight

"If you want to be treated like an adult, you have to act like an adult."

This wasn't the reaction Rebecca was hoping for from Trevor. "Criticize me while I'm down, why don't you?" She stormed from the kitchen and marched back to the office, ready to resume painting again.

"I'm not taking Susie's side against you."

She shot him a cold look. "Could have fooled me."

"Your sister may not have said what you wanted to hear just now, but her motivation in coming over here, and trying to help you out, was genuine."

"Don't you get it?" Rebecca pried open the lid on the paint can, gave the primrose yellow enamel a stir. "That's just the problem. Susie and my father didn't trust me to handle the situation with Grayson Graham without their behind-the-scenes protection, and they don't trust me to be able to pull off this business venture without their intervention. Nothing has changed and it probably never will."

He eased onto a low stack of book boxes. "It won't if you keep up that attitude. There's nothing wrong with accepting a little help and advice."

Rebecca stirred with a vengeance. "You're telling me

you let your dad and/or your brothers come over and tell you how to run the Wind Creek?"

Trevor stretched his long legs out in front of him. "I listen to their advice. Particularly when they have something to say that will help me. Then I decide what it is I want to do and do it."

Rebecca picked up a brush. "No hard feelings."

"None required. None meant, either."

She painted with long, even strokes. Gritted her teeth. "You make it sound so simple."

"It is simple."

She snorted.

"And there's something else, too."

Rebecca rolled her eyes. "Why is everyone so free with the advice where I'm concerned?"

"Just because Grayson Graham betrayed you, doesn't mean every other guy will."

She set her paintbrush down and wiped her hands with a rag. "Are we talking about every other guy or you?"

"Me." Trevor took her into his arms.

She splayed her hands across his chest. "I can't do this now."

His eyes glimmered with mischief. "What?"

She gasped as he sat back down on the box, taking her with him. One minute she'd been standing, the next draped across his lap. "Get involved with you."

He anchored one arm around her waist, tunneled his other hand through her hair. "Is that a choice to make?" His lids lowered to half-mast. "Or something that happens despite our intentions?"

Rebecca had told herself the next time he kissed her she would be prepared, she would have all her defenses up. That buffer fled the moment his lips made contact with hers. It wasn't so much the soft, sure feel of his mouth moving on hers, although that was tantalizing. Or the way his tongue dallied provocatively with hers, finding every sweet spot with ease. It was the way he took charge and dominated the moment, and her. The way he deepened the kiss and slid his tongue over the plump curve of her lower lip. The way he made her feel so ravished and cherished all at once.

As if she was meant to be with him, meant to do this. Meant to take this risk. Which was why of course she had to come up for air and say, "I've got so much on my plate right now…. Trevor…I can't risk…"

He nuzzled the side of her neck, finding the nerve endings just beneath her ear. He turned his attention to her lips again, kissing and caressing her with even less reserve. "Sure about that?" he murmured.

Rebecca was sure about one thing, as she allowed herself to melt into his touch, one last time before she forced herself to get back to work. No one had ever kissed her like this. No one had ever held her so close, and given so much or made her want to deepen the connection between them so very badly.

Which was why when the kiss finally halted, and the amazing intimacy ended, she felt stunned and bereft. Elated and confused.

"I've got to go back to my place, and finish up there," Trevor told her hoarsely, his expression reflecting her reluctance to get back to business as usual. "When I'm done, I'll be back to help you with all this."

"Oh, yeah?" Embarrassed to have revealed so much about her desire so readily, Rebecca vaulted off his lap. Stalked away. "And what's that going to cost me?" She willed her knees to vanquish their trembling. "'Cause if you're looking for another home-cooked dinner..." She spun around to face him.

Or, heaven help them both, more of this...

His expression said, Game over.

"Don't you get it?" He caught her hand and pulled her against him, so there was no mistaking the desire dominating his lower half or the pounding of his heart beneath his shirt.

He paused to kiss her again, slowly, lingeringly, until she believed—as did he—they had something special, something neither could ignore.

He rubbed his thumb across her lips, looked deep into her eyes. "The pleasure of your company is gift enough."

TREVOR RETURNED about the time she had finished putting her herd in the barn for the night. He brought with him a picnic supper of cold fried chicken, potato salad, coleslaw, two bottles of ice-cold beer, a thermos of coffee and another plate of his homemade ranger cookies.

The fiercely independent side of Rebecca would have liked to say thanks but no thanks and send him on his way, but the more practical part of her was starved for food, and hungry for his company, even if he was an insufferable know-it-all from time to time.

So she made a big deal of sighing, and invited him to join her, as he must have known she would.

Grudgingly ignoring his satisfied smile, she dragged a couple of lawn chairs into the twilight.

In the distance, she could see Vince Owen and his cowboys unloading yet another two cattle haulers into the back pasture. Which made her wonder just how many cows Vince was planning to run on the Circle Y? Two hundred? Three hundred?

No one in Laramie ran as many cattle on such small pastures.

Of course, Vince could build more fence. He had plenty of land—fifty acres or more—that wasn't currently being used for grazing, in front of and to the sides of his ranch house, which was set back a ways from the road.

Not that it was any of her concern.

She had her own problems to deal with.

At the center of which was what she was going to do with her considerable physical attraction to Trevor McCabe, now that he had nixed the idea of a one-time-only no-strings affair.

Figuring she'd better get her mind on something other than the emotional argument and passionate kisses they had shared earlier, she turned her thoughts back to the business at hand.

In terms of ranching, she knew there was plenty she could learn from him. And as long as it was her idea, any "help" she received from him on her own terms, at her request...

"How long did it take your ranch to turn a profit?" Rebecca asked Trevor when they finished eating and went back to the garage to pick up where she had left off.

Trevor started painting the half a dozen bookshelves she had primed and Rebecca went to work on the battered wooden file cabinets she'd picked up at office surplus. "About a year," he said.

"What'd you do until then? How'd you make ends meet?"

Trevor moved the brush back and forth with steady, rhythmic strokes. "I hired myself out as a cowboy to work other ranches, like my dad's, on a temporary basis."

Which was coincidentally exactly what her dad had suggested to her that very morning.

Rebecca tried not to wonder if he would make love

with the same slow, steady expertise he did everything else. "That didn't make you feel like a failure?"

He shrugged, his frayed chambray shirt molding the contours of wide shoulders and broad chest. "Work is work. Besides," he teased her gently, his gaze roving her lips before returning to her eyes, "haven't you heard…pride goeth before a fall?"

She flushed, aware her lips were tingling the way they did when they kissed. "I thought the whole goal of being a rancher was to be self-sufficient."

"It is. But everybody's got to start somewhere. And unless you're having your success handed to you on a silver platter, it's usually at the bottom."

"I WORRIED IT MIGHT BE too early to stop by," Meg Carrigan said at seven o'clock the next morning. She was wearing her nurse's uniform.

Rebecca shook her head. "I got up at five-thirty."

The two women hugged. "The question is, what time did you go to bed last night?"

Rebecca knew she had circles under her eyes. "One, maybe two."

"Oh, honey…" A wealth of love was in Meg's voice.

Rebecca lifted a hand. "I'm okay, Mom. I only need about four or five hours of sleep."

"You might be able to *get by* on that. You *need* seven or eight, minimum, to be truly rested."

"I'll work on that when I get my ranch up and running."

"So how are things coming?" Meg asked cheerfully.

"Let's look and see." Rebecca led Meg across to the garage. She opened up the doors. Meg gasped in delight at what she saw. Pale primrose-yellow walls, bookshelves, desk and files.

"You had built-ins put in already?" Meg asked.

Rebecca shook her head, pleased at the way the formerly rustic space was turning out. "All the furniture is used. I just cleaned it up and painted it a shade darker than the walls."

"Well, it looks marvelous. How'd you get so much done so fast?"

Rebecca thought about claiming superpowers but knew it would be pointless—Meg could read her like a book. "I, uh, had a little help." She saved them both the trouble of Meg prying the information out of her.

Unfortunately, Rebecca noted, as Meg lifted her brow, waited, that tidbit wasn't enough to satisfy Meg's need to mother her.

"Trevor McCabe was over here last night, painting, too," Rebecca said, doing her best to contain a self-conscious flush.

"Oh!" Meg looked thrilled.

Rebecca's brows climbed before any more conclusions could be leaped to. "He was just being neighborly."

"Oh?"

So her too-cool attitude wasn't working. Rebecca propped her hands on her hips. "Mom, please..."

"I gather this means the two of you are no longer quarreling."

Rebecca tensed at the assumption in Meg's eyes. "How'd you hear about that?"

"Amy said Sunday..."

"Amy needs to learn to be quiet."

Meg merely smiled and blessedly let it drop. "I brought you something. My laptop computer and color printer. And several reams of business stationary in the ranch's new signature color, Primrose yellow. I can use your father's, and/or my computer at the hospital, so I'm not in any hurry to get them back."

Rebecca's eyes misted. "Oh, Mom. Thank you."

"You're welcome."

"This is going to help me so much."

"I'm glad. In return, I want you to cut your father and Susie some slack."

Rebecca propped her hands on her hips. "Is there anything you don't know about?"

"Very little, as it happens. And I mean it, Rebecca. It's past time this feud between the three of you ended."

Rebecca began carrying the gifts to her office. "I'd be happy to call a halt if they'd quit trying to run my life."

"They mean well."

Rebecca set both on the desk. "Meaning well and doing well are two different things."

"So, they screwed up again by doing and saying the exact wrong thing. It doesn't mean they don't love you because they do—every bit as much as I love you, and yet you're never mad at me."

They went back to get the rest of the stuff from Meg's car. "That's because you know how to be supportive."

"Or because I leave the heavy lifting to them." Meg's voice gentled. "Listen to me, darling. It's true. I don't usually assume the role of bad cop because your father does it so well. And let's face it, it's more fun to be the good cop, but that doesn't mean I don't worry about you, too."

Rebecca refused to let her agitation show. "Your point?"

"Families are made up of people who are human, and that makes them inherently flawed institutions."

"Or in other words," Rebecca ruminated on a belea-guered sigh, "there is no such thing as a perfect family."

"Any more than there is a perfect person." Meg squeezed her hand. "You appreciate me because I don't expect you to be perfect, honey. I'm telling you, if you ever want to be happy, you have to stop expecting others to be faultless."

REBECCA WAS STILL THINKING about what her mother had said to her when she saw the parcel post truck rumbling up the drive. Before she could do much more than step outside the office, he had dropped a big box onto her porch, lifted his hand in a wave and driven off.

Wondering what it was—she hadn't ordered anything—Rebecca went over to investigate.

The box bore her address all right—but Vince Owen's name. The package had been sent from a Dunnigan Dog Food care center in Dallas. Rebecca sighed. She could call Vince and ask him to come pick it up. Or she could run it next door herself, and leave it on his front porch.

Tossing the big cardboard box into the bed of her pickup truck, she climbed into the sweltering cab, put the windows all the way down and drove over, the unseasonably hot spring air wafting over her.

There were no pickups parked at the Circle Y.

Rebecca cut the engine, hopped out of the cab and ran the box up to the front porch. She had just dropped it when she heard a lot of loud, eager barking. Coming around the side of the house, she spotted a portable chain-link kennel, approximately six by ten feet, positioned beneath the shade of a tree.

Spying her, Coco got even more excited. She barked harder, running back and forth along the fence.

Unable to leave without at least saying hello to the puppy, Rebecca headed Coco's way. "Hey, girl, calm down now," Rebecca said, noting how hard the little dog was panting.

Rebecca knelt down beside the fence.

Whimpering hard, Coco stuck her tongue through the steel links, trying hard to lick Rebecca's hand, and nearly catching a baby tooth on the metal in the process. Rebecca looked around. Saw no one.

"I really shouldn't do this without at least asking permission," Rebecca told Coco, standing and walking over to the gate. "But what the heck…"

She slipped inside.

Coco took a flying leap, trying to jump into Rebecca's arms.

Coco whimpered harder, louder. Her rough eager tongue bathed the underside of Rebecca's chin. Her little body quivered as she settled in Rebecca's arms. Then she abruptly settled down, cuddling against Rebecca's chest and panted even harder.

Figuring she had time to comfort the lonely pup, Rebecca settled in the grass and stroked Coco's head, rubbing behind her chocolate-brown ears.

"Now, listen, little one, you've got to settle down," Rebecca soothed. "Running around like that in this heat can't be good for you, even if you have some shade. See that little doggy igloo over there in the corner? Yes, that one." Rebecca chuckled as Coco licked her hand. "It's nice and cool, and there's even a cushion in there for you to lie on. You've got two great big bowls of water and two more of food, so you're all set there. There's even a chew bone for you in the corner over there. And a corner of the grass that I can see you've been using for your own private potty. So you really are okay."

Coco turned her big dark eyes to Rebecca, whimpered more, then got up and walked on wobbly legs to her water bowl. She drank thirstily, emptying nearly half of it, before coming back to Rebecca's lap. She climbed back on and settled in, as if for a long nap.

"Oh, baby, I wish I could stay here and cuddle you all day long," Rebecca said, as Coco began nosing Rebecca's shirt and pants, in a way that told Rebecca Coco was picking up the scent of the alpacas on her clothing. "But I can't. I've got to get back and finish putting my office together, and see my herd has enough water in this heat—although like you they go right for the shade—and then get them inside the barn and settled for the night before the thunderstorms that are predicted for this evening appear."

Coco's expression turned alert and apprehensive.

Rebecca wondered if the pup had ever weathered a storm. Rebecca hoped she wouldn't have to do so alone and outside.

"I'm sure Vince or one of his two cowboys will be back by then," Rebecca said.

As if on cue, some of the cattle started mooing. Coco turned her gaze in the direction of the cows in the two big pastures that bumped up against Rebecca's pastures two and three.

"You agree with me, don't you, Coco?" Rebecca murmured, studying the wall of beef cattle. "There are way too many animals on those two patches of grass." Oh, they had plenty of water all right. Feed and water troughs lined the entire perimeter of the aging split rail wooden fencing that fronted the Circle Y ranch house and barns. The problem was, some of the cattle seemed to be having trouble getting to it, as the biggest steers were blocking their way.

"Oh, well, it's not my problem," Rebecca said. "Nor, sadly, are you." Reluctantly, Rebecca stood and set Coco down.

Coco turned mournful eyes to Rebecca.

"Your owner will be home soon," Rebecca reassured gently. She leaned down to pat the pup on the head, and then quickly let herself out of the kennel.

Coco let out a bark in protest, then ran after Rebecca, jumping and leaping against the fence.

Knowing there was nothing she could say that would comfort the lonely little puppy, who like as not had many such days ahead of her, Rebecca grimaced and turned and headed for her pickup truck, empathetic tears running down her face.

Rebecca spent the rest of the afternoon unpacking her books and papers and trying not to think about Coco. She filled her bookshelves and file cabinets, set up several lamps and the floor fan that was going to have to do until she could install a window air conditioner, then unpacked the rest of the personal items in the moving boxes and carted those up to the house.

She had just finished with the last of the clothing, when she heard a weird trumpeting sound.

What the...

The noise got louder.

It was now accompanied by a fierce, barking that sounded all too familiar. *Coco.* Rebecca raced down the steps, through the kitchen, out the back door, just in time to see chaos erupt.

TREVOR WAS DEEP in conversation with one of his business customers when he heard what sounded like a mini riot erupting. "I'm going to have to call you back," Trevor said, setting down the phone.

He raced for the door.

Midnight-blue clouds were gathering on the horizon with the typical speed of Texas weather. His herd was stamping and moving restlessly in response to the chaos on the next two ranches over.

A weird trumpeting sound pierced the air like a civil

defense siren. On the Primrose, he could see the alpacas racing around the pastures like racehorses in training.

That couldn't be good.

On the Circle Y, dust clouds rose, and the Black Angus cattle moved toward the perimeter like a herd during roundup.

Trevor didn't have to think. He hopped in his truck and drove to Rebecca's as quick as he could, bumping along, avoiding fence and cutting through their front yards. By the time, he got there Rebecca was racing back and forth, shouting and calling at the cause of the commotion in vain.

"Coco! Stop it now! Do you hear me! Stop it!" she shouted, tears running down her face.

The puppy either didn't hear her—highly plausible given all the aggravated mooing and alpaca trumpeting going on—or was too worked up to mind. Didn't matter. Blue Mist was running around frantically, trying to get away from the dog, who was chasing her.

"You get Blue Mist!" Trevor shouted above the din. "I'll get Coco."

Trevor hopped the split rail fence and headed for the dog.

Thinking it was a game of chase, Coco tried to evade Trevor.

Trevor hunkered down, held his arms wide, waited.

The puppy ran back and forth, still barking, but clearly tempted. Trevor stared straight at him and waited some more.

With a joyful yelp, Coco raced straight for Trevor and leaped into his arms.

On the other side of the pasture, Rebecca was still trying to calm Blue Mist.

Figuring she knew the animal best, and would likely have better luck with that, Trevor took the puppy toward the Primrose ranch house.

He carried her inside, set her in the laundry room, shut the door and headed right back out.

Coco resumed barking. It hardly mattered.

Trevor had another emergency to attend.

Rebecca's alpacas were still stampeding. The storm was ever closer, lightning flashing in the distance, thunder rumbling.

Wincing against the piercing warning call of the alpacas and the deeper mooing of the fiercely upset cattle, he raced for his truck, got a lasso and returned.

"Head toward her and be ready to comfort her," Trevor shouted over the cacophony.

To his relief, this once Rebecca bowed to his expertise in such matters and obeyed. He threw the rope. It landed around the top of the alpaca's legs. He tightened the lasso just enough to cause Blue Mist to stumble. Rebecca was right there. She caught the stunned alpaca in her arms.

And that was when, unfortunately, all hell really broke loose.

REBECCA HAD JUST REMOVED the lasso from Blue Mist's body and started leading her by the halter toward the safety of the barn when the earthshaking rumbling started.

Only it wasn't a quake.

And it wasn't a tornado.

Or even the fierce-looking thunderstorm drawing ever near that set her other nine alpacas into a frenzy. It was the sight of two hundred Black Angus cattle breaking through the barrier of the aging split rail fence between the properties.

The already-galloping alpacas were no dummies. They knew they were outweighed ten to one by the steers. Unable to get past the mesh Trevor had put up on the other side of the Primrose–Wind Creek property line, they headed for the only way out.

Spare minutes later, the two herd-sires barreled through the aging wooden fence line at the rear of Rebecca's property. The seven female alpacas broke through the fence separating pastures two and three and zoomed after the herd-sires, just ahead of the rampaging cattle.

Fortunately, the alpacas were lighter and faster than the Black Angus cows coming after them.

Unfortunately, all were running straight into the quick-approaching thunderstorm.

Blue Mist—perhaps exhausted from the ordeal—or perhaps just accepting the fact she now had a halter snapped to her lead, stayed with Rebecca.

"Take her to the barn and put her in a stall!" Trevor barked as the noise abated and animals scattered. He already had the cell phone out of his pocket. "I'll call for help!"

By the time Rebecca came back out of the barn, the skies had opened up, rain was pouring down. "My alpacas," Rebecca whispered, standing under the safety of the roof line, getting wet anyway.

Looking as if he didn't mind the drenching, Trevor gave her shoulder a reassuring squeeze. "We'll round 'em up. Don't worry. I've got half a dozen cowboys coming."

"How?" Rebecca trembled as the sky lit up with a jagged yellow flash, aware she could lose everything, including her precious alpacas. "How are you going to round them up?"

Trevor's jaw set. Determination radiated from him. "Any way we can. Most likely, horseback. But first we're going to have to wait for the thunderstorm to subside."

The thought of all that open countryside and the lightning flashing overhead terrified her. Glad Trevor was there, to see her through this, she bit her lip. "What if…?"

He shook his head, cutting off the thought. "They're animals, Rebecca. They'll know instinctively to seek shelter." He waited for a break in the lightning to push her toward the house, shielding her with his body as they ran.

He stopped just inside the door. "Meanwhile, I'm going to drive over and alert the ranches and country homes due south of us to the problem."

Glad he seemed to know just what to do, Rebecca nodded. "I want you to stay here and work the phone. Call the sheriff's department, and the office of the Laramie County Rancher's association and let them know what's happened, too. Have them help put out the word. Given all the cattle that are on the loose, we're going to need all the help we can get." Trevor stepped outside.

Rebecca caught his sleeve and pulled him back. "What about Vince?"

None of this would have happened if not for him.

Trevor grimaced. "I called him on his cell. He and his two hired hands are in Fort Worth—picking up more steers, if you can believe that. It'll be two hours or more before they can get back."

THE NEXT FEW HOURS were the tensest in Rebecca's life.

Help came from more people than she ever could have imagined.

Trevor's father, Travis McCabe, his two younger brothers, Kyle and Kurt, and his brother Teddy all showed up. They each brought half a dozen friends, and more vehicles, flashlights, lassos, cell phones and two-way radios than anyone had a right to expect. Neighbors and several members of the sheriff's department, helped out, too.

Before long, Rebecca started getting reports of alpaca sightings. With each alert, another alpaca was found or several more Circle Y cattle were rounded up.

Stacks of sandwiches and coolers of soft drinks were brought in. Rebecca made an endless supply of coffee.

By midnight, three quarters of the Circle Y cattle had been rounded up and pastured safely on other ranches. Rebecca had all but one of her herd back in the stable. And it was when the last one was being brought in that she first noticed something was wrong—really wrong—with Blue Mist.

Chapter Nine

Knowing from the way Blue Mist was alternately pacing her stall and hopping restlessly up and down the birth of her baby cria was near, Rebecca raced back to the house through the pouring rain. Relieved the lightning and thunder had stopped, she got another stack of clean towels from the linen closet, the first aid kit Jeremy had given her the day she moved in and the book she had on birthing alpacas. She had read it cover to cover several times during the year she was planning the start-up of her ranch.

Heart racing, she carted the birthing manual back out to the barn. Blue Mist was still hopping up and down. Rebecca saw the cria's head had begun to crown.

She donned sterile gloves and stepped into the stall.

With a groan, Blue Mist lay down and rolled onto her side, panting and pushing hard.

Rebecca let her strain a few more minutes, until the head and the front hooves were all the way out.

Following the directions she had memorized, she broke the sack and cleared the airways.

The cria blinked, looked straight at Rebecca. But did not seem to be any closer to coming the rest of the way out of its mama.

Rebecca touched the alpaca's shoulders gently. "Come on, Blue Mist, push a little more. You can do it."

Blue Mist strained, quivered.

The cria was making no progress.

Not sure how long the baby alpaca could stay that way, worried that the body of the cria was somehow wedged awkwardly in the opening, Rebecca reached in and began to gently work its front legs out.

One inch, two...

As soon as the front legs cleared, the rest of the cria's body came out. Rebecca made another check of the airways, was rewarded with a weak, mewling sound that was music to her ears.

Trembling with joy, she used a towel to wipe it clean and another to dry it off. She had just cut and tied the cord, dabbed the stub and area around it liberally with iodine, when she heard the rumble of a pickup truck, and the clanking of a cattle hauler, dragging behind.

Short minutes later, Trevor strode in, her herd-sire on a lead beside him. He was clad in a long yellow rain slicker. His hat looked drenched, as did his face and hair. "Got the last one here," he told her, looking over the top of the stall. A smile split his handsome face. "Hey, who is this?" Trevor said softly.

"Little Blue," Rebecca announced.

Positioning the cria close to Blue Mist, she stepped out of the stall, took the lead from Trevor. "Keep an eye on them for me a minute, will you?" she said.

"Sure." Trevor leaned against the outside of the door, while Rebecca grabbed a towel, and led Black Onyx down to his stall. She rubbed him down, checked for injury, and blessedly found none.

"You ever done this before?" Trevor asked.

Rebecca gave the herd-sire food and water, then walked back to where Trevor was standing.

"Birthed a cria? No. It was my first time."

"Looks like it's going pretty well so far," Trevor observed as Blue Mist got back on her feet.

Rebecca watched the alpaca sway back and forth, in much the same way she had earlier. "She's yet to finish her delivery and Little Blue has to stand on her own and nurse."

"That'll all happen, in due time," Trevor predicted.

Sure enough, Blue Mist began slowly but surely to deliver the placenta.

Seeing all was going exactly as it should, Rebecca turned back to Trevor, "Listen, about what you did for me tonight—"

He shushed her with a look. "It's nothing you wouldn't have done for me."

Rebecca checked on her alpaca, then turned back to him, "You were right about the fence."

Trevor's expression turned grim. He took off his hat and swept a hand through his damp hair. "I would have preferred not to be."

"How many cattle are still on the loose?"

Trevor undid the snaps on his coat. "Thirty or so is the rough estimate. Once steers get spooked like that, well, they can run pretty fast and far."

Glad the northern front moving through had forced the temperature down into the very comfortable low seventies once again, Rebecca asked, "What about Vince? Did he really bring more cattle back with him?

Trevor shook his head. "Nowhere to put 'em now. He sent them to another of his ranches, with the two hired hands he employs at the Circle Y."

"What about the rest of his cattle now?"

"The cattle ranchers with nonorganic herds are taking them in, five or ten here, five or ten there. It'll have to stay that way until he gets his fence fixed."

"Look," Rebecca whispered.

Little Blue was getting to her feet. Though wobbly, she was able to stand and find her way to her mama. Rebecca touched Trevor's arm. "I think she's going to nurse."

Little Blue rooted around, making that soft urgent sound, until she found what she was looking for. She fastened her lips over her mother's teat and began to suckle, awkwardly at first, then more and more confidently.

Rebecca and Trevor watched in silence, taking in the wonder of the moment.

Eventually, Trevor wrapped his arm around her shoulders. "You look tired," he said.

"I know. But I can't rest yet."

"Vince come by or send anyone to pick up Coco?" Trevor asked.

Rebecca shook her head. "I've been taking her out to go to the bathroom—on a leash—every couple of hours. I guess I should have tried to call Vince and let him know I have her, but I haven't really had the time."

"Morning is soon enough," Trevor said. "Meantime, can I get you anything?"

"Coffee would be great. But I gave the last of it away. There's none made."

"I'll go put on a fresh pot, and see to the pup," Trevor said.

He slipped from the barn.

Rebecca continued to watch the cria nurse until the little alpaca had finished and both mother alpaca and cria lay down to rest.

Exhausted, Rebecca headed for the house.

TREVOR WAS JUST POURING the coffee into two mugs when Rebecca stepped through the door. She looked gorgeous—tousled, exhausted and wet through and through. "Had I known you intended to make a run for the ranch house I would've left you my slicker."

She flashed a weary smile. "Then you would've been soaked to the skin."

Better than seeing her standing there, shirt and jeans clinging wetly to every delectable curve, Trevor thought.

She wiped her face on a dish towel.

Her hand trembled as she reached for the coffee.

His heart filled with a depth of feeling he didn't expect. "You've got to get some rest," he told her gruffly.

"I need to keep checking on Blue Mist and Little Blue for the next few hours, make sure they nurse again."

Trevor consulted his watch. "Tell you what. It's one-thirty now. I'll hang out in the stable, keeping watch over them while you catch a quick nap. I'll wake you at three-thirty. Or sooner, if need be. Tell you where things stand."

Her lips slid out in the stubborn pout he was beginning to know so well. And could never stop wanting to kiss.

She tilted her head at him, independent as ever. "It's not your job to watch over the animals on my ranch."

Just as it wasn't his job to want her so bad he ached. Trevor shrugged, adjusted his stance to ease the pressure building at the front of his jeans.

He turned away from her, and looked at the rain still coming down in torrents. It drummed against the house and ground and filled the dark of night with a repetitive hush.

It was the kind of night a man and a woman should be huddled under the covers. Wrapped in each other's arms. After first...

Trevor swallowed so much coffee, he nearly burned his throat.

He really had to stop thinking like this.

Aware she was watching him over the rim of her cup, he told her the truth. "I'm too wound up to sleep for a while anyway. So I might as well be doing something productive." *Other than seducing you.*

Rebecca ran her hands through her hair, thinking. She sank into a kitchen chair, then started suddenly as the next thought hit. "Oh my…I forgot to ask. What about your herd, Trevor…?"

Finally, some good news. "All fine," Trevor was pleased to report. "Fence held. Didn't lose a one, although half a dozen of my white Charolais came nose to nose with some of Vince's Black Angus." At her surprised look, Trevor explained, "Generally, cattle herd together in a storm for protection. Especially when lightning and thunder are involved. Fortunately there was a double row of fence between them."

Rebecca propped her chin on her hand. "Why didn't yours stampede the way Vince's cattle did?"

Trevor grimaced, aware the whole calamity this evening could easily have been prevented with proper management. "I had far fewer animals housed in each of my pastures that adjoin your three. The cattle didn't feel they were trapped to begin with. Trapped cattle tend to be more nervous, kind of the way people are in crowds."

Rebecca worried her bottom lip with her teeth. "I know what you mean about that. I hated some of the tours that had us packed in like sardines in a can."

Trevor pulled up a chair next to her. Their knees touched under the table. She didn't move away. "What was the worst?"

A rueful expression crossed her face. "I had a group of senior citizens who had always wanted to see the ball drop in Times Square on New Year's Eve, and they insisted on being right out in the middle of the melee." Rebecca made a comical face, recalling. "Of course they got too cold and had to use the facilities and some of them eventually needed to sit down and there was no place to sit down."

"I'm sure you handled it with aplomb." Just like the catastrophe tonight.

Rebecca flashed a weary smile. "I got everybody through it. And then swore never again. If a senior tour was crazy enough to try it, they'd have to get another guide."

"And did they?"

"Oh yeah." She sat back in her chair and stretched her long legs out in front of her. "There's no limit to people doing wild and crazy things."

If she stayed here much longer he was going to pull her into his arms, and he had no business putting the moves on any woman who had been through what Rebecca had this evening.

He stood and moved away. "I thought you were going to get some rest."

She exhaled slowly and stood, too. "You sure you don't mind?"

Although it took every ounce of willpower he had, he put his hands on her shoulders and pivoted her in the direction of her bed. "I don't mind."

TREVOR SHOULD HAVE KNOWN she wouldn't do as he ordered. Half an hour later, Rebecca stepped back into the barn. It had finally stopped raining and the air smelled as fresh and clean as she looked. He couldn't help it; he was glad to see her. "You showered."

She pirouetted so he could see her clean navy T-shirt and boot-cut jeans. "I'm glad you could tell."

"Well, I've got some good news for you." Trevor inclined his head at the stall that housed Blue Mist and Little Blue.

Blue Mist was standing patiently.

Little Blue was positioned beneath her, head tilted toward her mama's tummy, nursing contentedly.

Rebecca sauntered nearer. Hands in her pockets, she rocked back on her heels and observed. She had dried her hair, and left it long and loose, instead of putting it up. He appreciated the way she looked in braids but he liked her honey-blond hair this way, too, silky straight, swinging against her shoulders.

Reluctantly, Trevor turned his attention back to the activity in the stall. "That's a good healthy suckle," Trevor said.

Rebecca nodded, moving close. "Amazing how quickly they're up and running around, compared to human babies, isn't it?" she asked softly.

Sharing in her wonderment, Trevor wrapped his arm about her shoulders. "That's what comes from traveling on four feet instead of two." He appreciated the way she leaned into him. "Takes baby birds a mite longer, for instance."

She turned to face him, the warm abundance of her breast brushing his chest. "You're a regular font of information."

Trevor pushed away the urge to explore her soft womanly curves. "I did major in agriculture in college."

She released a beleaguered breath. "Bet you never figured you'd be helping a neighbor out by tracking down her alpacas."

"Actually," Trevor admitted reluctantly, "I was worried

about that," which was why he had put up the double fence where he could, "but I never figured it'd happen the way it did."

Without warning, Rebecca's eyes filled with tears. Embarrassed by the show of emotion, she stepped away.

Guilt came, swift and hard. "I'm sorry."

"You didn't do anything to cause it." She wiped her lashes with the pad of her index finger.

He wrapped her in a comforting hug. "I didn't have to remind you of the enormity of what nearly happened right now, either."

"Damn, Trevor. I could have lost everything." Her voice was muffled against his chest. He felt the warmth of her breath through his shirt.

He sifted his fingers through the shimmering softness of her hair, lifted her face to his. "But you didn't," he said gruffly.

"Thanks to you." A hiccup caught in her throat, and then all the emotion she had been holding back this entire time came pouring out. She cried long and hard, the silent sobs shaking her chest. Her arms came up to wrap around his neck. He folded her closer still. Continued stroking one hand through her hair; the other gently massaged her back.

"Thanks to an awful lot of people," he added.

She sniffed. "But you're the one who rescued most of the alpacas."

"Only because I left the cattle finding to everyone else," he said, aware he had never felt like anyone's hero the way he did right now.

She looked up at him gratefully. "You saved my ranch, Trevor. You saved me."

She sounded so distraught he couldn't bear it. "You

saved yourself with your cool head and ability to marshal all the help we needed to get the situation under control." He stroked her shoulder to quiet her.

"But the point is, I couldn't have done it without you, Trevor. If you hadn't been here to clue me in, taught me that ranchers help each other, told me whom to call tonight, I wouldn't have known where to start. I might have lost precious time. Might have…" Her voice broke.

She started to cry again.

And this time Trevor couldn't help it.

Couldn't not follow his heart and gut any more than he could have not helped her this afternoon when all hell broke loose.

"No more argument," he told her, gruffly glancing over his shoulder. "Little Blue and her mama are fine. We're getting you back to the house."

"Trevor."

Not about to let her argue her way out of what common sense dictated she needed—sleep, and plenty of it—he slid a hand beneath her knees and swung her, still crying, still protesting, up in his arms. He carried her out of the barn, across the yard. Clouds were dispersing. The hint of a crescent moon and a sprinkling of stars shone overhead. Everything smelled brisk and new.

He propped the door with his foot, then his back, and carried her on inside, not stopping to put her down in the kitchen as she probably expected, but moving deliberately through the house, on up the stairs, to the big four-poster bed she had bought along with the house.

He set her down beside it. "No argument. You're getting two hours of sleep. Right here. Right now."

Holding on to her with one hand clamped to her shoulder, he leaned across her to toss back the covers.

"Now can you take it from here, or am I going to have to strip you down, too?"

She angled her chin at him, anger sweeping away her tears. "You are so hilarious, Trevor McCabe."

Trevor noted with pleasure his bold move had achieved something. "Well, at least you stopped crying," he noted in satisfaction.

Her golden-brown eyes sparked again—with an entirely different emotion.

"Only—" she went on tiptoe, surprising him as much as he had just stunned her "—so I could do this."

OKAY, REBECCA THOUGHT, so this was not what she should be doing right now. Not nearly.

But she couldn't help herself.

She had been wanting to kiss Trevor ever since he had strode into the stable tonight, bringing the first two recovered alpacas with him. By the time he'd arrived with Black Onyx, some six more search and rescues later, she was so enamored of the strong courageous, generous-to-a-fault man Trevor McCabe had grown up to be she could barely stand it.

She had thought she didn't want or need any man to rescue her. She'd said she didn't want to be involved, physically, emotionally, or any other way with anyone right now. And she could hold to that decision easily, except when Trevor was around. And it was darn near impossible to force back the rush of emotion inside her when she was in his arms like this, feeling his mouth moving over hers.

He kissed her like there was no tomorrow. As if yesterday had always belonged to them, the future theirs for the taking. All she had to do was muster the courage to see where this blossoming friendship and fierce physical attraction between them led.

And that wasn't hard to do, either, not when his tongue was playing with hers, his hands were moving in her hair, the powerful muscles of his chest abrading her breasts. One arm slid down her back, flattening her against him, thigh to thigh. In the feminine heart of her, she could feel the tingly heat starting, her knees weakening, her whole body swaying as she threw herself into the kiss.

He stopped kissing her long enough to say, "This isn't…"

She caught his face in her hands, looked deep into his eyes, and whispered, "Yes, it is."

They were celebrating life. Victory. Over the elements. Over fear of intimacy. Over just about everything, because when she was in his arms like this, when he was sliding his hands beneath her T-shirt, over her ribs, to gently cup her breasts, she knew there was nothing finer, nothing more exciting or satisfying than the potential of making love with him.

"I want you." His lips left hers to take a thorough tour of her neck.

A shiver of want went through her. "I want you, too."

She parted the edges of his Western-style work shirt with a single jerk, sending the metal snaps flying.

He stopped kissing her long enough to grin as she smoothed her palms over the warm, satiny muscles of his chest. His pecs were tight, his nipples just as hard as hers.

Rebecca had never gotten why people in books and movies got so caught up in the touching, discovering.

Now, finally, she knew.

She couldn't get enough of him. The salty taste of his skin. The hardness of him, pressing through his jeans. The tenderness of his hands, as he divested her of her shirt, too.

Her bra went next.

His eyes darkened. She had never felt more beautiful than at that moment, seeing herself reflected in his gaze. "I knew it would be like this," he whispered, bending her backward from the waist. His lips touched where his hands had been.

Fire swept through her.

Aware this was every fantasy she had ever had come true, she gasped as his hands undid the snap and zipper on her jeans.

Holding her against him, one of her legs caught between both of his, he eased his palm beneath the elastic on her French-cut panties.

Quivering as he found her, Rebecca lifted her mouth to his. Kisses poured out of them, one after another. Feelings built. Desire exploded in liquid, melting heat. By the time he had her jeans and boots and panties off, she thought she was going to die if he didn't take her soon.

She helped him undress, too.

The first sight of him made her mouth go dry and her heart beat all the harder. "Oh. My."

"Why, Miz Rebecca, I think you're pretty sexy, too."

He searched his wallet, finally coming up with a rumpled condom packet that looked as though it had been there a while.

Grinning, he tumbled her onto the bed.

"Let me." Feeling sexier, more adventurous than she ever had in her life, she tore the wrapper with her teeth. Slowly, seductively helped roll it on. And then there was no more waiting. He was shifting her onto her back, parting her thighs with his knee, making sure she was as ready as he, and then one slow smooth motion later, they were one.

The first connection of body to body was magic. Their kisses only amplified it. And then there was no more waiting, no more patience, only white-hot heat, urgent need and passion and satisfaction unlike anything Rebecca had ever felt.

TREVOR COULDN'T BELIEVE it was over so soon. He'd waited a lifetime to find a woman like this, a woman who could turn his world upside down, make him want, make him need, make him feel as if he could be everything to her, knowing damn sure she was all to him.

Fearing he was too heavy for her, he shifted off and away from her, taking her with him as he moved.

"I'm sorry," he murmured against the tousled silk of her hair.

Rebecca stiffened. She pushed herself up on her elbow so she could look at his face. "For…?"

Trevor let his hands sculpt the beautiful lines of her face, all the while holding her searching gaze.

"What else?" He flashed her a lopsided grin. "Rushing." He bent to kiss the curve of her shoulder, the U of her collarbone, the uppermost curve of her breasts. "When this happened, I had figured to really take my time. Make it last."

Rebecca sighed, stretched, glanced at the clock. "It is three-thirty in the morning," she reminded him.

Trevor wasn't using that excuse.

"The time doesn't have anything to do with it."

Trevor cupped the weight of her breasts in his hands, laved the tender pink tips with his tongue.

"I just couldn't wait to bury myself deep inside you. But now that we've taken the edge off, so to speak…"

Appreciating the way she quivered when he touched her, Trevor paid homage to her other breast. "We can do it all over again, and this time, sweetheart—" he paused to blaze a trail that went lower still "—I am really planning to take my time."

TREVOR HADN'T BEEN KIDDING when he said he wanted to take his time making love to her, Rebecca thought half an hour later. If the first time they had made love had been all speed and heat, sheer male-female aggression and possession, the second time was all soft, hot languid kisses and tender-sweet caresses; it was finding a way to satisfy each other without bodies joining; it was finding humor in the lack of protection they needed to be really, truly together again.

Nevertheless, satisfaction came, for both of them, and they fell asleep wrapped in each other's arms.

Rebecca woke at four-thirty as Trevor was climbing back into bed. She lifted her head.

"I went to check on Blue Mist and her cria. Both are doing fine. When I left the barn, Little Blue was nursing again."

"Oh, good."

"I took care of Coco, too, so you've got another hour or two you can spend sleeping again. I suggest you use it."

And use it Rebecca did, snuggling right back into Trevor's arms.

She loved the way he felt pressed up against her, loved the warm safe way he made her feel.

Common sense told her she would be a fool to get too used to it; after all, they weren't even dating, but for the moment she intended to accept what joy came her way.

When the alarm rang at five-forty-five, she shut it off and eased out of bed.

To her relief, Trevor barely stirred.

Now that the tumultuous lovemaking was over, she needed time to sort out her feelings.

The sun rose in the east as she stepped outside and made her way across the yard, to the barn.

The herd was restless, but Rebecca didn't know what to do about pasturing them. The fence was broken down in all three sections. She had no rails to fix it. No mesh fence to put up. Meantime, thanks to Vince's neglect of his new puppy, she still had Coco to watch over, too.

Rebecca went back in the house, snapped a leash on the dog and took her out to the front yard, well away from the barn.

She was standing there, waiting for the chocolate lab to sniff out just the right spot, when Vince's Escalade turned in to her drive.

He parked, got out and came toward her. His eyes were bloodshot, his face rimmed with beard, his usual smug, superior attitude nowhere to be found.

"I heard you had my pup." He knelt down to pet Coco. Then stood. Shook his head. "I also heard she caused the stampede."

"It was a lot of factors," Rebecca said bluntly, not about to cut him any slack. "All combined, they led to disaster."

Trevor had been right, if she was going to pasture alpacas next to their cattle, they needed better barriers between the three ranches.

She—a novice rancher—might not have known better, but someone with Vince's experience and background probably had.

Rebecca looked at Vince. "What are you going to do about the fence?"

Vince straightened. His glance touched on Trevor's pickup truck, still sitting next to her house. No expression readily apparent on his face, he turned back to Rebecca. "I'm going to put in barbed wire. It's the cheapest, most efficient way to keep 'em apart."

Rebecca stiffened in alarm. "I can't have barbed wire next to my alpacas."

Vince shrugged, unconcerned. "So double up on fence along the property line between the Primrose and the Circle Y. You can do whatever you want on your side, use mesh or more split rail. That's your business and your decision. But I've got to worry about my own. And right now I've got cattle penned up all over the place. I have to bring my herd back as quickly as possible. It's as simple as that." He took the leash from Rebecca.

The pup looked back at Rebecca, her expression sad as could be.

"What are you going to do about Coco?" Rebecca asked. If she'd dug her way out once, she could do it again. The Lab pup was lucky she hadn't been stomped to death in the resulting melee.

Vince shrugged. He patted the pup's head before putting her in his Escalade. "I'm going to do the only thing I can at this point—put her in the house, in a steel crate, and hire a dog walker to come by and care for her every day."

"IT'S A GOOD PLAN, a reasonable one. Why are you upset?" Trevor asked over breakfast. "I'd think you'd have enough to do, just seeing to your own concerns."

Rebecca set a platter of fluffy golden-brown biscuits on the table. "He doesn't love that puppy."

"Vince isn't mistreating her, either."

"Coco's lonely." Rebecca sat down and took a stab at her eggs.

"She has a way of making friends. She'll find someone on his ranch—a cowboy, someone—to give her the affection she craves."

Rebecca tried to take comfort in Trevor's certainty— and worried anyway.

"And if she doesn't?" Rebecca found she had lost her appetite.

Trevor leaned over and fed her a bite of melon. "She will. Anyone who loves dogs is going to love that lab. They won't be able to help themselves."

Rebecca returned the favor, by hand-feeding Trevor a strip of bacon. She tilted her head. "So you think she's a cutie, too."

Trevor's brow lowered in gruff warning. "She's not our dog. Spend your time worrying about Blue Mist and Little Blue and the rest of your herd."

Another vehicle rumbled up the drive.

They looked out the window in tandem, saw Greg Savitz, the insurance agent stepping out of his car, a camera in his hand, a grim look on his face.

This, Rebecca thought, could not be good.

Chapter Ten

Greg Savitz strode toward Rebecca and Trevor. The thirty-year-old married man was dressed for business in a shirt, tie and slacks. He had a camera in one hand, a clipboard in the other. "Heard you had a little trouble here yesterday."

Rebecca nodded.

Greg paused to shake hands. "I'm going to have to inspect the damage."

Rebecca had figured as much. "Will my policy pay for a new fence?"

Greg shook his head. "The coverage you selected only covers the outbuildings, the house and the herd."

Rebecca sighed. "That's what I thought." She led him into the barn. "Luckily, my alpacas are fine."

"You were able to recover them all?" Greg asked, pausing to make a few notes.

Rebecca looked at Trevor, unable to contain her gratitude for all he had done. "With other ranchers' help, yes."

"Well, that's good," Greg said, studying the rafters overhead. "What about a mister and fan cooling system for this barn?"

"I purchased one. I'm going to install it as soon as possible."

"Yourself?" Greg gave her a surprised look.

"Yes," Rebecca said, trying not to think how difficult it was going to be to mount the turbofans on the ceiling, along with the low-pressure water nozzles, temperature gauge and PVC pipe.

Although it appeared to be costing him not to jump in and offer his help for that, Trevor let Rebecca conduct her business and remained silent.

Greg's brow retained a skeptical tilt. He took a few photos, then walked out of the barn to the latter two pastures, where the broken, splintered fence was evident. He examined the weak, weathered wood and took a few more pictures. Frowned.

"I can feel the bad news coming," Rebecca rocked forward on her heels. "You might as well spit it out."

"I screwed up by not getting out here to inspect the property at the time the policy was issued. I assumed everything was in order. I shouldn't have."

Dread pooled in the pit of her stomach. "What are you talking about?"

Greg rubbed at the back of his neck. "The incident yesterday indicates mismanagement on your part, Rebecca. As per the terms of the contract you signed, your insurance coverage has been suspended until a new fence is put in and a proper cooling and ventilation system installed in the barn."

"She's not going to need that temperature-wise for at least another month," Trevor put in, on her behalf.

"You and I know that," Greg agreed, "and had the fence been in satisfactory condition and the stampede yesterday not occurred, we would let that slide. But there was a big catastrophe here yesterday that could easily have been avoided. The insurance company can't overlook that."

Rebecca wanted to make sure she understood. "So

you're leaving me without any coverage until those items are fixed?"

"I'm sorry, Rebecca. I've got no choice." Greg frowned. "And there's one more thing."

How could it possibly get any worse? Rebecca wondered.

"Because of the incident last night, the Primrose alpaca operation is now considered high risk, and your rates are going up another fifty percent, effective immediately."

"I DON'T KNOW WHAT I'm going to do." Rebecca paced back and forth. "I can't even take the alpacas out, except on a leash. I have nowhere to safely pasture them, now they know they can break through the existing split rail fence without much effort at all." Miraculously, the aging wood in the first pasture was still intact on all four sides. But she couldn't put all eleven alpacas in the same pasture at the same time, and she couldn't risk so much as a stray cat or dog getting into the pasture with them and causing another stampede.

She'd been lucky yesterday; she hadn't suffered any loss of life. Rebecca couldn't count on being that fortunate again.

Trevor regarded the water logged land with a pensive expression. "I've got to see to my own herd, but after that I can go into town and get some mesh fence. If we were to subdivide this first ten-acre pasture into three sections, you could put them all in here for now. There's plenty of room."

Rebecca had been thinking the same thing, but to hear it from him, rankled. He was speaking—and acting—as if he ran this property. And he didn't. She went toe-to-toe with him. "Don't you think that's my decision to make?"

Trevor gave her the same look Rebecca's father gave her whenever Luke thought she needed to acknowledge her inability to manage on her own and accept Luke's help. Trevor's lips formed an uncompromising line. "I don't want to play games with you, Rebecca."

One night of passion, and already he was trying to tell her what to do! She jerked her chin at him. "And I don't want you trying to take charge of my life."

His eyes narrowed. "You didn't seem to mind me helping you out with your problems last night."

"That's because it was an emergency situation and I had no choice!"

He stepped closer yet. "And this isn't?"

The heat from his body engulfed her. "I can manage my own affairs, thank you very much."

Unhappiness darkened his hazel eyes. "What are you trying to say to me?"

She swallowed, figuring he would not take this well. "I think last night was a bad idea."

Trevor's gaze raked her slowly and deliberately. "The me saving your ranch for you, or the part where we made love?"

The needling sarcasm in his low tone had her flushing self-consciously.

Determined not to back off from the boundaries she'd set, she said, "Both."

Ignoring the slight curl of resentment to his lips, she continued resolutely, "It was great of you, Trevor. I appreciate it."

He braced his legs apart and folded his arms in front of him. "The taking charge of the alpaca rescue part."

"Yes. That part was wonderful. But—" Rebecca twisted her hair into a long rope and knotted it on the back of her head "—we shouldn't have started anything else no matter how grateful I was."

"Grateful," he echoed in disbelief.

She gestured listlessly. "You know how overly emotional I was after the birth of Little Blue."

His voice turned husky with the memory. "You were ecstatic. You had every right to be."

Rebecca turned her gaze to the sun climbing over the rain-drenched meadow.

The last twenty-four hours had been a roller coaster of emotion. "But my joy over that was no reason to tumble headlong into your arms." She was speaking as much to herself as to him.

"So you're saying that's all it was," he said as he searched her face. "A reaction to catastrophe and elation."

That was all it could be. "It was a lot to handle in one night."

He said nothing. He didn't have to—it was clear he didn't believe a word of what she was saying. She inhaled deeply and tried again, knowing even if she wasn't saying it right, their lovemaking had been too much too soon. "I've got enough on my plate already. I can't start a relationship." Especially with a man who could easily come in and take over every aspect of her life.

She didn't want to be told what to do.

Judged by what she did not do.

Abruptly, he looked as satisfied as he had when they'd climaxed together that last time. "So you admit it wasn't just a fling on your part?"

She admitted she never had flings.

Working to keep him where she needed him—at arm's length—Rebecca swallowed and said, "I admit it was a mistake, one I have no intention of repeating."

THE IRKED BUT undefeated look on Trevor's face as he walked away uppermost in her mind, Rebecca went back into the barn and set about giving all her alpacas food and water. Satisfied the herd was okay for the moment, Rebecca went back into the house. She put in a call to Tyler, telling him that Little Blue had entered the world, healthy as could be. The vet said he would be over later that day to check on the cria and again the following day to give Little Blue a CDT shot, Vitamin A and D, and a selenium shot.

Rebecca thanked him and telephoned her brother, Jeremy. "Are you working at the hospital today?" she asked.

"You know I have Wednesdays off, at least for now."

"Plans?"

"I'm going to look at ranch property for myself. See if I can't find something in my price range."

Rebecca knew his price range, fresh out of residency. If he wanted land with the house, whatever he could afford was probably going to be a fixer-upper, in the extreme. Although why Jeremy—who had zero interest in either crops or cows—was insisting on being a gentleman rancher, she did not know. "Can you put that off and come over and help me out? I've got to fix the fence. At least part of it, so I can put my alpacas outside."

"Yeah, I heard about that, but Susie is the one with the know-how in that department."

"She's mad at me."

"So apologize to her. You know you owe her."

"She'll think I'm only doing it to get her to help me."

"Well, if that's the case, I wouldn't blame her for not helping you." *Click.*

Rebecca stared at the phone. She couldn't believe Jeremy had hung up on her. Then again, that was typical for him, too. If he thought someone needed to do something, he would not help him or her avoid it.

Sighing, Rebecca stared at her phone. She dialed again. Grimaced.

Susie picked up on the second ring. "Carrigan Landscape Architecture."

"Hi, Susie."

"Rebecca."

At the sound of her older sister's stiff, cordial tone, Rebecca closed her eyes and rubbed at the bridge of her nose. She couldn't believe she was actually doing this, after making such a big to-do about being able to handle everything herself.

"Rebecca?" Susie said again, gently this time.

Rebecca drew a breath, tears of exhaustion pricking her eyes. "I need your help."

Susie was there an hour later with a roll of mesh fencing similar to what Trevor had strung along the property line, a sledge hammer and two bundles of metal fence stakes in the back of her pickup.

"There's no way we can do all three of your pastures," Susie said. "But we can at least get a half-acre run set up in the pasture closest to the house. You can rotate your herd in and out, until you have the time and resources to replace and repair all of the fencing."

"Thanks. I'm really going to owe you."

"No problem." Susie turned away without looking at her sister.

Rebecca caught Susie by the arm. "Susie. I really am sorry."

This time Susie looked Rebecca in the eye.

A mixture of guilt and embarrassment prodded Rebecca to continue. "It's not you, it's me. I'm the one who hasn't gotten over what happened before, with Grayson Graham."

Susie drew on her leather work gloves. As always, she did not suffer fools. "Don't you think it's about time you did?"

"Yeah, I do. Life is too short to dwell on what happened then."

"No kidding," Susie muttered in a way that reminded Rebecca that her older sister had been given her share of life-altering events to deal with, too, starting when Susie was sixteen. And yet somehow had come out all the stronger.

The two began to work, setting up stakes and rolling out fence. "This is really going to look bad at the Open House on Sunday, isn't it?" Rebecca said, after a while.

Susie wouldn't lie. "Yes. Having a temporary fence and pasture set up is only going to reinforce the word around town this morning."

"Which is…?" Rebecca asked, in dread.

"The Circle Y and The Primrose ranching operations are already out of control."

Rebecca knew she deserved at least some of the criticism. "What's the best way to repair the damage to my professional reputation?"

Susie pounded in a stake, then held it while Rebecca fastened the mesh fencing on the post. "Delay the Open House another month or so."

Together, Susie and Rebecca moved farther down the line. "I can't do that. I've got to be able to get some outside investors to put down money on Sunday if I want to pay off the balloon payment due next week on my operating loan."

Susie set up the next post with the casual expertise of someone who worked outdoors for a living. "You can't refinance?"

Rebecca made a face. "Not without insurance. Which was suspended until I get my mister and fan cooling system set up and all the fence repaired."

Susie sighed. "I wish I had the crew and the materials to help you, but I'm totally booked. Everyone wants new landscaping this time of year."

Rebecca told herself the sweat trickling down the back of her neck was due to the heat of the spring sunshine. "I'll figure something out."

"You sure?" Susie paused, all heart. "Because if it's just a question of money…"

Rebecca held up a hand. "I got myself into this mess. I'll get myself out."

Knowing time was of the essence—she now had less than four days to prepare for the Open House—Rebecca spent the afternoon rotating her herd-sires, females and nursing mother and cria, in and out of the single fenced pasture. It wasn't an ideal situation, but at least she was able to get the animals out of the barn for a few hours.

By the time evening came, she was exhausted.

And lonely as could be.

Part of her had expected Trevor McCabe to call or come by. He hadn't done either. It was what she wanted, for the two of them to maintain separate lives. So why was she so unhappy?

THURSDAY PASSED with no word from Trevor. Rebecca saw a lot of activity on his cattle ranch, though. For a good part of the day, his livestock had been loaded up and driven off for parts unknown. When Trevor wasn't doing that, he was out on his ranch, moving his remaining cows around.

Around dinnertime, she saw Tyler drive down to Trevor's place and walk out to the pasture with him, vet bag in hand.

Eventually, Tyler left the Wind Creek and drove over to The Primrose. "Everything okay over at Trevor's place?" Rebecca asked as she escorted him to the barn.

"No, unfortunately. Trev's got a real mess on his hands."

Alarm stiffened her spine. "Why? What's wrong?"

Tyler frowned. "He's got some sick cattle. We're hoping the whole herd hasn't been infected, but it's too soon to tell."

Maybe she shouldn't feel hurt Trevor hadn't called her to tell her what was going on over there—especially given how unhappily they had parted. But she did. "Is that why he's been taking cattle off the ranch today?" Rebecca asked.

"Using Miss Mim's binoculars again?" Tyler teased.

Rebecca blushed. Caught red-handed.

"Trevor told me about that," Ty said.

Rebecca shrugged. "They do come in handy. Seriously, what's going on?"

"Looks like some of Vince Owen's cattle infected Trevor's with an antibiotic-resistant bacterial disease."

Tyler's tone told her how serious the malady was.

"Can it be treated?"

"Yes. That's the good news. The bad news is the hit Trevor is going to take financially because of the exposure." Briefly, Tyler explained, finishing, "This could severely impact his profits for the year. Worse, the other ranchers who rounded up and temporarily housed the Circle Y cattle are suffering the same fate with their own herds. This strain of bacteria wasn't present in Laramie County prior to this."

A fact which must make Vince Owen very unpopular, Rebecca thought.

"It could be an epidemic," Rebecca murmured.

Tyler nodded. "Starting to look that way."

Hating the one-sided turn their relationship had just taken—as if Trevor was good enough and smart enough to help her, but she wasn't viewed in the same way,

Rebecca choked back her disappointment. "How's Trevor holding up?"

Tyler McCabe looked at her as if he knew there was a lot going on between her and Trevor. "You want to know that," Tyler said drily, "you need to ask him yourself."

The men in Laramie, Texas had a lot in common, Rebecca thought, after Tyler McCabe had given Little Blue and Blue Mist clean bills of health, and left.

They were always pushing a woman to do what they thought best.

Yet she couldn't just stand by and do nothing in Trevor's hour of need, especially given the way he had come through for her. So she did the neighborly thing. Whipped up some dinner and headed over to the Wind Creek, wicker basket in hand. After all, what was it he had told her, neighbors didn't have to like each other or even get along, to lend a helping hand?

Only after she arrived and heard the outdoor shower outside the barn going did she realize she should have called ahead, to let him know she was dropping by.

Too late. Trevor stepped out, dripping water, a large bath towel wrapped around his waist. The look on his face told her he had known it was her. He strode past her, through the grass, toward the ranch house. "I gather you heard the bad news."

Trying not to recall how that hard masculine body had felt pressed up against hers, Rebecca struggled to keep up. "That Tyler had to administer medicine to your sick cattle, which decreases their value substantially?"

His features were grim. He held the door to the mission-style ranch house. "Can't sell a cow as organic if it's had antibiotics."

Admiring the whitewashed walls and red tile roof,

Rebecca stepped inside. The U-shaped home was built around a shaded outdoor patio. It had a beamed cathedral ceiling, a wall of windows overlooking the central courtyard. A masculine family room with oversize leather furniture and a big stone fireplace comprised the front of the home.

Rebecca handed over the picnic basket, watched as he set it down. "You're sure your cattle got it from the Circle Y cattle?"

"Oh, yeah." Trevor led the way down one wing, his bare feet moving soundlessly across the muddy-red ceramic tile floor, to the laundry room off the kitchen.

He plucked a pair of navy blue briefs and a clean pair of jeans off the top of the clothes dryer. "They were nose to nose with my herd the night of the storm. Vince puts antibiotics and growth hormones in his feed, which makes his Black Angus grow bigger, faster and increases their value, since beef is sold by weight. But it also leaves them vulnerable to infection from some pretty harsh strains of bacteria."

Rebecca turned away seconds before the towel hit the floor. "Which is what your cattle have."

She heard, rather than saw, Trevor clothe his lower half. "I hauled off all the sick ones—they're now getting treatment at Tyler's ranch."

Trevor strode past her, looking mighty fine without shirt or shoes.

Heartbeat accelerating, Rebecca ventured only as far as the entrance to the kitchen. "Tyler uses his ranch for treating sick animals?"

Trevor ventured into what appeared to be a bedroom. "Yep, Healing Meadow Ranch is primarily a large animal veterinary facility, or the closest thing we have to a large animal vet hospital in these parts." He returned, buttoning up a long-sleeved burgundy twill shirt.

Telling herself she most definitely did not want to kiss him again, Rebecca asked, "How long before the cows get better?"

Trevor shrugged. "Couple weeks, probably, before they get a clean bill of health and I can sell them."

"You have to do that?"

Trevor nodded, a mixture of fatigue and disappointment showing on his face. "They're no longer organic, and I can't risk infecting the rest of the herd. Unfortunately, they're not going to bring a market price like what they would have had they not gotten sick."

"That's awful."

His expression did not change. "It's life."

Rebecca edged closer, taking in the soap and fresh-air scent clinging to his skin. "Has this ever happened before?"

A flash of anger glimmered in his hazel eyes. "Not anywhere near this degree."

Wishing she could comfort him physically, the way he had her, without it meaning anything, Rebecca asked softly, "How much of your herd are you losing?"

He shifted his gaze to her lips. "Roughly a third."

She felt herself flushing with heat. "No wonder you're upset," she said. "Is there anything else I can do for you?"

Any hint of Texas hospitality faded. He moved brusquely toward the door. "I thought you said we weren't going to do that anymore."

Rebecca had no choice but to follow. "Y-you know what I meant," she stuttered.

"No. I'm not sure I do."

She took a deep breath. "I'm trying to be a friend."

"I can see that." He opened the doorway. Hand to her elbow, he ushered her on through. "I'm not sure I'm ready to be 'just friends.'"

"SO THAT'S HOW YOU ended it, just walking away," Teddy McCabe said, an hour later.

"What choice did I have?" Trevor opened up a soft flour tortilla and layered it with strips of grilled fajita-style chicken and grated cheddar cheese. "I'm not going to pretend I don't want to be in her bed again. I do."

Teddy added salsa, lettuce, sour cream and guacamole to his. "You could try giving her a little room."

Trevor opened two longnecks of Shiner Bock, and handed one to Teddy. "The last thing a woman like Rebecca needs is 'room' to run away."

"You think that's what she's doing?"

How the heck should he know? "She doesn't want a man in her life." Not the way he wanted to be…

"Any man or just you?" Teddy grinned.

Trevor exhaled roughly. "Both."

"You could pursue her."

Trevor hadn't been brought up to take advantage of a woman. "I'm not going to twist her arm to get her in bed with me again."

"No. You'll just leave that to Vince Owen."

Trevor lifted his head. "What are you talking about?"

Teddy scooped salsa onto a chip. "He's still telling everyone in town that Rebecca is going to be his woman by the end of the week."

Trevor savored a bite of the delicious dinner and tried not to think how much better it would have tasted had Rebecca been here with him. "That'll never happen," Trevor said.

Teddy shot him a skeptical glance. "Are you sure?"

Trevor set his jaw. "Rebecca's not that much of a fool."

"Then why is Vince Owen running around bragging like it's already a done deal?" Teddy asked.

Why indeed...?

"And why did he tell everyone the romance is starting tomorrow night?"

"How BAD IS IT?" Amy asked, the following morning.

Rebecca had called her as soon as she'd opened the morning's mail, and Amy had stopped by on the way back from delivering a flatbed of plants to several of Susie's landscape projects. Rebecca knew that Amy—who had started her own nursery business from scratch, would not only understand—she might be able to offer some concrete business advice.

"Pretty bad." Rebecca handed the letter to Amy. "The investment group that now owns my mortgage and operating loan says they are sending out a representative Monday morning at 10:00 a.m. My balloon payment of twenty thousand dollars is due before my temporary operating loan rolls over into a permanent one."

"It also says you must show proof of insurance before the loan can go to the next phase."

"Which is a problem, because my coverage was suspended until I can get the fence in, the mister and fan cooling system up in the barn."

"And you have the Open House on Sunday, too."

Rebecca nodded, feeling so overwhelmed she barely knew where to start.

"Everyone is busy with their regular jobs during the week, but I can round up a crew to help you with the fence and the misting system over the weekend," Amy said.

But would it be too little too late to try and do all that on Saturday? Rebecca wondered.

"Any chance Elliott Allen can help you out with a refinancing package?"

"I talked to him on Monday. He said he might be able to, if I were to come up with a better business plan."

"So what's stopping you?" Amy asked.

What indeed?

Rebecca spent the rest of the morning running the numbers. She was going to have to lease out all seven of her female alpacas for pregnancy, and convince investors to use her two herd-sires for studs… She could borrow money from Susie for her ongoing operating costs until she got her situation straightened out. But that would confirm her father's opinion that she was not capable of running a business on her own.

Rebecca could take Elliott Allen's advice and ask Trevor for help putting together a better prospective for the Laramie bank. But with Trevor still ticked off at her for deciding the two of them needed to go back to being just friends that didn't seem a palatable option, either.

Rebecca walked out to the pasture, where Blue Mist and Little Blue were taking a turn, grazing and basking in the warm April sunshine.

"So that's the new one," a low voice stated behind her.

Rebecca turned to see Vince Owen walking up to join her. He looked as though he'd had a little sleep, a shower and a shave. His clothes were expensive and neatly pressed.

Behind him, two more pickups with his ranch insignia rumbled up the drive. Eight dusty, sweaty cowboys got out. Two more trucks—an electrician's and a plumbing truck—parked behind them. Two additional technicians got out.

Rebecca noted the beds of the pickup were piled high with wooden split rail fencing, similar to what had crumbled under the weight of the stampeding cattle, and rolls of mesh, similar to what Trevor and Susie had already put up.

"I've been thinking and I feel awfully bad about what happened the other night. It was my fault for not keeping Coco inside the house. I know you've got this Open House coming up, and you can't expect to do much business if you've got pastures with big sections of broken-down fence. I was going to just go with barbed wire on my side, but after thinking about it, I can see your point. That won't look right on The Primrose, and it might be hazardous to your alpacas. So I'd like to make amends by having eight of my hired hands repair the existing wood fence, run mesh inside of that, and the electrician and the plumber put up the mister and fan cooling system in your barn. So what do you say?"

Rebecca would have liked to turn Vince down.

But he was right.

She did need help. Now.

Did it really matter where that aid came from?

What was it Trevor said to her? *"You don't have to like your neighbor or even know 'em to lend a hand. Ranchers help each other out. That's the rule."*

What Vince was doing would go a long way to repair the damage done. "I'll pay for all of the materials and go half with you on the fence labor. And I'll reimburse you for the installation of the mister and fan cooling system in the barn, but I'm going to have to do it over time."

"No problem. We can work out a payment plan later. Even barter for it, if you want."

No way was she cooking dinner for Vince. Rebecca regarded her next-door neighbor warily. "Like what?"

Vince shrugged. "You could take care of Coco for me—walk her and care for her—when I'm away from the Circle Y."

That, Rebecca wouldn't mind. She loved the little

puppy. And if she could bring love and affection into the chocolate Lab's life…it would not only be a good deed, it would ease Rebecca's mind. "Sounds good," Rebecca said. "But even if I were to groom and board Coco, it would take years to pay off the labor charges that way."

Vince looked unconcerned. "Then we'll add other stuff, as well. The point is, we can sit down and figure all that out later."

Rebecca didn't want that hanging over her any more than she wanted to be endlessly in debt to anyone. "We'll negotiate suitable compensation as soon as the labor is done and we know what all the charges are," she said. "Tomorrow morning okay with you for that?" That would give her the night to think of ways to repay the debt that did not involve her coming up with a great deal of cash.

"Sounds great to me." Vince stuck out his hand, to conclude the business. As they clasped palms, he smiled. "Now, what else can I do to help you get The Primrose up and running?"

Chapter Eleven

"I'm over at The Wagon Wheel restaurant," Tyler told Trevor at seven-thirty that evening. "You'll never guess who's here."

"And I probably don't want to," Trevor grumbled.

"Rebecca is having dinner with Vince Owen."

Trevor tensed, aware this was his worst nightmare coming true. He shoved a hand through his hair. "And that's my business because?"

His brother's voice dropped a goading notch. "Don't pretend you don't care." Ty paused, then reported, "He's really turning on the charm."

Trevor's misery multiplied. He rubbed the back of his neck and struggled to keep his emotions under control. "Rebecca's a grown woman, Ty. She can have a meal with whomever she pleases." *Even if it twists my gut into knots.*

Tyler grunted. "You know as well as I do that she would not be having dinner with him if she knew about the wager Vince Owen tried to make about her."

That was true enough. Trevor still didn't want to hurt or embarrass Rebecca that way. He knew how sensitive she was, how vulnerable her pride, which had already taken a huge hit. He wasn't sure she could stand up and make her sales pitch at her upcoming Open House if she knew what had been said about her, behind her back, even if only one man had been doing all the boasting. Best, he figured, to continue to spare her that humiliation.

Trevor studied the collection of frozen dinners in his freezer, the meager contents of his fridge. "Rebecca's not foolish enough to fall for Vince's line." He took out the lone carton of milk and upended it, drinking the remaining tablespoon or two of milk.

"That's what you thought about Jasmine. And she sure fell for it, hook, line and sinker. Or am I remembering incorrectly?"

The memory stung. Nevertheless, Trevor refused to overreact. "It's probably just a business dinner."

Tyler scoffed, his disbelief evident. "You come over here and take a look for yourself. And then tell me that." *Click.*

Trevor told himself he wasn't going to go.

And he kept vowing that even as he grabbed his wallet and strode out to his pickup truck.

It wasn't as if Rebecca was his woman.

Or any of his concern.

She'd made it clear to him that despite the days of spending time together and helping each other out that culminated in a night of powerhouse lovemaking, nothing concrete had changed. The two of them weren't going to be more than friends.

He didn't owe her anything.

It wasn't his job to protect her.

Nevertheless, twenty minutes later, he found himself walking in to The Wagon Wheel restaurant.

Rebecca was still sitting with Vince.

It didn't look as if she had gone to much effort for the outing.

She was clad in a long-sleeved white T-shirt, denim skirt and boots. Her hair was in two loose braids. Her cheeks were pink. Her eyes were on Vince.

They appeared to be disagreeing about something, albeit very quietly.

Trevor watched as Vince leaned forward persuasively, took Rebecca's hand, in his. She offered a tight smile—the kind a woman gave when someone was hitting on her, in unwelcome fashion.

Trevor looked Rebecca in the eye. "Sorry I'm late," he fibbed. He turned to her companion. "Vince." Then back to Rebecca. "Ready to go?" he asked, pretending they'd had other plans that trumped whatever she was doing now.

Recognition flickered in Rebecca's eyes. "Oh. Yes." She eased her hand from beneath Vince's. She looked Vince Owen in the eye. "Thank you so much for the drink and appetizer."

"Your parents are expecting us," Trevor said.

"Right." Rebecca clasped her handbag, and stood. "I'll get back to you tomorrow with that list," Rebecca told Vince.

Vince smiled as if he hadn't had his date stolen out from under him. "You do that," he said.

Trevor slid his hand beneath her elbow. He escorted her from the restaurant.

She didn't speak until they reached the parking lot behind the building and climbed into his pickup. Her cheeks pink with embarrassment, she waited until he had eased behind the steering wheel before she inquired coolly, "I assume you were fibbing about the meeting with my parents?"

Trevor started his truck and backed out. "You assume right."

She shot him a withering glare as he paused to turn right. "Don't expect me to thank you for getting me out of there."

As it happened, Trevor thought as his foot hit the accelerator, that was exactly what he had expected. Along with a heartfelt hug of gratitude and a kiss or two. "Wouldn't dream of it." He pushed the words through his teeth.

An uneasy silence fell between them as they drove through town, and out onto the country road leading to their ranches.

She clamped her arms in front of her and stared straight ahead. "I can handle Vince Owen."

Trevor released a short, humorless laugh. "Sure about that?"

Rebecca turned her glance to the passing scenery. "At least he doesn't try to kiss me every time he sees me."

Trevor inhaled the juniper fragrance of the soap and shampoo she used. "Maybe not yet," he allowed.

Rebecca whipped her head around. As she turned to face him, her left knee came up on the bench seat between them. He didn't even know why he was trying to warn her off and/or talk sense into her. Or why the sight of her bare calf above the boot should be such an incredible turn-on. Except that he knew how soft and smooth and toned her body was.

"What's that supposed to mean?" she demanded.

French-cut cotton panties weren't that much of a turn-on, Trevor told himself. *Unless, of course, Rebecca was wearing them.*

Aware Rebecca was still waiting for an answer, Trevor bit out, "Nothing."

Rebecca put her boot-clad left foot back on the floor with a resounding stomp. "Obviously, you charged into The Wagon Wheel, intent on rescuing me. From what? The evil clutches of that madman?"

A more apt description couldn't have been made. Well, maybe it was a little over-the-top.

"Just promise me you'll be careful," Trevor insisted.

Rebecca threw up her hands, clearly not believing a word he said. "Of what exactly?" she snapped in mounting frustration.

Trevor knew the words sounded ridiculously paranoid even as they came out of his mouth. "Vince Owen is not a man you can trust. In fact, the more generous and helpful he seems, guaranteed—the less trustworthy he is."

"You sound jealous."

Trevor feigned cool. "You think so?"

"I know so!"

"Well, then." Trevor steered over to the side of the road, into the grass and put the truck into Park. "If I've been tried and convicted in your eyes," he drawled, releasing the catch on his safety belt, "I might as well do this."

Trevor hit the emergency blinkers and moved across the bench seat. Ignoring the astonished look on her pretty face, he took her into his arms, and covered her mouth with his.

He expected her to put up a fuss. But the deeper he kissed her, the more passionately she kissed him back.

His tongue touched hers. She met him stroke for stroke, parry for parry. He groaned, crushing her closer against his chest, and heard her soft telltale whimper of acquiescence. And that was when the Escalade slowed, passed by, moved on. But not before they both got a look at the driver.

VINCE OWEN'S FACE, turned straight at them was all the reminder Rebecca needed. Letting loose with a most unladylike word that perfectly summed up the situation, she extricated herself from the warm, hard cradle of Trevor's arms. "I hope you're satisfied!" she fumed.

Looking as if he wanted nothing more than to haul her back in his arms and resume kissing her with even more passion, Trevor stayed where he was. He lifted a querying brow.

"Obviously what happened just now was all for your rival's benefit," Rebecca stormed, her emotions vaulting completely out of control.

"Like I knew Vince was going to drive by here and catch us!" Trevor scoffed.

Rebecca tapped a lecturing finger against the hardness of his chest. "First of all, *you* were kissing *me,*" she pointed out.

"And you were kissing me right back!"

Her temper skyrocketing, she ignored that obvious truth. "And second of all, if he were going back to his ranch, he would have had to take this road to get there." A fact Trevor obviously knew.

"If I had wanted Vince to see me kissing you, I would have laid a big one on you in the restaurant."

Working to slow her thundering heart, Rebecca shrank against the window. "And sacrificed your reputation as a Texas gentleman? I don't think so."

Trevor shook his head, his expression unerringly grim. Without another word, he fastened his seat belt, put the pickup truck in gear and steered back out onto the road.

Rebecca would have liked nothing more than to continue arguing with him.

Afraid they'd end up kissing again if she did so, she kept quiet until they arrived at The Primrose.

"Thank you for the ride home," she said politely.

"You're welcome." Trevor got out, too.

She dropped her purse inside the back door, then headed across the yard. "I'm not inviting you in."

Trevor looked as though he was settling in for the long haul. "So we'll talk out here."

Deciding the best thing to do was ignore him, Rebecca went in to the barn.

To her amazement, the fan and mister cooling system was up. A flick of the switch next to the door and a raft of cool air went flowing through the barn.

Aware they wouldn't need the system this evening, she turned it back off. Walking up and down the stalls, she checked on her herd. All had eaten their evening meal and still had plenty of water. Little Blue was nursing content-edly while Blue Mist stood by patiently, every bit the gentle, protective mama alpaca.

Satisfied all was well for the moment, Rebecca strolled back out of the barn. Flashlight in hand, she walked through all three pastures. The broken-down fence in pastures two and three had been completely repaired, sturdy mesh placed inside the perimeter.

Best of all, the Black Angus that had been moved back onto the Circle Y had been pastured on the other side of the ranch, well away from Rebecca's property line. That could only help her when she held her Open House on Sunday afternoon.

"I'm sorry I didn't get around to helping you with all this," Trevor said eventually, as they cut through the land-scaped backyard, toward the ranch house.

Was that what he thought this was all about? Shocked, Rebecca turned her glance to Trevor. "I know you've had your hands full with sick cattle, and all that."

They stopped at the gazebo.

He sat down on one of the stone benches, gestured for her to do the same. "Sorry I messed up your date with Vince."

It was her turn to scoff. "No, you're not."

He flashed the sexy grin that turned her inside out. He rubbed his jaw, lifted his shoulder in a hapless manner.

"Okay, I'm not." He watched as she settled a safe distance away from him. "Are you dating him?"

"No." Rebecca told herself she was glad they had the width of the gazebo between them. "Course not."

"Then why were you having dinner with him?"

She flattened her hands on either side of her and stretched her legs out in front of the bench. "He wanted to talk ranching."

Trevor watched her tug her skirt as low as it would go and cross her legs at the ankle. "And you wanted to listen."

Rebecca ran her fingers across her denim-clad thigh. "I felt I owed him that courtesy after he provided the labor for the work that had to be done around here."

"And?" Trevor's gaze seemed fixed on her hand.

Rebecca swallowed and looked Trevor in the eye. "It was a mistake. The way Vince does business will not work for me—it's too close to the financial edge. He's all about taking whatever shortcut he can find to get whatever goal he's set, regardless of whoever else he might mow down in the process. He seems to think that's just the cost of doing business, ranching or otherwise."

Trevor did not look surprised. "That sounds like Vince."

"And there's something else," Rebecca found herself admitting. She studied Trevor's expression. "The whole time Vince and I were in the restaurant, we were getting funny looks from the other diners. Or at least the men that were there."

Trevor shifted his gaze toward the house.

She knew a man avoiding answering when she saw one.

"Why? Did you have spinach and artichoke dip on your chin?"

Rebecca stood and walked over to stand next to him. "I'm serious, Trevor. Even before you showed up to publicly spirit me away, people were looking at me like I was…really stupid…for being there with Vince."

Trevor shrugged and turned his attention to the stars and the full moon shining overhead. Slowly, deliberately, he got to his feet. "Maybe they think you can do better, too," he said eventually.

Rebecca had to tip her head back to see into his face. "By dating you?"

He tilted his head down, slanted her a look. "There are worse things."

He had a point there. Rebecca sighed. "Like sleeping with you and telling myself it'll be okay."

"It would be all right," he countered softly, "if you'd let it continue."

A shudder of awareness swept through her, weakening her knees. "Friends and neighbors shouldn't make love on a whim," Rebecca insisted stubbornly.

"You're right about that," Trevor said.

Rebecca looked at him, unable to hide her surprise.

"But what if it's more than a whim?" Tenderness emanating from him, he sifted both hands through her hair. "What then?"

REBECCA KNEW, even before Trevor shifted her close and flattened a hand against her spine, that he was going to kiss her again. Gently, this time. Inquisitively. And that sensual exploration turned out to be even more devastating than the caress he'd laid on her when their passions were stoked, and their tempers were raging.

Sheer physical desire she might have been able to resist.

She definitely could have turned away any attempt to dominate her through sexual expertise.

But gentleness—wanting—were something else, especially when his emotions so closely mirrored hers. She hadn't been able to stop thinking about the way he'd made her feel, so cherished, so desired. Beautiful. Womanly. She hadn't been able to stop thinking about the expert caresses of his fingertips searching out all the pleasure points of her body, or the way he seemed to know intuitively what she needed.

She moaned as he cupped her face in both hands and held her head under his. She trembled as he caught her bottom lip between his teeth, and worried it gently with the edge of his tongue. And then he was kissing her full-out again, pushing her back against one of the white stone pillars, the warmth of his body blanketing hers.

Dampness pooled low, mingled with tingling heat. When he urged her up on tiptoe, inserted his knee between her thighs, she complied. His lips slid down her neck, even as his hands slipped beneath her T-shirt, to find the clasp of her bra. "I've missed you so much."

His confession thrilled and comforted her, and prodded her to honesty.

"Me, too." She stretched sinuously, as his palms kneaded her swollen flesh. "Too much."

Which made her wonder why she was fighting him, fighting this, anyway….

She felt his smile against her ear. Softly, he declared, "No such thing."

She gasped and he took her mouth again, hotly, decisively.

His thumbs traced the tender crests, rubbing back and forth, creating a hot, aching need.

"Oh, yes," she said, between slow, sipping kisses that had her arching wantonly against him. "There is."

She caught her breath as his hands found their way to the hem of her denim skirt, lifted it slightly, eased beneath.

"Not where we're concerned," he told her gruffly, in a way that almost had her believing it.

And then he was kissing her, again and again. His hands slid up her thighs, found their way between.

The next thing she knew, her panties were easing down. He was touching her there. Creating ripples of fire, of need.

She caught her breath as the sensations mounted, spread.

Trembling against his hand, she felt herself begin to slide inexorably toward the edge.

"Not…without…you," she said.

She struggled to find his zipper, pushed it down, even as the heat of his kisses spread outward, through her chest, across her shoulders.

The scent of his soap and cologne filled her senses as he brought her to the brink, and she tortured him, too, first with delicate touches, then full-out exploration.

Wild with sensation, caught up in the recklessness of the moment, they drove each other into waves of passion, until neither could stand it anymore.

Catching her by the hips, he lifted her against the stone. The chill at her back contrasted with the heat in front of her, the rumpled clothing crushed between them.

And then he was part of her again, searching, taking.

Bringing her closer yet.

Both hands cupping her bottom, he held her right where he wanted, right where she needed to be, and then there was no more thinking, no more holding back, only hot, wet kisses and hotter pleasure.

She trembled and cried out.

He caught the sound with his mouth, and then, he, too was moaning, shuddering, thrusting ever deeper.

Together, they surrendered to the inevitable, to each other, to whatever this was, and would always be.

REBECCA CAME BACK to reality slowly.

She couldn't believe she had done this again.

Couldn't imagine *not* doing it again.

He set her down gently, brought up her panties, lowered her skirt. A kiss to the side of her neck, her ear, her temple. Then he was zipping up, fastening his belt. "Let's go upstairs to your bed."

Trembling, Rebecca armed herself with her only defense against him—humor.

She flashed him a crooked smile that belied the vulnerable way she felt inside. "You always want more."

Emotion trembled in his voice. "I want you."

"Trevor…"

He clasped her shoulders. "I want you, Rebecca. And I know you want me."

Rebecca tried to deny it. But when he put his lips to hers, when he kissed her like that, and swung her up into his arms, and carried her across the yard, all her excuses, all her defenses, began to fade.

"We're going to have to talk about this," she warned.

He swept through the door. "In the morning."

"Trevor—"

He strode up the stairs. "Talking about this always gets us into trouble, Rebecca."

He had a point there, she conceded reluctantly.

He made his way down the upstairs hall, to her four-poster bed. He deposited her next to it. "Feeling on the other hand, acting on those feelings, always leads to something good."

Rebecca trembled with a mixture of anticipation and need. "Lovemaking, you mean."

"And feeling close to you. And being close to you. And having you close to me."

Close felt good, Rebecca noticed as he divested her of her clothing, and helped her remove all of his. Close felt very good.

Giving in, Rebecca let him lead her where he wanted her to go, and in return, she led him, too.

By the time they fell asleep, she felt sated, secure and, much to her surprise, very much as if she was falling head over heels, deeply, irrevocably in love.

"YOU PROBABLY DON'T WANT to talk about this," Trevor said, the next morning. Nixing the idea of having breakfast together—and not so coincidentally, conversations just like this—Rebecca had dressed and headed straight to the barn at the crack of dawn. Figuring, hoping, he'd take the hint and go on back to Wind Creek.

He hadn't.

"Then I'm guessing we shouldn't," Rebecca replied, pasturing the last of her herd.

She didn't want anything ruining the wonderfully wild and passionate night they'd shared.

She was afraid if they talked too much, something would.

"I have to know."

Obviously not finished lending a hand, Trevor walked back to the barn with her.

"What kind of deal did you make with Vince Owen for all that labor on the fence, and the cooling system in the barn?"

Still doing her best to chase him away, Rebecca donned her leather work gloves. "Are you worried I might be offering him home-cooked dinners?"

Briefly, sheer male possessiveness flashed in Trevor's eyes.

Ignoring her hint, he pushed the wheelbarrow to the last stall. "Did you?"

Rebecca shoveled waste from the stall floor. "No. Of course not."

Trevor moved from stall to stall, right along with her. "Then what did you offer him?"

Rebecca welcomed the fresh morning air, moving through the barn, dispersing the fecund smell of animals quartered overnight.

She set her jaw. "And this is your business because…?"

Trevor's steady gaze never wavered. "I care about you."

Care. Not love.

He helped her empty the contents into the compost pile Susie would later pick up, to turn into fertilizer.

"I don't want to see you in a bad situation," Trevor continued.

Now he was sounding like her dad, and Susie, way back when. They'd tried to protect her, too. "You really don't trust me, do you?"

"In what sense?"

Hooooo boy. Not a question the rancher should have asked.

"I'm not worried about you being unfaithful to me," he said.

His confidence both thrilled and annoyed her. She wanted him to be possessive in a sexual and romantic sense. Yet she wanted her freedom to do as she pleased, without worrying over his reaction, too. "That's good." She paused to wet her lips. "Although…"

He lifted a brow.

Throwing caution to the wind, she finished her thought. "I don't recall anyone saying anything about being exclusive."

"We're exclusive, all right," he told her gruffly, the same kind of passion in his hazel eyes that was there every time he took her into his arms.

Rebecca knew, as a fiercely independent woman, she should have resented the assumption on his part.

She didn't.

Maybe because…although he hadn't told her he loved her, the way she now knew she loved him…his attitude was still a step in the right direction. The direction she wanted them to go.

"Then what are we arguing about?" she asked, perplexed.

He brought his arms up to hold her close. "You. Being in over your head."

Resentment rankled in her heart once again. "And not having the sense to know it?" She elbowed her way out of his embrace.

He caught her to him once again. "I didn't say that."

She planted her hands on her hips anyway. "But you think it."

"Look." Trevor sifted his hands through her hair, tilted her face up to his. "I know Vince. He's never been the kind of guy that gives something for nothing. There isn't a philanthropic bone in his body. Yet he lends you eight of his hired hands, brought in from all three of his ranches, to make the necessary repairs."

Rebecca sighed. About that much at least she had a very plausible explanation. "Vince said they were in the area anyway, to move cattle to his other two ranches. He also said he felt bad about Coco digging out and causing the stampede that caused the damage, and he wanted to make reparations."

Trevor stepped back and away from her. "That sounds good on the surface."

Rebecca studied him. Suddenly, she had the same strange feeling she'd had at the restaurant last night, as if she was the only one not in on the joke. "Is there something you're not telling me?" she asked quietly.

Now it was Trevor's turn to look and act uncomfortable with the direction the conversation was taking. He walked over to the first pasture, now divided into thirds, and looked out to Blue Mist and Little Blue. "I just know how devious he can be when he wants something."

Rebecca watched the nursing cria and patient mother with the same wonder she felt when she'd delivered Little Blue. "You're thinking about what Vince did to you and Jasmine, to break the two of you up."

Trevor acknowledged this was so with a slight dip of his head.

"He's made no secret he's interested in me. I've made it clear I'm not interested in him that way."

Trevor rested his palms on the top of the rail. "That's what has me worried."

Rebecca studied the large capable hands that had made sweet, wonderful love to her throughout the night.

Sighed.

"The sick competition thing again," she guessed.

Trevor shrugged. "Vince's going all out for you that way doesn't make sense on a rational level. When it comes to me, Vince isn't reasonable."

Rebecca rubbed the toe of her boot on the soft green grass. "I still don't get what that has to do with the work his men did on my property."

Trevor directed his gaze from the rest of her sedately grazing herd, back to Rebecca. His attitude was as blunt as his voice. "Did you or did you not make a deal with him to reimburse him for his help?"

A little taken aback by how strong Trevor was coming

on, Rebecca found herself admitting, "Vince and I agreed to work it out later, by cash or barter or whatever combination seems to work."

Trevor's frown increased. "Barter?" he repeated.

Rebecca's exasperation grew exponentially. "It's no big deal, Trevor. We talked about me taking care of Coco when Vince is unavailable. I'm *not* going to be cooking any meals for him. In any case, he's going to send me a detailed write-up for the labor charges."

Not appeased in the least, Trevor ordered, "When you get it, I want you to let me know what the amount is. I'll loan you the money. You can pay him off."

Rebecca harrumphed in contempt. "That would be like robbing Peter to pay Paul." *I think I've done enough of that already.* She started to turn away.

Trevor clasped her elbow lightly, pulled her back. "Listen to me, Rebecca. You don't want to put yourself in a position of being indebted to Vince Owen, in any way."

She wrested free of him, threw up her arms and stomped backward. "What I don't want is you telling me how to run my ranch or deal with my neighbors!" She gave her words a moment to sink in, then stared him right in the eye and continued, "I'm a grown woman, Trevor, perfectly capable of figuring out the right and wrong thing to do."

He stopped grimacing long enough to open his mouth.

She held up a hand before he could interrupt.

"I know I'm going to make errors, Trevor. Every rancher does in the start-up process. But it's up to me to overcome whatever mistakes I render. All I want from you—all I *insist* that I have from you—is respect! And if you can't give that to me—" she paused to draw a last, enervating breath "—then you shouldn't give me anything at all!"

Chapter Twelve

No sooner had Trevor left to care for his own animals than Vince knocked on Rebecca's door.

Fresh from the shower, her hair still wet, she had on no makeup. She felt oddly vulnerable as she opened her front door.

Vince's glance took in the fine fabric of her stone-colored slacks and notch-collared blouse. "Business meeting today?" he asked her.

For reasons she didn't want to examine too closely, Rebecca did not want to tell him her plans.

"Something like that."

She nodded at the file folder of papers in his hand. "Is that the labor charges for the work yesterday?"

"Yes." Vince handed her the manila folder. "I wrote it up, just like you asked."

Rebecca leaned against the banister.

Her eyes widened as she perused the figures.

"Five thousand dollars?" she asked.

"I employ the best in the business," he said. "Their contract states they get paid double time for anything not in their specific duties. And, of course, the plumber and electrician who put in the mister and fan cooling system each charge two hundred dollars for emergency calls plus last minute rates, which are substantial. And then there were the materials."

Trevor had been right to mistrust Vince Owen.

Rebecca stared him down. "This is awfully steep."

Vince flashed an unsavory smile. "Are you backing out on the deal we made?" he asked.

"No." Unfortunately, it was too late for that. It was her own fault, Rebecca knew, for not having talked money and got a firm estimate before one minute of work was done by anyone. Had she done that, she wouldn't be in this mess now. "But I'm going to need a day or two to figure out what kind of repayment schedule I can handle."

"I'm a patient man," Vince said. He looked past her. "Is that coffee I smell?"

Her deeply ingrained Texas manners forced her to smile and ask, "Would you like a cup for the road?" *Before I do what Trevor said I should have done in the first place, and boot you out of here on your tail.*

Once again, Vince Owen was all genial charm. "That would be very nice, thank you. Unless you could join me for one now?"

"I'm afraid not. I've got an appointment. But I'll be glad to get you a cup to go." Rebecca led the way into the kitchen.

"I have to tell you," Vince continued, "I was very sorry our dinner ended so abruptly last night."

Rebecca had only agreed to have a drink with Vince, and then only because that was the only way he would discuss ways she could improve her business plan.

It did not appear that it would be helpful to point that out to him.

"I should have told you about my previous engagement."

"You should have told Trevor that you and I weren't finished, and advised him to go on without you. Where was it you said you were going? To your parents?"

Caught in an obvious fabrication—albeit a social, romantically motivated one—Rebecca flushed. "Turns out we had the wrong night for that."

Vince flattened a hand on her kitchen counter. "You don't have to lie to me, Rebecca."

That was about all she and Vince agreed upon.

"All right. I won't." Rebecca paused. "You might as well know anyway. Trevor and I are…seeing each other."

Vince's expression turned droll. "I gathered that when I saw his truck pulled over on the side of the road, the two of you going at it like a couple of love-starved teens."

Rebecca handed Vince his coffee. "I think you should go."

Vince accepted the travel mug full of coffee that had been on the warmer far too long. Looking in no hurry to go anywhere, he folded his arms in front of him. "Aren't you the least bit curious about the group that holds the mortgage on this place now?"

Rebecca tensed at the clever cruelty she saw in his eyes. "I know who they are, that they specialize in buying up high-yield, unusual investments."

"Do you know who owns Edge Investments?"

Rebecca gestured inanely.

"Perhaps," Vince advised her in a low, silken tone that sent a chill down Rebecca's spine, "you should find out."

Rebecca would have liked to go straight to the library to research Edge Investments but she had a handful of invitations to deliver, including one to Trevor's uncle Wade

McCabe, a multimillionaire who had made his wealth by investing in growing businesses, in addition to the oil wells his wife, Josie, a wildcatter, had founded.

Figuring if anyone in Laramie would know just what kind of outfit Edge Investments was, Wade might, Rebecca stopped by their ranch first.

After inviting the handsome older couple to the Open House the following day, Rebecca filled Wade McCabe in on the recent turn of events regarding her property loan. "The new mortgage holder is sending a representative out to collect the balloon payment, Monday morning. I'd like to know what to expect."

"Trouble, is my guess. I'm sorry, Rebecca. That outfit is known for snapping up high-risk, high-value investments and forcing the property owners into bankruptcy and foreclosure."

Rebecca let out the breath she had been holding.

This was getting worse with every moment that passed.

She should have listened to her father, and gone a more conventional route for her financing and started her alpaca operation much more slowly.

She should have listened to Trevor and stayed the hell away from Vince Owen.

But she hadn't done either, and now she was in a mess from which she wasn't sure she was going to be able to extricate herself.

"Are you feeling okay?" Josie Wyatt-McCabe asked.

Rebecca nodded. "Do you know who owns the company?" she asked.

Wade shook his head.

"Edge Investments has such a bad reputation within the Texas investment banking community, I don't think the real owners want their names associated with it. They have a CEO, of course, sitting in the Dallas office, but he's only twenty-four, and nothing more than a figurehead."

"Maybe Miss Mim can help me find out more," Rebecca said.

Wade paused. "I hate to see anyone taken advantage of, Rebecca. If you find yourself in need of rescuing…"

The magic words she did not want to hear.

Rebecca forced herself to appear a great deal more confident than she felt. She declined their generous offer, smiled and shook hands with both. And headed for the next person on her list.

By noon, she had personally dropped off a dozen more invitations.

At Laramie Gardens Home For Seniors, Miss Mim and the other residents were eagerly awaiting her arrival.

"Thanks for letting me practice my sales pitch in front of you," Rebecca told the group assembled in the meeting area.

She set up a projector and passed out copies of the information packets she had prepared. Then she began her prepared spiel.

The senior citizens were generous in their comments and suggestions on where she needed to improve. Rebecca accepted them in the helpful spirit in which they were given. Consequently, her second run-through was much better. Clearer, more concise. Energetic. "I just wish you all could see the alpacas in person, particularly Little Blue and her mama, Blue Mist," Rebecca said, as she packed up her stuff for transport back to the ranch. "They are so sweet. You'll never see a more adorable ranch animal."

"Maybe we could do a field trip," Miss Mim suggested.

"That would be wonderful." Rebecca smiled.

"Tomorrow afternoon okay with you?" Miss Mim asked.

"You'd be willing to sit through this a third time?" Rebecca asked in amazement, as everyone nodded.

"It'd give us a chance to see the darling alpacas. And enjoy the flowers and the beautiful April sunshine and refreshments."

Refreshments! Oh heavens, Rebecca hadn't even thought about that.

"You do have food and drink planned, don't you, dear?" Miss Mim asked.

I will have, Rebecca thought.

"Because if not, I could…"

Rebecca lifted a staying hand. "There's just one favor I need you to do, Miss Mim," she asked the former librarian. "And it's a big one."

TREVOR HAD JUST FINISHED his morning chores when the phone rang. "I'm glad I caught you. We need to talk," Luke Carrigan said.

Trevor knew if Luke was summoning him, he wanted to talk about Rebecca. "When and where?"

"My office in the hospital annex. How soon can you get here?"

Trevor consulted his watch. "An hour."

Saturday afternoon, the waiting room was deserted.

Luke ushered Trevor into his private domain. He motioned for Trevor to take a chair and settled behind his desk. As Trevor had expected, Luke wasted no time in getting to the point. "I want to know your honest assessment of how Rebecca is doing."

"Fine." Better since they'd made love again and spent the night wrapped in each other's arms.

Not so good since they had disagreed that morning, over his efforts to protect her from whatever Vince Owen was going to pull next. And Trevor knew Vince was up to something.

"Meg and I were out of town at a medical conference, but we heard about the stampede and the trouble that followed the moment we got back."

"It was a harrowing experience, but she got through it with flying colors in the end. Even delivered her very first alpaca, Little Blue, on the ranch, all by herself."

"That's great."

"I know you've had your doubts about Rebecca being a rancher. I had mine, too, but I have to tell you, your daughter is amazing."

"She's got what it takes to make a go of it?"

"In spades, sir."

Luke rubbed the corner of his mouth with his thumb. "I know the Open House is tomorrow afternoon."

"Yes, it is."

"And Rebecca's invited everyone she knows who might possibly be interested in investing."

"That's right," Trevor said, proud of the audacity Rebecca was exhibiting.

Luke drummed his fingers on his desktop. "She hasn't come right out and said so exactly, but her siblings think she's got everything she owns on the line this weekend. Is that correct?"

Trevor looked Luke in the eye. "These are questions you should be asking Rebecca."

"I would if I thought I'd get a straight answer."

Trevor knew what Luke meant. Rebecca was pretty prickly when it came to doing this by herself, for herself. "She hasn't discussed the financial particulars with me, either. But I know she would appreciate your moral support. And anyone else you can wrangle up to be there."

"Meg and I talked last night." Luke rocked back in his swivel chair. "We're prepared to write a check that would cover her expenses and immediate debt. We have no idea how much that is."

Trevor understood Luke's intentions were good. They were still dead wrong. "I think that would be a mistake. Rebecca would resent it and completely take it the wrong way."

Luke rocked forward once again. "We want to take some of the heat off so she can relax and enjoy her Open House and not feel pressured to sell, sell, sell."

Beginning to see why Rebecca got so aggravated with her successful physician father, Trevor exhaled slowly. "First of all, she's in business to market her alpacas. Tomorrow's event will be good experience for her. She may or may not meet her goals—although given how hard she's been working, not to mention how much she loves caring for her animals, I think she just might. In fact, I think she's going to surprise a lot of folks with her expertise. I know she did me."

Luke scowled. "I don't want her to be embarrassed."

Trevor shrugged amiably. "Then don't do anything to embarrass her."

Silence fell as Luke thought about that.

"Speaking of embarrassment," Luke continued eventually, "what was the deal between you and her and Vince Owen at The Wagon Wheel restaurant last night?"

Trevor swore silently to himself. He had hoped Luke wouldn't hear about that.

"A patient who saw it said Vince looked furious when you waltzed in there and stole his date."

"It wasn't a date, it was a business meeting," Trevor corrected irritably. "They were just having a drink."

"Apparently, Vince Owen didn't see it that way. He was madder than a hornet when he paid his bill and stormed out after the two of you left. Probably because he thinks you're interfering with that boast he made, about making her his woman before the month was up."

Trevor winced at the memory. "I'm sorry to hear Vince Owen's ire made other diners uncomfortable."

"But you're not sorry Rebecca's taken a shine to you, are you?"

No, couldn't say he was.

Deciding discretion was the better part of valor, Trevor met the older man's searing gaze. "What precisely are you asking here, sir?"

Luke sobered. "What every good father wants to know. What exactly are your intentions toward my daughter?"

"GIVEN THE WAY WE PARTED company this morning, I wasn't sure how glad you would be to see me," Trevor drawled.

Very glad as it happened, Rebecca thought, her pulse jumping at the sight of him.

Her intellect, however, was a lot more cautious.

Rebecca knew they needed more than passion and friendship to take their relationship to the next level. They needed to trust each other deeply.

And trust was the one thing she struggled most with. She wasn't used to getting what she wanted in the romance department, and she had never dreamed she could want a man as much as she wanted Trevor McCabe, or be cared for so intensely in return.

The deep satisfaction and joy she felt whenever she and Trevor were together had her waiting—wrongly or rightly—for the next catastrophe in her life to occur.

Trying not to notice how good he looked in the casual

shirt and jeans, she replied, "That all depends whether or not you're ready to give me the respect I deserve."

The look in his eyes gentled. "I've never disrespected you, Rebecca."

Hurt trembled deep inside her. Stubbornly, she reminded, "You haven't believed I could handle everything I need to handle on this ranch, either."

To her relief, he held up both hands, looking genuinely contrite. "My mistake. One I promise not to make again."

Wanting to be perfectly clear, in hopes they'd never have a similar argument again, Rebecca said, "I can handle all the challenges in my life. Including the ones you'd rather I not have to deal with." *Like Vince Owen.*

"Fine. Although I should remind you that you're back in Texas now, and Texans do *whatever is necessary* to take care of their women."

"Even giving them free rein?" Rebecca teased.

Trevor stepped across the portal and took her in his arms. "In your case, I guess I'm going to have to." He lowered his head for a steamy kiss.

Rebecca kissed him back with all the affection building up inside her.

"So how's the work going?" he asked, when they finally broke apart.

Rebecca took him by the hand and led him into the living room. "You know how I was worried last night because I hadn't received that many RSVPs?"

"I believe you mentioned it twenty or thirty times." He settled on the sofa beside her.

"They started coming in today, by phone and e-mail." She showed him the list. "Trevor, I've got seventy-five acceptances!"

"That's great."

"And fifty more maybe's!"

"Even better," he said cheerfully.

If only it were that simple, Rebecca thought, with an inward groan. "And not nearly enough food or drink to give them."

"No problem. I can make a grocery store run."

She made a face. "This isn't a poker party, Trevor. I can't just give them potato chips and soda."

Trevor looked at the cookbooks spread across the coffee table. "Obviously, you had more in mind for the reception part of the afternoon."

"Hot hors d'oeuvres. Fancy little desserts. Finger sandwiches. Texas beer. Wine. Plus, someone to organize the spread while I concentrate on talking business with my guests. If I could afford to call a caterer, it'd be no problem. But…"

He put a silencing finger to her lips. "Phone your siblings. Ask them all to bring something. Same with your mom and dad. I'll call everyone in my family who can cook. It can be their ranch-warming gift to you. And don't give me that I Want To Do Everything Myself look, Rebecca. Yes, you're begging for favors, but these are acts of kindness we will return in spades, because that's what family and friends do for each other. There's no shame in asking for help when you need it."

"How come you're always on the giving end and never on the receiving end of things, then?"

"Because I've already been through the start-up phase of my ranching career. As you soon will be, too."

Rebecca made another face at him.

He pulled out his cell phone. She picked up hers. They started dialing.

Fifteen minutes later, Meg Carrigan and Annie Pierce

McCabe had both volunteered to set up and oversee the buffet tables, and they had the beginnings of a spread that would make Martha Stewart proud.

"Everything will be here an hour before the guests arrive. Guaranteed." Trevor handed over the list of items being donated to the event.

Rebecca added it to hers and perused them with a satisfied sigh. "I still need beverages and ice," she stated with a frown.

"Make me a list. I'll go get it and while I'm in town, I'll pick us up some dinner."

Rebecca couldn't help it. She felt that she was imposing far too much. "You really don't have to do all this," she told Trevor softly.

To her surprise, he agreed with her. "You're right. I don't."

Her heartbeat sped up. "Then why are you?"

He smiled, shifted her onto his lap and kissed her again. Deeply, irrevocably.

She was trembling when he let her go.

"That's why," he told her softly.

Because he wanted to make love to her again? she thought. Or for a deeper, more emotional reason?

She knew what she was hoping for, but no more confessions were forthcoming as Trevor smoothed the hair from her cheek, looked deep into her eyes. "Besides, there's something I forgot to do in town, too. And I better hurry before it's too late."

He touched his lips lightly to hers, and slipped out of the ranch house.

Her lips still warm and tingly from his kiss, Rebecca watched him go. It was hard to believe how much she had come to care for Trevor McCabe in so little time. Harder still to imagine her life without him, ever again.

The telephone rang.

Seeing from the caller ID it was Miss Mim, Rebecca picked up the phone. "Tell me you found out who owns Edge Investments," she said.

"I did," Miss Mim replied. "But you're not going to like it."

That, Rebecca noted, an earthshaking five minutes later, was the understatement of the century.

Figuring there was no time like the present to confront the most underhanded person she had ever come across, she got in her pickup and drove to the Circle Y.

Vince opened the door.

Coco shot past him and went straight for Rebecca. Rebecca bent to pet the chocolate Labrador retriever. Coco responded by licking Rebecca's arm, and wagging her tail so hard she nearly fell over.

"I figured you'd be stopping by this evening," Vince said casually, motioning her inside.

Rebecca remained on the porch of the Circle Y ranch house.

Reluctantly, Rebecca turned her attention from the love-starved pup, straightened slowly. "I'd prefer we talk out here."

"Suit yourself." Vince shut the door. Waited, an expectant look on his deceptively handsome face, while Coco sat on Rebecca's foot, her weight braced against Rebecca's leg.

Wishing she could just take the puppy home with her once and for all, Rebecca forced her thoughts to remain on the disturbing problem at hand, and the neighbor who might just be trying to ruin her. "You own Edge Investments."

Vince smirked at the way the eager puppy turned, and tried to climb up Rebecca's leg. "That's right."

Feeling a little canine protection might not be a bad idea, Rebecca picked the twelve-pound puppy up and cuddled her against her chest. "You purchased the loans on my property deliberately."

Vince noted the way Coco settled down immediately, before returning his impassive gaze to Rebecca's face.

"I had the feeling you might need my help."

Rebecca recalled the letter she had gotten in the mail.

"Is that what you call it?" She worked to keep the emotion from her voice.

"Threatening to foreclose on me if I don't have my insurance in place and the balloon payment on Monday morning?"

"I helped you get the property back to an insurable state."

Vince was acting as if she should be *grateful* to him.

"The question is why if you intend to try and foreclose on me?" Just how sick was this man?

"I don't want to force you from your property, Rebecca," Vince told her calmly. He stepped toward her, took the puppy, opened the door and pushed Coco inside. "I'd like nothing more than to have you living next door to me and Trevor McCabe."

"Providing?" Rebecca ignored the heart-rending barking on the other side of the closed door.

"You let the world know—starting tomorrow, at your Open House—that you're my woman." Vince turned and frowned as the ruckus continued.

"But I'm not your woman," Rebecca pointed out, a great deal more tranquilly than she felt. Inside the house, the barking turned to pitiable whimpers.

Vince folded his arms in front of him and continued. "I'm a much better companion for you. You'd know that, if you gave me half a chance. Plus, I can afford to give you anything you need, including money. If you're with me, Rebecca, you and your ranch will want for nothing."

Rebecca stepped back, away from him. She propped her

hands on her hips. "I can't believe this," she muttered, not bothering to hide her revulsion.

His persuasive smile faded. Coco raced to the window and began barking there. "Then you better start," Vince warned, his low tone as chilling as it was matter-of-fact. "I'm through playing around, Rebecca. Finished losing you to an idealistic loser like Trevor McCabe. I want you in my life and in my bed."

Trevor had been right—Vince Owen took "unhealthy competition" to a whole new level.

Rebecca forced herself to ignore Coco's pitiful whimpering. Not easy when the sound alone was enough to break her heart. "Why?" she asked Vince. "So you can parade me around Trevor like a red flag in front of a bull and stick it to him that way?"

Vince's expression hardened. "Trevor McCabe needs to understand once and for all that I'm superior to him in every way." He paused, continued smoothly, "You can help me accomplish that."

How could she not have realized how vicious Vince Owen was? "You understand that not only am I not physically or intellectually attracted to you, that I also find you extremely loathsome?"

Excitement gleamed in Vince's eyes. "The fact you find me personally despicable will only make it that much more thrilling in the bedroom."

Feeling as if she was going to be sick, she stepped completely off the porch. "Information garnered from personal experience, no doubt."

He shrugged and made no apology.

Rebecca clenched her fist, her keys digging into her palm, as the puppy began barking hysterically once again. "I'm not going to let you blackmail me."

Smugness creased his features. "You've got a night to think about it. I trust by morning you'll have figured out your ranch means more to you than whatever it is you think you have going with Trevor McCabe."

Rebecca told herself the tears of anger and frustration welling behind her eyes were for the puppy, not herself and the unholy mess she had just gotten herself into, all by not listening to Trevor's cautions. "And if I don't?"

Vince lifted his hands in the most casual of gestures. "Then you better have a twenty-thousand-dollar check for Edge Investments on Monday morning, to make that balloon payment, as well as some sort of repayment schedule set up for the five thousand dollars labor charges you owe me," he told her with a cool, satisfied smile. "Or your days on The Primrose Ranch are going to be over, sooner than you think."

Chapter Thirteen

"I know it's early, but you all need your beauty sleep tonight," Rebecca told the female members of her herd as she snapped leashes on all their halters and prepared to lead them, en masse, from the pasture to the barn for their nightly feeding and bedding down.

Refusing to let Vince Owen's threats throw her off course or depress her, she went right back to the work schedule she had set for herself.

"We've got a big day tomorrow, and I'm counting on every one of you to look and act especially adorable to dispel the rumors of your waywardness earlier in the week."

Pewter Percy, one of the herd-sires snorted in reply, as Rebecca passed his stall. "Yes, I know it wasn't your fault. You didn't start that stampede, and given the size of the Black Angus cattle running toward you, you had no choice but to run for your lives, as far and fast as you could. The way I see it, that just proves how smart alpacas are, what survivors you are. And I'm a survivor, too," Rebecca continued, stabling one female alpaca after another. Enough of one to overcome even the toughest opponents, without running to anyone else for help.

She was an adult—perfectly capable of handling this all on her own.

Black Onyx tilted his head, skeptical as always. The fact he happened to be male doubled her irritation. "Now, don't look at me like that, big fella. I know it looks bad on the surface." Like Vince Owen might actually take everything from her if she didn't capitulate to his demands and sleep with him, just to tick Trevor off. "But I know what I'm doing. And the fact of the matter is, we're almost there." Rebecca finished stabling the animals and took all the leather leads and hung them on a hook near the door. "We just have to hold on a little longer."

"Of course I know Trevor would help me. If Trevor knew what happened tonight, he'd probably go over and punch Vince Owen in the nose and help me get the money to pay off the sleazy jerk, to boot. But that wouldn't be right." Rebecca moved on to the stall closest to the door that contained the newest member of her herd.

Little Blue edged closer, drawn to the emotion in Rebecca's low tone. Blue Mist looked equally concerned. She knelt down to check mother and cria. "That would be letting him solve my problems for me, and although it's tempting to let him do that—you don't know how tempting—I got myself into this mess. It's up to me to get myself out. And I can do it, too." Satisfied all was well, Rebecca stood.

Blue Mist nosed her cria into the corner of the stall.

Getting the message, Little Blue began to nurse.

"All I have to do is let people know what a good investment alpacas are, and get them to sign up for leases tomorrow. Then I'll have the money to make the balloon payment on Monday morning and time to refinance the balance with a reputable banker like Elliott Allen, which is who I should have gone to in the first place. And I'll be able to concentrate on building this place up to be the best alpaca ranch in Texas…."

"Telling bedtime stories to the herd?" Trevor asked, strolling in.

Rebecca smiled, her heart quickening, as always, at the sight of him. She hated keeping things from him, but this was her problem. "Something like that," she drawled.

He looked around in admiration. "It's amazing, how far you've brought this place in just two weeks."

Rebecca made no attempt to contain her pride and contentment. "Thank you."

"I'm serious. You're turning out to be one heck of a rancher, Rebecca Carrigan."

Now if she could just figure out how to get Vince Owen out of her and Trevor's life, once and for all.

Pushing aside the guilt she felt for not confiding her latest challenge to Trevor, she adopted a deceptively light tone. "I'm glad you finally figured that out."

"After tomorrow everyone else in Laramie County will know it, too."

Rebecca drew a breath. "I hope so."

"I know so." The corners of his eyes crinkled. "Ready for a surprise?"

She loved it when he looked at her like that, as if she was the best thing that had ever happened to him. Determined to stay in the moment, she edged closer. "That all depends. What is it?"

"Come and see." Trevor took her by the hand.

Propped up against his pickup truck was a large, rectangular-shaped present.

He stood back to watch. "Open it."

Rebecca pulled at the ribbon and tore off a corner. It

didn't take her long to discover what it was. A big wooden sign in the signature ranch color of Primrose yellow. Bold black letters proclaimed, The Primrose Ranch. Huacaya Alpacas for Lease, Sale and Boarding.

Emotion clogged her throat. She determined not to cry.

He edged closer. "I noticed you didn't have a business sign next to the road. I figured we could put this one up for now. Then if you wanted to change it out for something else later—"

Rebecca let go of the sign, wreathed her arms around his neck and silenced him with a kiss. "That's the best present I've ever received! Thank you so much!"

Twenty minutes later, Trevor pounded a stake into the ground next to the mailbox. The elegant-looking sign was attached.

Trevor and Rebecca stood back to admire it in the fading daylight. "I should get a camera," Rebecca said.

"We'll do that tomorrow," Trevor promised, lacing an arm about her waist, shifting her close. "Meantime, we've got dinner to eat. And knowing you, probably a hundred last-minute details to tend to," he said.

He wasn't far off.

Rebecca still had investment brochures and information packets to print and put together. Individual pictures of the alpacas to arrange in the slide projector she had borrowed from the public library. White folding chairs to arrange in the office, where the presentation was to take place.

Finally, near midnight, there was nothing more that could be done.

Trevor came up behind her, wrapped his arms around her and buried his face in her hair. "You've got to get some rest," he murmured against her ear.

Happiness unfurled inside her. "I know."

He turned her to face him, tenderness etched in his expression. "Do you want me to go or stay?" he asked her gently.

How had she ever lived without him in her life? Without this? She smiled, rose on tiptoe, wreathed her arms about his neck. "What do you think?" she whispered.

He rubbed his lips on hers. She opened her mouth to the pressure of his, encouraged his tongue to dally, even while hers did the same. "That kiss feels like a yes."

She drew back, already working free the first button on his shirt. "It's also an invitation to shower." Her fingers touched warm, muscled skin.

He playfully touched his nose to the bridge of hers. He leaned forward, his forehead touching hers, and held her face between his hands. "With or without you?"

Lusty images filled her head. The knowledge he wanted her as much as she wanted him was almost as powerful an aphrodisiac as her growing feelings. "Your choice."

He grinned unabashedly and looked deep into her eyes. "Then you know what I choose." Hand in hand, they started for the ranch house.

No sooner had the door closed behind them than he found the corner of her mouth, and the center, exploring until the need pooled deep inside her. Her nipples ached for his touch. Her lower half strained against him. "We're never going to get upstairs if you keep kissing me like this," she warned, as his hand closed over her breast, claiming the soft flesh and teasing the nipple through the smooth cotton T-shirt.

"Oh, we'll get there," he promised in a low, husky voice that heightened her anticipation all the more, the hard length of him pressing into her. His eyes were slightly glazed. "One article of clothing at a time."

She had time to draw a breath, and then his mouth was on hers again, and they were kissing as if the world was going to end. She lost her boots in the kitchen, along with his. Her T-shirt next to the stove. Her bra in the hall. Not to be outdone, she got his jeans off in the foyer. His shirt at the bottom of the stairs. By the time they had reached the bedroom, they were breathing erratically, and skin to skin. Her inhibitions fled, dwarfed by the need to make hot, soul-searing love with Trevor McCabe. And judging from the way he was looking at her, kissing her, touching her, he wanted to take his sweet, lovely time with her, too.

Legs trembling, body aching, Rebecca bypassed the bed in favor of the shower. She'd had far too few moments like this in her life….

And nothing…nothing…even close to Trevor McCabe.

He grinned as she turned on the spray and pulled him in along with her. As always, it took a moment for the water to get warm. They laughed and shuddered as the cold spray hit their bodies. Shivering, she came toward him. The unique male scent of him filled her senses. He clasped her to him, his palms spreading heat across her skin. By the time the kiss ended the moisture pelting them was warm and enticing.

"Allow me." Rebecca grabbed the bar of juniper-scented bath soap, and rubbed it across his chest, back, down his thighs, between. He groaned as she rinsed with the handheld attachment.

"My turn." Eyes darkening, he backed her against the wall. Took his time lathering her body, even longer rinsing. Her nipples budded. The skin between her thighs grew slick.

She arched against him, impatient now, longing for the ultimate closeness. She'd never felt more alive, never felt so safe, warm and protected. Loved, even though he had never said the words out loud.

The thing was, she realized, as she kissed him back, her hands caressing every inch of him, she loved him, too.

He gripped her bottom and stroked her where their bodies met. Drawing her leg up, she settled against him. "Uh-huh," he said. "In the bed."

It took forever to towel dry, even longer to get situated between the sheets. Wild with yearning, she rolled onto her side.

He lay beside her, stroking, caressing, taking his time. Kissing her slowly, completely. Demanding the same. Until he was on top and her legs were wrapped around his waist. Holding her arms pinned above her head, he pushed inside her, timing his movements, building their pleasure, taking her with him to the very depths. Focused on one seductive plateau after another, she clenched around him, gasping his name, and then there was no more time, no more playing, no more holding back. They were pushing toward the edge, falling, racing, feeling. Climaxing together in mind-blowing passion. Floating freely, slowly…coming back down…shuddering together… holding each other… loving…kissing…and starting all over again.

"I HAVE TO TELL YOU, Rebecca, what you've done here is downright amazing," Elliott Allen said.

Rebecca had asked the Laramie banker and her ranch insurance agent, Greg Savitz, to arrive early for a private tour. They had viewed the barn, visited all eleven of her alpacas grazing sedately in the pastures, taken in the new ranch office in the old garage and ended up in the gazebo, where a small refreshment table had already been set up.

Rebecca poured iced tea for Elliott, lemonade for Greg.

"Does this mean my insurance is now reinstated?" she said.

Greg nodded. "In fact, everything now looks so good, I'm going to talk to the home office about bringing your rate back down to where it was."

"Thank you." Things were so tight financially, every little bit was going to help.

Greg went off to join Trevor, who was standing in the yard, talking to his father and hers, who had shown up early, along with Annie and Meg. Banished from the kitchen, the men set up folding tables and chairs in the shade.

Now for the real test. Rebecca turned to Elliott. "Have you had a chance to look at the new business plan I faxed you last night?"

Elliott nodded. "I reviewed it before I came over here. It looks good, Rebecca. If you can meet your financial objectives today, I'll have no problem getting the loan committee to approve a new financing package for The Primrose."

Rebecca smiled.

Finally, it seemed everything was going her way.

She had the ranch she had always dreamed of owning, an alpaca operation and a man who made her happier than she ever imagined she could be.

All she had to do was stand up to Vince Owen and show everyone she could handle anything that came her way—even a deliberate attempt to ruin her newfound romance and drive her into ruin—all on her own.

TREVOR KNEW SOMETHING had been bothering Rebecca the previous evening. She had been too quiet one minute, chattering like a magpie the next. It could have been just nerves over the official opening of her business, all the guests she was expecting, the fact, with all eyes on her, she really wanted to succeed.

That was a lot to handle for someone who had only been in the ranching business for two weeks.

His gut told him it was more than that.

There'd been a reckless-to-the-point-of-desperation quality to their lovemaking. As if one of them had been going off to fight a war…. And then there was the way she had been holding on to him last night, in her sleep. Not just snuggling close, the way she had before. Holding on for dear life.

Something had happened to change her mood during the time he'd gone into town to get her ranch sign, and the other items she needed. What, he didn't know.

He'd find out.

But it would have to wait until after the Open House, when she had accomplished the goals she had set out for herself.

Fortunately, he had a lot to keep him busy.

Trevor's brothers arrived just ahead of feed store owner, Nevada Fontaine, Dave Sabado and tractor salesman Parker Arnett.

Trevor had just said hello to the group when Vince Owen sauntered over.

Not surprisingly, given the havoc his substandard ranching practices had caused earlier in the week, Vince got a polite but cool reception from the group of men. A fact, Trevor noted, that seemed to push him to further ruthlessness.

His expression smug, Vince tipped his hat back, and abandoned even the pretext of politeness. "You all ready to see me win my bet?"

Trevor tensed.

This was the lowlife he knew, the one who had dogged him all through his university days.

Glances darkened as the men closed rank around Vince. "You can't have a bet if no one agrees to wager," Nevada Fontaine reprimanded, mocking Owen's tone.

A distance away, Trevor saw Rebecca glance over. Tense.

Because she knew the history between the two men and intuitively anticipated Vince might try and make trouble with Trevor today? Or had something else happened…something he knew nothing about?

"And the way I recall it," Dave Sabado continued, oblivious to the dark nature of Trevor's thoughts, "you got no takers."

Parker Arnett put in, "Besides, seems Rebecca Carrigan is already spoken for."

It was time to stake his claim. "They're right. Rebecca is with me now," Trevor announced flatly.

"Really?" Vince taunted, rocking back on his heels. He regarded Trevor with arrogant derision. "Is that why she rushed over to my place last night, the moment you left for town?"

Trevor knew Vince well enough to ascertain when he was telling the truth. Or at least the part of it that Vince wanted Trevor to know.

And there was fact in this.

Which was probably why Rebecca had been so single-minded and hyperactive last night. Because Vince had said or done something to try and upset her. And knowing Rebecca, she had determined to handle whatever it was on her own.

Tyler and Teddy McCabe stepped forward in a way that reminded Trevor of their "Triplet Threat" days. In true "One for all, and all for one" fashion, Teddy glared at Vince. "We don't want any trouble here today, Owen."

Tyler flanked Vince's other side. "We'd hate to have to

bodily throw you off the property, but if you don't behave yourself, starting now, we'll do just that."

Trevor nodded, glad he had his brothers for backup. "No one is ruining this day for Rebecca." *Not even you. Snake belly.*

Vince held up both hands, backed off. "Fine." His complacency remained unaltered. "We'll just see what happens."

Vince strolled off.

It was all Trevor could do not to throw him off The Primrose, anyway.

Rebecca walked briskly up, what Trevor imagined was her tour-guide smile fixed firmly on her face. "What's going on?" she murmured, taking Trevor by the elbow, and leading him over to the side of the house, by the back door, well out of earshot of the guests roaming the property.

"The usual." He clamped down on his temper. "Vince was just trying to get under my skin."

Worry darkened her eyes. "What did he say?"

Trevor figured he could ask Rebecca about Vince's comment and find out what had really happened between Vince and Rebecca later. "Nothing that bears repeating," Trevor said, more concerned about her than himself. And at the moment, she was looking mighty pale. "You about ready to start?"

Rebecca nodded, took a deep, relieved breath and folded her arms in front of her in a defensive pose. "I just hope I can pull this off."

Trevor had the feeling her sudden anxiety had something to do with Vince Owen, which made him want to throttle the man all the more.

"Are you kidding? You're going to be fantastic," he said, giving her elbow a squeeze.

As it turned out, there were so many people there, Rebecca had to do her presentation three times, and each time, it was a standing-room-only crowd.

By the time the afternoon had ended, she had leased out all eight of her female alpacas for the next three years, she had eight orders for stud service, and Miss Mim and a group of other seniors had arranged to buy Little Blue outright and board her on the ranch. A dozen others were interested in leasing and/or buying arrangements, as soon as Rebecca was able to expand her herd. She collected ten percent of all monies owed when the contracts were signed, as per her business policy. Rebecca couldn't stop smiling as she said goodbye to everyone who had come by.

Finally, it was just Rebecca and Trevor.

And that was when Vince Owen chose to appear once again.

REBECCA HAD HOPED that when Vince realized she wasn't going to capitulate to his demands, that he would slink away to the hellhole from which he had risen. Apparently not.

He walked toward Rebecca, his expression ugly. "You made a mistake here today," Vince told her.

Rebecca put down the serving platter in her hand. "You're the fool, for ever trying to blackmail me in the first place," she muttered furiously.

Trevor looked at Rebecca.

Relieved to finally be able to tell Trevor everything without fear he would try and solve her problem for her, she explained, "A company Vince owns, Edge Investments, now holds the mortgage on this place, as well as my operating loan. Vince told me yesterday that if I didn't tell everyone I was his girlfriend today that he would foreclose on me tomorrow morning if I couldn't make the balloon payment." Rebecca turned to Vince. "But thanks to my success this afternoon, I'm going to be able to pay that off. Then I'm going to refinance and never have to worry about being blackmailed by you again."

To her dismay, Vince smirked as though he still held the high card. "It's not that simple."

Trevor moved closer to Rebecca. "Sure it is," Rebecca said.

Vince's seedy grin faded. "There's the matter of the five thousand dollars labor and material charges you owe me. I expect immediate repayment on that, too. Or I'll be forced to take you to collections and sue you for nonpayment of debt."

Rebecca's spirits sank like a stone in the bottom of a pond. She'd thought she was finally in the clear financially!

"That wasn't our agreement and you know it," she stormed.

Vince stared her down victoriously. "I've got eight cowboys, a plumber and an electrician, who saw us shake hands on it, before work ever commenced."

Shock reverberated through her. "You said I could have as much time as I needed for that. That all you wanted from me today was some sort of repayment schedule, which I have!"

"Funny—" Vince rubbed his jaw "—I don't remember it that way. In fact, the way I remember it, *the entire payment is past due.* You were supposed to give me a check at the time I presented you with the bill yesterday morning. You didn't. Being the generous man and neighbor that I am, I gave you another opportunity to pay me again last night, and again you refused."

The lie was so outrageous it took her a moment to recover. Trevor looked as if he was about to take Vince's head off.

"I'm not going to let you get away with this," Rebecca said through her teeth.

Vince smiled at both of them and slowly dropped his hand to his side. "You're not going to have any choice. You can't refinance with a lien on your property, and I plan to put a lien on this place first thing tomorrow morning. After that, I'll use your nonpayment of your debt to trash your credit rating, which will make it impossible for you to refinance with anyone else. And your drastically lowered credit rating will force me to up the interest rate on your mortgage, as per terms of your original loan agreement. By the time I'm done with you, you'll be begging me to foreclose on this ranch and put you out of your misery. Of course, all that could change if you agree to go on a few dates with me."

Rebecca threw her hands up in frustration, paced a distance away. "What is it with you? Why are you fixated on this dating thing? When you know I'm not the least bit attracted to you?"

"Because," Trevor told her grimly, "he can't stand the thought of not winning the wager he tried to make about you the first day he came to town."

Rebecca blinked, sure she hadn't heard right. But apparently from the looks on both men's faces, she had. "What bet?" Rebecca asked warily.

"He said he would make you his before the month is out," Trevor replied in a low, bored tone. "And get a ring on your finger, too. The dates he wants are a precursor to that."

"Well, it's not going to happen." Rebecca whirled back to Vince. "I don't care what you threaten me with."

"We'll see about that." Vince flashed an evil smile and walked off.

"Unbelievable," Trevor muttered under his breath, watching him go.

When they were alone again, Trevor looked at Rebecca with calm self-assurance. "Don't worry about the five thousand dollars. I'll transfer funds to your bank account first thing tomorrow morning."

Rebecca struggled to take it all in. The demands, the betrayal, the fact that her finances, which looked so rock solid for the next six months a few minutes ago, were now tilting precariously again.

"You can pay me back whenever," Trevor continued.

Rebecca blinked. "That's your solution?" she said softly. *"To give me money?"*

Trevor shrugged. "If there's no lien, you can refinance."

She moved one hand slightly. "That's not the point."

His eyes narrowed. "Then what is?"

Feeling more of a fool than ever, Rebecca studied him. "When did you find out about the bet Vince Owen made about me?"

"Tried to make," Trevor corrected, irritation on his face. "No one at the feed store would wager with him. And I knew about it at the time. I witnessed it."

"And didn't see fit to tell me?" Rebecca asked, enraged.

Trevor regarded her calmly. "I didn't want to hurt your feelings."

Rebecca's anger mounted. "So instead you let me go on interacting with that sleazy lowlife without any knowledge of what Vince was doing and saying behind my back."

Trevor spread his hands. "I was protecting you."

She moved forward until they were only inches apart. "I don't want your protection! Who else knows about this?"

"All the men in town."

Rebecca noted there wasn't an ounce of apology in his hazel eyes. "My father?"

"Yes," Trevor replied curtly.

Shame warred with humiliation. "When did *he* find out?"

"He knew about it the first day he came to see The Primrose Ranch."

As she recollected, it all made sense. "Which is what you two were talking about when he went over to your ranch to get the pressure washer," she said through her teeth.

"He wanted to discuss it with me, yes."

"And *he* didn't tell me, either!"

Trevor folded his arms across his chest. He did not try to conceal his irritation. "We agreed to spare you the embarrassment."

"How very kind of you." Rebecca flashed a saccharine smile. "Did it ever occur to you that I wouldn't be in the mess I am right now if you had only told me what was going on from the get-go? Had you told me that Vince tried to make a bet about me, had you warned me in advance about his substandard ranching practices in regard to his cattle, I wouldn't have given him the time of day, neighbor or no, I would have known to install fencing right away."

"If you recall, I tried to talk to you about that. You wouldn't listen."

Rebecca went on as if Trevor hadn't spoken, "And I certainly wouldn't have accepted his offer of help with the new fencing and the installation of the cooling system in the barn!"

"So you made a mistake—"

Tears burned behind her eyes. "That could cause me to lose my ranch!"

"I told you," Trevor corrected with exaggerated

patience. "You're not going to lose The Primrose. I'm not going to let you lose your ranch. And neither is your father. Although a lot of what just happened could have been avoided if you had waited for me to help you with the labor on the fence and the cooling system in the barn."

Rebecca reached out to steady herself on the back gate of his pickup truck. "You had all you could handle with your sick cattle. And time was running out."

"I would have organized a group of guys to help me get it all done before the Open House and you wouldn't have been charged anything. And—" his voice dropped an accusatory notch "—I could have prevented what happened just now if you had told me that Vince was blackmailing you!"

Rebecca spun away from him. She shoved her hands through her hair. "It wasn't your problem!"

Hand on her shoulder, he whirled her back around. "Don't you get it?" His hold on her tightened possessively. "Everything that happens to you is my concern."

Blinded by equal parts hurt and fury, she shoved away from him. "Next thing I know you're going to be challenging my competence and telling me how to run every aspect of my life."

He gave her an if-the-shoe-fits look, and said, his voice soft as silk, "Just admit you were wrong not to come to me for help and tell me what was going on with Vince at the time it was going on, promise me you won't shut me out like that again, and we'll let it go."

The hell of it was, he didn't even realize he was being condescending. But she sure as heck did. She stepped forward, not sure whether to deck him or kick him in the shin; she only knew she wanted to wound him the way he had her. "We'll let it go?" she repeated on a soft, bitter laugh.

He nodded, still ready to forgive and forget.

She wasn't. And might never be. Rebecca balled her fists at her sides. "You're unbelievable, you know that?" When he didn't react, not in the slightest, she let her voice drop to a feral growl. "Get off my property."

His brow arched as if her words did not—could not—compute. "You're throwing me out?"

She scoffed, too devastated to continue. "What else would you expect me to do after the way you've undermined and disrespected me—not just today, but from the very moment we met up again in the feed store?"

His contriteness faded. "I'm not going to apologize for protecting you."

That was the problem. He just didn't get it. Pretending she'd seen this coming all along, Rebecca replied sadly, even as the happily-ever-after she'd wanted for them slipped through their fingers, "I didn't think you would."

Chapter Fourteen

"What in the world is going on over there?" Susan asked.

Amy moved to the kitchen window overlooking the Circle Y Ranch. Rebecca's two sisters had spent the night with her, alternately consoling her and brainstorming ways to immediately come up with the five-thousand-dollar labor charges she needed to pay off Vince Owen, and keep a lien that would damage her credit rating from being attached to her property.

Rebecca didn't know how she would have lived through the last twelve hours without them.

Her sisters were not just stellar independent business-women, with a lot to teach her, as it turned out, they were also very sympathetic when it came to the sheer stupidity of men in general, and Trevor McCabe in particular.

Rebecca only wished she had called on them sooner, instead of insisting on sorting out all her financial problems herself, her own way, without any family help.

Maybe if she had let Susan and Amy closer, she would have been so busy hanging out with them, she wouldn't have gotten so involved with Trevor McCabe.

And maybe not. Rebecca sighed.

Even now, as furious as she still was with Trevor, there

was just something about him that made her heart go pitter-patter and turn her world upside down. And honestly, how foolish and naive was that?

How ridiculously romantic?

"It looks like a parade of pickup trucks." Amy sipped her coffee.

"I see a few SUV's and sedans in the mix," Susan noted.

"As well as a coupe or two." Amy's nose wrinkled in perplexity. "What do you think it means?"

Susan and Amy turned to Rebecca.

As if she should know.

"I have no clue. And when it comes to Vince Owen, I really don't care. Let's just get these papers signed, the checks written, so I can run them to the bank before ten o'clock."

The three women sat down.

One last time, they went over the business contract their cousin, Claire McCabe Taylor, a Laramie attorney, had helped them draft via phone and e-mail, the previous evening.

They had just finished signing when they heard a parade rumbling up Rebecca's drive.

Admittedly curious, the three women stepped out onto the front porch of The Primrose ranch house. Cowboys and prominent business people of all ages poured out of vehicles and congregated on Rebecca's front lawn. Neighboring ranchers; all three of the McCabe triplets; their two younger brothers, Kyle and Kurt; their father, Travis McCabe; as well as ranchers Brad McCabe, Shane McCabe; and the husbands of all four Lockhart sisters were among those standing together. Rebecca recognized a dozen other members, including the president of the Laramie County Rancher's Association.

But it was Trevor McCabe, stepping forward as leader of the group, who had her heart pounding.

"First off, every man here owes you an apology," Trevor began bluntly.

"Including me." Rebecca's father moved to the front of the group, to stand beside Trevor.

Traitors both, Rebecca thought.

"We should have told you from the get-go about the wager Vince Owen tried to make about you two weeks ago," Nevada Fontaine said.

Dave Sabado agreed, "You're one of us, Rebecca, same as any other rancher."

Parker Arnett added, "The fact you're a woman is neither here nor there. We should have leveled with you like we would have talked straight to any man."

Luke Carrigan nodded, his expression contrite. "We're all guilty here, and we apologize."

Teddy McCabe stepped forward, too, pausing only long enough to shoot an apologetic look at Rebecca's sister Amy, before continuing frankly to Rebecca. "We also want you to know that you don't have to worry about Vince Owen any longer."

That sounded good to Rebecca even as she determined not to show her relief, lest it be perceived as a sign of weakness.

"He's decided to leave the county, effective immediately," Tyler McCabe said, with the same practical gentleness he used on his veterinary patients and their owners.

Although she was more than capable of keeping Vince off her property, even if she had to get a shotgun to do it, Rebecca knew getting him to leave the county was more than she could have wrangled on her own. "How'd you manage that?" Rebecca asked warily.

Travis McCabe looked at the group around him with paternal authority, "I'm thinking maybe we all should let Trevor explain that to Rebecca."

Amy and Susan got the hint.

"Good idea." Her sisters were off the porch in no time flat.

Before Rebecca could voice "Wait!" everyone had scattered. Truck doors were slamming. Engines starting. Vehicles were rumbling off in the same orderly fashion they had driven up the driveway.

Once again, she and Trevor were very much alone. Pretending her life was just fine without him, she faced him. "You want to tell me what's going on?" She made no effort to hide her cantankerous mood.

He stopped a few feet from her and looked into her eyes, his tone as flat and pragmatic as hers was curt and emotional. "I called everyone for an emergency meeting last evening, explained what Vince Owen was trying to do to you. This morning, we let him know as a group that we didn't need his kind around here."

Rebecca knew when she was getting the cleaned-up version of events. "Vince Owen wouldn't just leave because he found himself unpopular."

"You're right. He wouldn't. But he *would* depart to avoid multiple lawsuits lodged against him, due to the spread of livestock illness and property damage the gross mismanagement of his cattle caused."

Trevor withdrew a sheaf of legal papers from his back pocket. He handed them over, managing not to touch her in the process.

Trying not to feel bereft at the loss of personal contact, Rebecca scanned them quickly. "This affidavit states that Vince—not I—is the person responsible for the five-thousand-dollar labor charges on my property, and that he incurred them as fiscal reparation for the damage to my property, caused by his stampeding Black Angus cattle."

"Right. So the threat of any lien being placed on your

property is now gone. Should he so much as think about trying anything else, we all have our lawsuits ready to go. And they'll stay that way, until the statute of limitations runs out."

Which meant they'd have years.

Realizing this would also mean she would no longer see Coco, Rebecca sighed, and forced herself back to the business of the day. "I still have to make the balloon payment."

"Yes, but now you'll be making it to my uncle, Wade McCabe."

Rebecca lifted a brow.

"He and his lawyers are over at the Circle Y right now, completing the sale of the mortgage on the Primrose to one of Wade's investment groups. They're paying cash. So as soon as the papers are signed that threat will be gone, too."

Rebecca wanted to berate Trevor for doing that, too, but figured it would be hypocritical when the reality was, she felt nothing but relief she would not have her fate in the hands of Vince Owen in any way, and none of this was anything she could have managed on her own.

Still, the idea of being beholden to a McCabe, when she had just broken up with a McCabe…

She swallowed. "I had planned to refinance with Elliott Allen, at the Laramie Bank."

Trevor nodded respectfully. "And you can still do that, no problem, hopefully under much better terms than your old mortgage. In the meantime you won't have to worry about Vince. He no longer has any hold on you, financial or otherwise."

Finished, Trevor started to walk away.

Once again, too much was happening, too soon.

Rebecca strode after him before she could stop herself. "Trevor!"

He turned.

"Why did you do all this?" Rebecca asked, her heart in her throat. "Especially after the way we parted yesterday."

Was it because he loved her, after all? Because—like her—he was beginning to realize he couldn't bear the thought of a life without the passion they'd shared and the intimacy they'd found?

Trevor rocked back on his heels. He rubbed a hand across his mouth and chin. "Because I owed you," he said, lowering his voice to the soft, seductive lilt she knew so well. "You were only in this mess in the first place because Vince wanted to use you to get to me," he told her sorrowfully. "And because what he tried to do to you just wasn't right."

"WELL, HIS EXPLANATION makes sense," Jeremy said to Rebecca several hours later when he stopped by to see how she was doing.

Rebecca stared at her only brother. She had been hoping he would shed some light on the situation, him being a guy and all. "It was so matter-of-fact."

Jeremy paced back and forth, checking out the alpacas grazing sedately in the grass. He looked at her over his shoulder. "Would you have preferred to have him crying in his hankie?"

The depth of her exasperation made her tense. "You know what I mean."

"Yeah, I do." Jeremy smiled the way he had when they were kids. "You're still sweet on him."

That, Rebecca didn't want to hear, think or feel. She gave her brother a quelling look. "Trevor and I are over." She slid her hands in the pockets of her jeans. "The truth is, we never should have started anything up."

"Yeah, I can see how you'd think that." Jeremy leaned

on the pasture fence. "He just moved heaven and earth to get you out of trouble you never should have gotten yourself into, because he doesn't care a lick for you."

Rebecca rolled her eyes and corrected Jeremy's way-too-romantic version of events. "He rounded everyone up to chase Vince Owen out of Laramie because Vince Owen is nothing but trouble and it was the right thing to do for everyone, not just me!"

Jeremy chuckled. "You keep telling yourself that."

"Now he has nothing to feel guilty about," Rebecca continued stonily, studying the beautiful blue of the Texas horizon. *Except breaking her heart into a hundred million pieces.*

"Probably not." Jeremy strolled amiably closer. He tugged one of her braids. "You, on the other hand, are a different story."

Rebecca arched her brow at Jeremy.

He scolded her with a shake of his head. "Here you go again, letting your stubborn pride get in the way of your happiness."

She folded her arms over her chest, over her heart. "That's what *you* think I'm doing."

"Not just me, Rebecca. Everyone in the family knows what a mistake you're making, refusing to forgive Trevor for trying his hardest to keep you from being hurt."

Put that way, her actions did sound stupid.

Had Trevor given her the slightest sign that he still cared for her, she would have been back in his arms in two seconds.

The problem was, he didn't call her. Not that day. Or the next, or the next.

Didn't e-mail.

Didn't come by to check on Little Blue and Blue Mist and the rest of her herd.

Didn't bring her dinner or invite himself to dinner, in return.

He worked his ranch.

She worked hers.

Days passed. One after another.

Vince Owen packed up and left, just as he said he would.

Rebecca refinanced her property with the Laramie bank.

And she missed Trevor McCabe more and more every hour, every minute, that passed.

Finally, the following Saturday evening, she mustered up her courage, baked a batch of ranger cookies, got herself gussied up and drove over to his place.

Lively country-and-western music filled the air as he answered the door. While she had been pining away, Trevor McCabe looked as if he'd never felt better.

Obviously just out of the shower himself, he was clean shaven and nicely dressed, in a white Western shirt, dress boots and jeans.

"Here to congratulate me?" he said with a sexy smile.

Actually, to make a peace offering. But now that he'd mentioned it... "For what?" Rebecca asked.

"Purchasing the Circle Y."

Which was, coincidentally, a property he had wanted all along, Rebecca realized with a start. The only thing missing from his equation of perfect happiness was the Primrose, which she still owned.

"So your ranch is now twice the size," she affirmed.

"That's right." Pride and contentment radiated in his low tone.

"And you've got two houses."

"I'm planning to turn the one at the Circle Y into a business office."

"Congratulations," she said stiffly. *Now she was*

*buffeted on both sides by Trevor McCabe land, which
was going to be nothing but a constant reminder of all
she'd had, and then lost.*

Trevor tilted his head, studying her aggravated scowl.
"I thought you'd be happier for me."

I would be if I thought you still cared.

"Happier to know you've got a neighbor on both sides
you can rely on," he continued, a questioning look in his
hazel eyes.

She caught a whiff of the slow roasting beef brisket, the
yeasty smell of fresh-baked bread. Unable to totally keep
the jealousy from her voice, she thrust the peace offering
at him and backed slowly toward the door. "I feel like I'm
interrupting."

The sparkle was back in his eyes. "You're right," he
agreed cheerfully. "I'm not alone."

Rebecca bit down on an oath. "You've got a date." Why
was she surprised? Just because the thought of *her* going
out with anyone else was incomprehensible did not mean
he was as foolishly single-minded.

He made a seesawing motion with his hand. "More like
a lifetime commitment."

The notion rocked her back on her heels. She'd thought
they would have time to make amends, to see if they
couldn't get past this and pick up where they'd left off.
"You're engaged?"

His smile was as soft and enticing as his kisses had once
been. He took her hand and tugged her close. "Why don't
you come and see?"

Rebecca liked to think of herself as a mature adult, but
this was too much. She put up a palm to keep him from
coming any nearer. "Thanks, but no."

He came closer, anyway, wrapping an arm about her

waist. When she would have pushed away, he held fast. "The thought of me with another woman really bothers you, doesn't it?"

Rebecca regarded him with haughty cool. "I just think it's a little soon."

"Mmm." His voice was a sexy rumble in his chest.

She tried not to notice how warm and solid and enticingly masculine he felt. Or how good he smelled, like soap and cologne. "You don't seem surprised."

"Why would I be?" he asked compassionately and calmly. "I feel exactly the same way about seeing you with anyone else."

Feeling a chink in her emotional armor, she wrinkled her nose at him. "And yet you haven't called, haven't e-mailed, haven't dropped by."

His gaze remained on hers, as steady and strong as his presence. He cupped her face in his free hand. "I was waiting for you to come to me."

Her heart began to pound. Hope rose deep within her. "You were so sure that would happen?"

"I know what you feel for me," he told her in a low voice, husky with emotion. "I know how rare it is." He paused to give her a long, hot kiss. "I know a love like ours doesn't come along every day." He paused to kiss her again, deeper, more soulfully. "And I know there is no way on this earth that I am ever going to be anything but more in love with you each passing day."

She blinked, wanting to be sure she hadn't imagined this. "You—?"

"Love you," he said, the depth of his contentment sweeping over them both. "Yes, Rebecca, I do. Just as you love me."

She couldn't help it—she began to smile, even as her

stubborn independent nature reasserted itself. "I never said that," she reminded.

He grinned, triumphant. "You didn't have to." He held her tight and buried his face in her hair. "It was in your eyes every time you looked at me." He leaned back slightly. "It was in every kiss, every caress, and it was certainly there in spades every time we made love."

She bit her lip, savoring the way his arms felt around her. "Then why didn't you come after me?"

His expression gentled once again. "I knew you needed time to sort out your business affairs, process everything that's happened and discover what was in your heart and mine."

Also correct. "And now that I know?" she asked cautiously, wondering where they went from here.

"I'm hoping you'll marry me." He held her face in his hands and kissed her tenderly. "Maybe not today, or tomorrow, but one day, when you're ready, I want you to be my wife."

Rebecca resumed breathing.

"But it's got to be on one condition."

She blinked back the mist of emotion. "Somehow, I knew there would be a catch."

He sobered, every inch of him resolute male. "You're going to have to let me do the man thing and protect you, just as I expect you to do the woman thing and watch over me. Because that's what people who love each other, who care for each other, do."

She flashed her untamable grin at him. "Spoken like a true Texan."

"Through and through. So is it a deal?" He waited.

But not for long. "Yes," Rebecca said firmly, looking him right in the eye. "I'll marry you."

"When?"

The man did not waste any time. But then he never had. "Six months from today."

That quickly, it was decided. Which gave them plenty of time to start kissing again. And kissing and kissing.

She was ready to head for his bed when he murmured against her lips, "There's just one more thing."

Of course.

"You're going to have to accept part-ownership of one of your wedding presents now."

He certainly planned ahead.

"Because it's very important we share in the responsibility." Trevor said soberly as he took her by the hand.

She went along willingly. "Now, you're confusing me."

He winked. "We've got room in our life for one more, don't we?"

Oh yes, back to the mysterious "guest" in his kitchen.

"That all depends on who it is," she cautioned wryly.

"Trust me. You're going to love her as much as she already loves you."

Rebecca certainly hoped so.

They rounded the corner.

Coco was curled up in a wicker basket in a corner of the kitchen, fast asleep.

"She was sold with the Circle Y ranch," Trevor said.

Rebecca wasn't surprised the puppy had been so readily given over. Vince Owen did not have the temperament or the time to successfully care for a puppy. Trevor, on the other hand, had love and patience in spades, as well as an amazing rapport with all animals.

Trevor knelt down beside the Labrador retriever. Gently touched the back of her soft chocolate-colored head. "Hey, sleepyhead, wake up."

Coco opened her eyes. Stretched. Saw Rebecca. And shot up like a stone coming off a slingshot. The next thing Rebecca knew she had her arms full of wiggling, happy puppy.

"I think she's as glad to see you as I was," Trevor drawled.

Rebecca could not stop laughing as Coco licked her beneath the chin. A fiancé and a puppy all in one night. "This is the best present I've ever received. My only question is how did you get her to sleep?" Rebecca rubbed behind the Lab's ears.

"Lots and lots of exercise. Or as Tyler told me, 'a tired puppy is a happy puppy.'"

The theory seemed to work. "Good to know."

Trevor bent and snapped on a leash. "What do you say the three of us go for a walk? Then we'll come back, have dinner, put her down for the night, and see if we can't find a way to amuse ourselves…."

"THIS HAS GOT TO BE one of the proudest days of my life," Luke Carrigan told Rebecca six months later.

"And to think," Meg Carrigan teased her husband with spousal affection, "she managed to find a man to marry without your assistance."

"Now," Luke stated, with a playful glance at his son and other two daughters, "if only her siblings could settle down, too."

"My medical practice and my ranch is all I've got time for these days," Jeremy said.

"No kidding," Susan teased. "That place of yours is in such bad shape it'll take light-years to fix up."

"You won't find any woman willing to share it with you, until it's at least somewhat habitable," Amy agreed.

"That's the plan," the energetic bachelor, Jeremy, grinned.

Luke turned to Susan. "Don't look at me," she said. "I'm not about to head down the aisle any time soon, except as Rebecca's maid of honor."

"I'd happily get married," the incredibly romantic Amy begged to disagree, "if I could only find someone to fall madly in love with, too."

"It'll happen when it's meant to happen," Meg stated with maternal confidence. She looked at her husband. "And not a moment before, no matter how much *meddling* anyone does. Meanwhile—" Meg stepped behind Rebecca to adjust her tiara and veil. The two women's eyes met in the mirror "—I want Rebecca to know how very happy I am for her, too," Meg said in a low voice so choked with sentiment it brought tears to everyone's eyes. "She's accomplished so much in such a short period of time."

Rebecca turned to face her family. "I couldn't have done it without all your support, though, the way you all lent a hand with the shearing and the Open House. Not to mention helping me figure out how to get more out of the land."

"It was your idea to reduce the size of the pastures to more manageable levels, and lease out the rest for planting," Amy pointed out.

"But you contracted for the property to expand your nursery business, and Susan brokered the deal and directed her landscaping crews to help refence the fields." Rebecca paused. "I couldn't have accomplished near as much without all of you."

"That's what family's for," Meg said.

The wedding planner knocked and stuck her head in the door. "Time to get the show on the road, folks," she said.

Wedding music sounded in the chapel beyond.

Jeremy escorted Meg to her mother-of-the-bride seat in

the front of the church. Susan paired up with groomsman Tyler McCabe. Amy stepped off with Teddy McCabe. Luke offered Rebecca his arm. Together, they walked through the pews of well-wishers, to the altar, where Trevor waited.

Rebecca had only to look into his eyes to know how beautiful she looked. And heavens, he was gorgeous, too.

Her heart brimmed as her father kissed her and gave her away and then she and Trevor stood before the minister, hand in hand, ready to pledge their future together.

"…I take thee, Trevor…"

"….as my lawfully wedded wife…"

"…joined together, let no man put asunder. Trevor," the minister finished, beaming, "you may kiss your bride."

And with Coco watching contentedly in the wings, on the end of a primrose-yellow lead, Trevor did.

* * * * *

The next book in Cathy Gillen Thacker's latest series is coming soon!

Watch out for
The Rancher's Family Thanksgiving,

available October 2008 only from Mills & Boon® Special Edition.

Mills & Boon® Special Edition
brings you a sneak preview of Marie Ferrarella's
Capturing the Millionaire…

It was a dark and stormy night…when lawyer
Alain Dulac crashed his BMW into a tree, and
local vet Kayla McKenna came to his aid. Used
to rescuing dogs and cats, Kayla didn't know
what to make of this stranger…but his
magnetism was undeniable…

Don't miss the fantastic third story in
THE SONS OF LILY MOREAU *series,*
available next month, October 2008, in
Mills & Boon® Special Edition!

Capturing the Millionaire
by
Marie Ferrarella

The first thing Alain became aware of as he slowly pried his eyes opened, was the weight of the anvil currently residing on his forehead. It felt as if it weighed a thousand pounds, and a gaggle of devils danced along its surface, each taking a swing with his hammer as he passed.

The second thing he became aware of was the feel of the sheets against his skin. Against almost *all* of his skin. He was naked beneath the blue-and-white down comforter. Or close to it. He definitely felt linen beneath his shoulders.

Blinking, he tried very hard to focus his eyes.

Where the hell was he?

He had absolutely no idea how he had gotten here—or what he was doing here to begin with.

Or, for that matter, who that woman with the shapely hips was.

Alain blinked again. He wasn't imagining it. There was a woman with her back to him, a woman with sumptuous hips, bending over a fireplace. The glow from the hearth, and a handful of candles scattered throughout the large, rustic-looking room provided the only light to be had.

Why? Where was the electricity? Had he crossed some time warp?

Nothing was making any sense. Alain tried to raise his head, and instantly regretted it. The pounding intensified twofold.

His hand automatically flew to his forehead and came in contact with a sea of gauze. He slowly moved his fingertips along it.

What had happened?

Curious, he raised the comforter and sheet and saw he still had on his briefs. There were more bandages, these wrapped tightly around his chest. He was beginning to feel like some sort of cartoon character.

Alain opened his mouth to get the woman's attention, but nothing came out. He cleared his throat before making another attempt, and she heard him.

She turned around—as did the pack of dogs that were gathered around her. Alain realized that she'd been putting food into their bowls.

Good, at least they weren't going to eat him.

Yet, he amended warily.

"You're awake," she said, looking pleased as she crossed over to him. The light from the fireplace caught in the swirls of red hair that framed her face. She moved fluidly, with grace. Like someone who was comfortable within her own skin. And why not? The woman was beautiful.

Again, he wondered if he was dreaming.

"And naked," he added.

A rueful smile slipped across her lips. He couldn't tell if it was light from the fire or if a pink hue had just crept up her cheeks. In any event, it was alluring.

"Sorry about that."

"Why, did you have your way with me?" he asked, a hint of amusement winning out over his confusion.

"You're not naked," she pointed out. "And I prefer my men to be conscious." Then she became serious. "Your clothes were all muddy and wet. I managed to wash them before the power went out completely." She gestured about the room, toward the many candles set on half the flat surfaces. "They're hanging in my garage right now, but they're not going to be dry until morning," she said apologetically. "If then."

He was familiar with power outages; they usually lasted only a few minutes. "Unless the power comes back on."

The redhead shook her head, her hair moving about her face like an airy cloud. "Highly doubtful. When we lose power around here, it's hardly ever a short-term thing. If we're lucky, we'll get power back by midafternoon tomorrow."

Alain glanced down at the coverlet spread over his body. Even that slight movement hurt his neck. "Well, as intriguing as the whole idea might be, I really can't stay naked all that time. Can I borrow some clothes from your husband until mine are ready?"

Was that amusement in her eyes, or something else? "That might not be so easy," she told him.

"Why?"

"Because I don't have one."

He'd thought he'd seen someone in a hooded rain slicker earlier. "Significant other?" he suggested. When she made no response, he continued, "Brother? Father?"

She shook her head at each suggestion. "None of the above."

"You're alone?" he questioned incredulously.

"I currently have seven dogs," she told him, amusement playing along her lips. "Never, at any time of the night or day, am I alone."

He didn't understand. If there was no other person in the house—

"Then how did you get me in here? You sure as hell don't look strong enough to have carried me all the way by yourself."

She pointed toward the oilcloth she'd left spread out and drying before the fireplace. "I put you in that and dragged you in."

He had to admit he was impressed. None of the women he'd ever met would have even attempted to do anything like that. They would likely have left him out in the rain until he was capable of moving on his own power. Or drowned.

"Resourceful."

"I like to think so." And, being resourceful, her mind was never still. It now attacked the problem of the all-but-naked man in her living room. "You know, I think there might be a pair of my dad's old coveralls in the attic." As she talked, Kayla started to make her way toward the stairs, and then stopped. A skeptical expression entered her bright-green eyes as they swept over the man on the sofa.

Alain saw the look and couldn't help wondering what she was thinking. Why was there a doubtful frown on her face? "What?"

"Well…" Kayla hesitated, searching for a delicate way to phrase this, even though her father had been gone for some five years now. "My dad was a pretty big man."

Alain still didn't see what the problem was. "I'm six-two."

She smiled, and despite the situation, he found himself being drawn in as surely as if someone had thrown a rope over him and begun to pull him closer.

"No, not big—" Kayla held her hand up to indicate height "—big." This time, she moved her hand in front of her, about chest level, to denote a man whose build had been once compared to that of an overgrown grizzly bear.

"I'll take my chances," Alain assured her. "It's either that or wear something of yours, and I don't think either one of us wants to go that route."

It suddenly occurred to him that he was having a conversation with a woman whose name he didn't know and who didn't know his. While that was not an entirely unusual situation for him, an introduction was definitely due.

"By the way, I'm Alain Dulac."

Her smile, he thought, seemed to light up the room far better than the candles did.

"Kayla," she told him. "Kayla McKenna."

* * * * *

Don't forget Capturing the Millionaire
is available in October 2008.